Needless to say, I heard about it first from Gus. I'd just
finished wrapping up a Ford Thunderbird for a customer in Leeds when I heard Gus's car outside. How
did I know it was Gus's car? Easy. Unless you work in

By the same author
Tinplate

DIE-CAST

Neville Steed

ST. MARTIN'S PRESS/NEW YORK

DIE–CAST

Copyright © 1987 by Neville Steed. All rights reserved. Printed in the United States of America. No part of this book may be used or reproduced in any manner whatsoever without written permission except in the case of brief quotations embodied in critical articles or reviews. For information, address St. Martin's Press, 175 Fifth Avenue, New York, N.Y. 10010.

Library of Congress Catalog Card Number: 87-29922

ISBN: 0-312-91197-1

First published in Great Britain by George Weidenfeld & Nicolson Limited

Printed in the United States of America

First St. Martin's Press mass market edition/September 1988

10 9 8 7 6 5 4 3 2 1

For Edward and Richard,
with love

One

"Now, sir, what other little gems do you have stashed away in your attic?"

His question took me by surprise. He had been browsing in my Toy Emporium for at least twenty minutes, and up to then had not wobbled his handlebar moustache to utter a sound.

"I'm afraid everything I have for sale I have on display," I rejoined, which wasn't entirely true, but true enough, I reckoned, to pass muster with him.

He moved slowly towards my counter, rubbing his chin with doubt.

"Come, sir, I thought every old toy dealer kept something rather special away in his attic, waiting for the next big international auction, or a customer with a Saudi Arabian-size bank balance."

His rather large and florid face was now uncomfortably close to mine, and I took a step backwards, which produced the kind of piercing shriek you don't normally have occasion to hear, outside a Turkish prison. I'd just, accidently, applied an eleven-stone pile-driver, alias my whole weight, on my Siamese cat's back paw. I bent down to apologize to the hapless Bing, but he'd vamoosed off into the house. When I rose again to counter height, I saw that my companion's bewhiskered face was a good deal less florid.

"Only my cat. I trod on him," I smiled. "But, anyway, what were you saying?"

He pulled himself together, and some blood began its return journey to his cheeks.

1

"I . . . er . . . was asking. . . ."

"Ah, yes," I interrupted. "Little gems in the attic, Saudi Arabian-size bank balances." I looked him in the eye. "Tell me first, Mr—er—"

"Truscott. Geoffrey Truscott."

"Mr. Truscott. What are you really after? What do you collect?"

He smiled, and suddenly I could see a little boy peeping out from behind the sixty-odd-year-old mask of his face.

"Rarities, sir. Rarities."

I began to rather like him, and not just because rarities in the old toy business mean the exchange of quite large numbers of bank notes.

"Car rarities? Commercial rarities? Ship rarities? Aircraft rarities . . . ?" He stopped me there.

"Aircraft, sir. Aircraft." He stepped back from my counter and swung around to point at the display cabinet which housed, or should we say hangared, my considerable collection of die-cast aircraft, mainly old Dinkies, but also French Solido, Danish Teckno, and pre-war Tootsietoy from the USA.

"Like those," he continued. "Only it's highly unlikely I would find what I want on public display. That's why I always ask about any gems in the attic."

I sighed audibly, because I was genuinely sorry not to be able to help him. The so-called gems in my attic did not include even one solitary aircraft. Some mint, boxed Britains Ltd soldiers, yes; a fine road-sweeping vehicle, and a pick-up truck made by the Citroën car company in 1928, yes; a beautiful tinplate paddle-steamer by Carette circa 1910, yes. All entered for, and awaiting, the next Sotheby's antique toy auction, where I reckoned they would attract far higher bids than I could raise by putting them on display in my Dorset seaside village shop in Studland.

"Can't help you right now, I'm afraid, Mr Truscott. I only have what you see on display. But if you tell me exactly what you're after, I can always let you know if I ever come across such an item."

2

The elderly Flying Officer Kite face moved closer to mine once more.

"I'll begin with a real *rara avis*, sir, a gem amongst gems, the stunning crown for any toy aircraft collection. . . ."

"The Dinky Avro Vulcan," I interrupted, almost certain that I would be proved right, for the precious few Dinky had ever made of that famous British bomber were only just beginning to surface on the market at huge prices, and all from Canada, where the entire production run had been exported.

He chuckled. "No, sir, not the Vulcan. A bird so rare that no one has yet tracked one down. No one. But they will, one day, they will. They said only one Vulcan had survived. Now we know of quite a few more. So there's hope, sir, there's hope." He looked at me with eyes afire with excitement. "I trust, sir, you know to what aircraft I am referring?"

I suddenly held on to the counter, as I realized there was only one that could live up to both his description and his obvious lust for possession, an aircraft that every avid aviation toy collector had dreamt of possessing one day, from the first moment they had seen its tantalizing photograph in the Dinky advertisements in the 1939–40 Meccano magazines. A die-cast toy, measuring all of four inches wingspan, that if ever found, could fetch thousands of pounds at auction.

"You can't mean . . . ?" I began, but he interrupted me.

"I do, sir. The de Havilland Flamingo air liner of 1940. The rarest bird of them all, would you not agree?"

I nodded feebly. What else can you do? The Flamingo is the King Solomon's Mines of the die-cast aircraft world, the Golden Fleece, the crock of gold at the end of the rainbow. Even that other bird, the Maltese Falcon of my favourite movie, would move aside for it.

"Well," I managed to offer eventually, "if my attic contained that, I wouldn't be running an antique shop, would I? I would be a wizard or a conjurer, a magician, a super-hero. With such an ability, I could probably also make gold out of

3

lead, cause the lame to run, the sick to pick up their beds. And maybe, just maybe, even make the trains run on time."

"You're laughing at me, aren't you, sir? All because, like so many, you don't believe Dinky ever produced a Flamingo, do you?"

He reached into the inside pocket of his blazer, and pulled out a very Asprey-looking wallet. I was impressed before I saw the American Express Gold card, the Harrods and Air Travel cards, and the comely clutch of fifty-pound notes, any one of which I could have done with right then. The old toy business is very cyclical. My present cycle had proved to have two flat tyres and a broken chain. I blamed it on the bad weather of the now thankfully past summer. From a small inside flap in the maroon leather, he produced the picture I knew so well, and handed it to me.

"They made it, sir. That's proof."

I shook my head. "It's not, I'm afraid. It's only proof they made a small wooden model for appraisal and photography, or, at best, a brass master. It's no proof they made dies from the brass master and went into production."

A liver-spotted hand took the clipping from me and tucked it back into its leather bed.

"Did you see the price in the advert, sir?"

"Yes, 'Dinky Toy 62f. Price 6d each.' Every serious toy aircraft collector knows the words off by heart."

"Well, that's proof in my book. Dinky never priced an item until they had made the dies and costed them. It would have been ludicrous commercial sense to do otherwise. Don't you agree, sir?"

I'd heard that argument before from other collectors, and it made sense. But, if that were true, what didn't make sense was that nobody had ever seen or found any trace of a Flamingo, or even its box or packaging in nearly fifty years. Still, I did not want to throw cold water over the glowing coals of his quest. It is a tonic to meet someone with such blinding optimism in these dark and rather dreary times, and especially someone of his age. I wondered where all his money had come from. One thing I did know—you didn't chance upon it by tilting at die-cast windmills.

"Well, I wish you luck. You could be right, and one day, you or someone like you will turn one up." I laughed, then went on, "I won't let you know if I find one. I won't need to. News like that goes through the old toy collectors' world like greased lightning."

He replaced his wallet in his inside pocket, and put his hand on the counter.

"Well, sir, I thank you. But to show you I'm serious, I'll tell you what I'll pay for a Flamingo in any paint condition as long as it is structurally complete." He took a deep breath, then whispered, "Fifteen thousand pounds."

Now it was my turn to take a deep breath—and whisper, "I'll remember that, Mr Truscott. I'll remember that."

His rather veined, moon-like face broke into another of his boyish smiles. "I'm sure you will, sir. I should add, my offer, of course, is not exclusive to you. I mention it to every dealer I come across in my travels. Today I was in Bournemouth on business, and was told about your shop by a competitor of yours in Boscombe; Second Childhood, I think the shop is called."

"That's right. Good shop. Nice things, especially tinplate."

"They speak well of you too, sir." He looked at his wafer-thin Piaget watch. "I must be away—I have another meeting in Bournemouth at five. No peace for the wicked." He grinned, gave me a card from his pocket and made to leave. At the door, he turned and added, "In case you're wondering if my offer is genuine, and I have that kind of ready spondulicks," (I hadn't heard that word for donkey's years), "let me tell you who I am. Since returning from the RAF some years ago, I arrange aviation armament deals for certain Arab states. They pay promptly and they pay well. Very well, my dear sir, I can assure you. So remember, anything rarer than a Vulcan. I have six of them already, you see—from Dinky, Tekno, Solido, prototypes, brass masters, mock ups. I'm sure you've got the picture."

He closed the shop door carefully behind him. Out of

curiosity, I came out from behind the counter, and went over to my front windows. I was just in time to see the long, sweeping shape of a Panther de Ville glide away from the kerb opposite, leaving a group of school children adrool with envy on the pavement. I looked down at the card in my hand. It said very simply in heraldic style script, "G.J. Truscott Esq, Purveyor of Defense Systems, Windlemere Manor, Windlemere, Salisbury, Wilts," plus two telephone numbers and a telex code.

I smiled a very sad smile, and wondered how many men, women and children had been killed by the arms he had sold to raise the money to keep him in the lap of luxury, and indulge the innocent and wide-eyed pastime of antique toy collecting at the very highest and most expensive level.

I slowly tore up the card, because, whilst I needed money, I did not need it that badly. I made my way back to the kitchen, where Bing was waiting with a very dark expression in his blue eyes. He watched me throw the pieces of card in the waste-bin, then couldn't resist sidling up. I stroked him and felt his back paw to make sure there was no injury, and, as I did so, I had a wild and wonderful thought that almost completely eradicated the unpleasant after-taste of Truscott's visit. Indeed, I began to regard our meeting as the start of a very promising new cycle for the modest Toy Emporium of Studland in the splendid and tranquil county of Dorset, with tyres and chain now mended, and, with luck, ten-speed gears to boot.

The continued absence of customers for the rest of the day—Truscott had been my only visitor—was rather compensated for by my enthusiasm for my newly minted business plan. And the peace and quiet enabled me to ponder on some of the problems I would inevitably face in its successful execution.

At ten to five, I decided such deliberation was best carried out in the comparative comfort of my own modest sitting-room, not on a hard chair behind a hard counter in an empty emporium. As I went to the door to lock up and swing my

"Open" sign to "Closed," I saw a familiar set of grizzled features at the shop window, and I recognized instantly the truth of that old adage, "The best laid plans of mice and men . . ." He came in, with that special kind of grin people wear when they want to trigger congratulations.

"A'ternoon, old son," he beamed. And it wasn't too difficult to see why he was beaming. He was hiding one arm behind his back.

"Okay, Gus. What have you discovered for me this time?" I asked in a tired voice.

He clumped over to the counter. "No, it's not like last time, Peter. I'm sorry about last time, but I think these might be more what you're after."

"Last time" was his so-called discovery of mint condition old Dinky toys. They turned out to be old Dinky toys all right, but every one was a repaint, expertly done, but repainting generally knocks the stuffing out of the value of small die-cast toys. Not that it was Gus's fault. He is a retired fisherman, best friend and pain in the arse by profession, and not a Sotheby's whizz kid. And the man who originally sold them to him in Swanage swore they were totally original. Contrary to popular belief, there *are* sharks round the Dorset coast.

Gus brought his arm round from behind his back and deposited a Marks and Spencer plastic carrier bag on the counter.

"Didn't know Marks and Sparks were into old toys now," I attempted as a joke. Gus treated it with the contempt it deserved, and plunged his huge hand into the bag. When it emerged, there was nothing to see. He cackled, then opened his fist. If he'd been almost anything but a six-foot, burly and weather-beaten old fisherman, I could have kissed him. Nestling in the life lines of his palm was a tiny, red tinplate car, all of three and a half inches long.

"Got more," he grinned. "Six altogether."

"All red?"

"No, all colours—green, blue, stony colour. Look."

He opened up the bag. Inside were five more cars, identical save for their colours, and all, bless 'em, had tiny Shell oilcans on their running boards, proving they were of genuine pre-war Minic manufacture. (Post-war ones had the cans deleted.)

"Where did you get them?" I asked, now rather excited, "and what's more important, how much did you pay?"

"From an old lady I put up some shelves for—in Osmington. She used to have a little sweet-shop there, sold toys as well. When she gave up, she forgot all about the unsold stuff in the attic, until I happened to mention my friend—that's you—who loved old toys. In a trice, she'd upped and got 'em. I didn't pay a brass farthing for them, neither." He winked. "Gave them for being so obliging." Old ladies seemed to do that with Gus. I never dared ask why.

"Know how much they're worth, Gus?"

He held one up and turned it over. "Marked '6d' on its bottom, see?"

"That's how much they cost pre-war. Mint Minic Fords like these are now worth sixty to seventy pounds each."

For a minute I thought Gus was going to faint.

"Gor—that's, let me see . . ." Maths was never the subject Gus had mastered *summa cum laude*, so I completed his calculation for him.

"Three hundred and sixty pounds, at least." Then I added, "Pity there are no boxes though."

Gus perked up again. "Oh, there are. I left them at her place."

I threw my hands up in the air. "But Gus . . ."

"I ain't going back, if that's what you're thinking."

"Why not?"

"Didn't do the greatest job on her shelves. They could be a bit wobbly by now. My screws weren't really long enough for her walls. Should have bought some others really."

I laughed out loud. It was typical of Gus not to buy anything new, if something he owned already could be botched to fit, albeit temporarily.

"Okay, Gus. Arabella and I are going over in that direction tomorrow evening. I'll pick up the boxes on the way."

"Where you going, then?" Gus wasn't exactly nosy, not in a nasty sense. He just reckoned that friends should tell each other every flipping thing. I'd grown to accept his attitude as quite normal. Love Gus. Love his questions.

"I told you the other day. It's film star night."

Gus rubbed his nose. "Oh, yeah. I remember now. That Lana-Lee Whatsit. . . ."

"Claudell."

"That's her. Well, hope you enjoy it, that's all."

"Why shouldn't we?" I asked with some trepidation.

"Nothing. Only her so-called husband-fella, Maxwell, I think his name is, hasn't half put people's backs up round here already. And he hasn't been in England five minutes neither. And she's such a nice lady—for an American. And a famous film star. Or so they say. Don't know why she had him back. I thought they'd been separated for years."

"They had been. I don't know why she allowed him back. Maybe it was in the interest of their eight-year-old—Tara-Lee, I think she's called. No business of ours really, though. I'll tell you what Maxwell is like after tomorrow night."

Gus pulled the only chair in the main body of the shop up to the counter. He sat down with a sigh. I knew now I'd got him at least until Arabella returned from her reporting for the *Western Gazette,* and probably for longer.

"Remind me how you got the invite. Me memory's not what it was."

I didn't correct him. His memory was exactly what it had always been. Either non-existent or highly selective, depending on how charitably one viewed it.

"Arabella met her when she went to the Manor for that big PR shindig for the launch of that new perfumery range by Reinhardt, bearing Lana-Lee's name."

"Oh yeah, Lana-Lee scents. Remember now. Knew it was something poncey or other. Took a shine to Arabella, I think you said."

I nodded, just as Bing jumped on to the counter, and began snorkelling between the stitches of Gus's old sweater for any traces of his last fishing trip. By the familiar aroma, his quest would not go unrewarded.

"Which is more than Arabella did to Maxwell. She only met him for a few minutes, but it was enough for her to understand his abysmal local reputation."

"Well, I expect he only came back to her to cash in on all the loot she must have got from Reinhardt for allowing her name and fame to be used."

"Could be. I gather his career as a motor racing commentator had ended and he's too old to race any more himself, so he's probably strapped for cash. But that's not the point. It's why someone as nice as Lana-Lee is supposed to be should let him back into her life at all."

"Funny, women are," Gus grunted. "Never know what they're going to do next." He looked across at me with one of his more penetrating looks. "Still, I expect they keep a good table. Plenty to drink too, wouldn't wonder."

I didn't rise immediately to the hint. I thought I'd keep him dangling for a second.

"It's a small party, I gather, not a dinner invitation, Gus. Arabella doesn't know her well enough for that. It'll just mean standing around making small talk about even smaller topics, I expect, with the odd canapé and glass of wine to make it half bearable."

"Well, old son, at least it will be *half* bearable." He grinned, and raised his right elbow off the counter.

"Okay, Gus," I capitulated, "come on in. I've got some Heinekens that suddenly seem to have your name on."

I ushered Gus behind the counter and into the house. But I didn't like the look in his eye. It spoke of many more Heinekens than were stacked in the frigidity of my Electrolux. And I could tell the intended deliberation on my new business plan would soon be drowned in the froth of their downing.

"What's on your mind?"

Her question startled me; I did not even know she was

awake. A soft shaft of moonlight caressed part of her left shoulder and breast as she rested on one elbow.

"Come on now, Peter. We've been together long enough for me to know when I've only got half of you." She traced an imaginary pattern on my chest with her forefinger. I smiled down at her.

"Which half of me is it?" I asked.

Arabella pulled herself into a sitting position, and the bed-clothes obeyed gravity. There was just enough moon sneaking in through the half open curtains to highlight a few nascent goosepimples around her nipples. I put my arm around her, and hugged her to me, for the night was distinctly cooler than usual for early October. But in reality, I'd take any excuse.

"Your left half," she grinned. "And I want to know where your right half has been ever since I came home tonight. It can't just be all the alcohol you and Gus consumed. There's something else, isn't there?"

I nodded. "Yes. I can't disguise anything from you, can I?"

"Would you want to?"

"No. Not really. I just wished to get things straight in my mind before I told you. That's all."

She gently broke away from my arm, and rolled on top of me. I did nothing to stop her.

"Well, I'm not getting off until you've told me."

Her mouth was now so near to mine, I could feel her breath tickling my two o'clock shadow. I made to kiss her, but she pulled back slightly. "Ah, ah, Mr Marklin. I made love with half a man earlier tonight. I'm not complaining about the physical virility bit, just the mental application. I'm not indulging again, until that other bit of you has decided to come down to earth. Come on, give."

"All right." I reached out and switched on the bedside light. I think more clearly when I can see the person to whom I'm talking. "I've had an idea, my darling, that's all."

"Goodness gracious," she smiled, "and what about? Us?"

"Not really. It's more about what supports us—or, rather, me."

"The toy business?" she said with a slight note of disappointment.

"Yes." I put my hands around her face. "How would you like me to add another string to my bow?"

"Sounds interesting," she laughed.

"I'm being serious," I persevered. "I'm planning a new enterprise." I made a noise as close to a trumpet fanfare as my mouth and throat could manage. "I'm setting up as a manufacturer."

She looked beautifully startled. "Of what, pray?"

"Dreams," I replied, dreamily.

"What kind of dreams?"

"Nice ones. And, what's more, dreams made reality—by yours truly."

"Let me guess," she smiled. "It has to be toys, knowing you. So you're going to become the 'Jim'll Fix It' of the old toy business." She thought for a second. "I know, you are going to try to remanufacture items that are in short supply."

I shook my head. "No. I'm going to make toys that are in shorter supply than that."

She looked extremely puzzled. I put her out of her misery.

"The toys I'm planning will never have been in existence before."

"Not *new* ones," she gasped in mock horror. "You've always maintained old toy buffs who trade in brand new toys are letting the side down, and all that."

"No, not new ones in that sense. I'm going to produce toys that have become famous for never having been discovered. That is, if I can find a model maker who's good enough to make the brass masters from which I can produce dies for small scale production."

"But if they've never been made, who will want them, Peter?"

"All the old toy fanatics who have seen the old advertisements for them, or heard about their planned production. Take the first one I'm thinking of producing, the Dinky Toy de Havilland Flamingo pre-war air liner. Perfect photograph of it appeared in Meccano magazines in '39 and '40, but no example of it has ever been found. There are thousands of die-cast aircraft collectors across the world who would give their eye-teeth for one of those. Same goes for a Dinky car shown around the same dates—a Triumph Dolomite Roadster. Again, a perfect photograph, but no actual car. Blueprints, however, have survived on that one. But not on the Flamingo, unfortunately."

"How did you suddenly come upon the idea?" Arabella asked, after a moment's mental digestion of my plans.

"Well, this ex-RAF type wandered into my shop this afternoon, and offered me fifteen thousand pounds if I could find an original. So I reckon I could charge around fifty pounds each for replicas. . . ."

The next quarter of an hour was taken up in a description of Truscott's visit, and a further amplification of the potential I saw for my new brainwave. Arabella, bless her, eventually seemed to see the same magic in it as I did.

"You're going to love doing this, aren't you, my darling? You're going to thrive on the active creativity of it all, in contrast to the rather passive role of just collecting and trading in vintage toys." She pulled the sheet around her shoulders and looked at me. "You've missed that a little, since leaving advertising, haven't you? The actual act of creation, I mean."

I'd never really thought about my recent life that way, so relieved had I been a few years ago to exchange the fickle, brittle world of an advertising agency for the quiet, gentle charm of developing my lifetime hobby of old toy collecting into a business that would just about support me. But, damn it, Arabella was right again. She seems to have a kind of sixth sense about people. Seventh and eighth too, I wouldn't wonder.

"Yes, I suppose so. I probably have missed that aspect."

"That could be the only fly in the ointment, then," she smiled. "For, over the next few months, I may have to go on putting up with only half a man, so obsessed I can see you becoming."

13

This time for a change, I rolled over on top of her, simultaneously switching out the bedside light in a mid-turn display of manual dexterity worthy of a Burt Reynolds at his seductive best.

"Right now, Miss Arabella Donna Trench, I'm just obsessed with you."

"All of you?"

"All."

"It had better be," she breathed. "Otherwise I'll sue that perishing Flamingo for enticement."

"We're not married . . . yet."

"Oh, that's true. . . ."

But by this time, we had again passed into that sensational land where rational argument has no place, and where nothing, but nothing, is done by halves—whatever Arabella imagines.

Two

The next morning I felt decidedly chipper, and not just because the autumn sun was pretending it was summer, and Arabella had more or less given her blessing to my enterprise, although that helped. In the eighteen months or so since we had first become lovers, I had grown to respect her judgement in no small way. (I think the feeling is roughly mutual, thank the Lord.) After, she'd kissed my marmalady mouth and driven off in her Golf convertible to the *Western Gazette,* where she was an on-staff reporter. No, they don't pay Golf convertible type money on that paper; Arabella's parents are oozing with acres up in Shropshire, and drop a little of the harvest her way.

I went to work on my Flamingo plan, for I did not intend to open up shop until the afternoon, and by lunchtime, I had worked out roughly everything that had to be done, but almost nothing about the exact means and cost of production. Still, I wasn't really worried. Others had trodden this kind of path before, and had reached their goal. In the last ten years, many toy collectors have begun to produce their own original models in small quantities, mainly in white metal, and usually of particular cars or commercial vehicles they admire, which have never been covered by the major toy manufacturers. And to me aircraft certainly seemed easier to cast than the intricate shapes of automobiles.

Basically, my scheme was simple: to produce the Flamingo exactly as Dinky had obviously planned around 1940. The twin-engined air liner would be in 1/200th scale, therefore just over four inches in wing-span. It would only carry surface detailing as indicated in the extant photograph and from other Dinky aircraft of the period. Painting would be a doddle, as the Flamingo was to have been all silver with black registration letters, G-AFYE, which I could probably get from Letraset, or have a transfer maker produce for me. I knew where I could get the tiny metal wheels, which were simply held in place by pins.

From my attic, I got down an old book I'd had for years, *Aircraft of the Fighting Powers Volume I* (revised edition published in 1943), which had fairly accurate 1/72 plans of the actual aircraft. They would then only need to be reduced to 1/200th scale by whoever was to make the brass master for the moulds. And there lay my major rub: who the blazes in Dorset was good enough to produce such a perfect brass master of the Flamingo? And how much would it cost?

Setting those problems aside for a moment, I went on to packaging. Its design was really decided for me. It had to be a square cardboard box, covered in matt darkish blue paper, with a printed description of the aircraft on the cover—exactly as all medium- and large-sized Dinky aircraft had been packed in the pre-war period. Not very inspiring looking maybe to a non-collector, but a magic design for the old toy buff, and a necessity if my reproduction Flamingo was to succeed. I dug out a spare Armstrong Whitworth Whitley box from my own collection as a reference for the box maker I would eventually choose.

By the time I did open up shop, I knew my very first priority was to find that model maker, for without him or her, I could not really proceed to the proper costing of my plan. The obvious solution, to ask one of my competitors to recommend someone, I eschewed, as I had no wish to alert them to my brainwave at this early stage, otherwise I might well get pipped to the post.

Curiously, that afternoon brought more customers than I'd seen for a week, so I had little time to brew on ways to track down my quarry. However, I wasn't grumbling. I needed the business to help pay for the obvious initial outgoings on the

Flamingo, and keep my bank manager from grabbing pen and paper.

A spotty youth in a studded, black leather jacket that had seen better days (and, I suspect, better youths) shelled out £35 for a Spot-On Fifties Humber Super Snipe. A bald-headed man with thyroid eyes and an equally prominent tie, parted with £60 for a French cij tinplate Renault Frégate, and an equal sum for the same manufacturer's Ford Vedette. And the big coup of the afternoon—£200 in fivers for a mint pre-war Dinky toy van with "Ovaltine" transfers on the sides, from a bachelor school teacher.

With £355 more than I'd started out with that morning, I felt even more chipper, and shut up shop at quarter to five to give me time to wash half Dorset off my old Volkswagen Beetle convertible, to make it decent for our evening drive to the Lana-Lee Claudell shindig at her reputedly magnificent manor house over Osmington way. It didn't look too bad by the time I had put away the chamois and the Turtle wax—even the rust seemed to shine—but I needn't have bothered. Obviously something I'd done, or omitted to do, that day, had upset the powers that be, for by the time Arabella, look-ing nonchalantly sensational with her newly cropped hair, boy's style (rich boy!), and sporting a slim-line version of a man's DJ and piped trousers, clambered into the Beetle, the heavens had opened with a vengeance. The raindrops were so big they actually hurt as I ran round to my side of the car —as if my new wing collar wasn't paining me enough with-out that.

By the time we had sloshed our way through the storm to Osmington, our spirits and our excited anticipation at being admitted to film star company, had been dampened some-what by the drops of water that seemed to permeate every other stitch hole in my Beetle's soft top. Arabella, by dint of holding an Ordnance Survey map of south Dorset over her head, arrived more dry than damp, but the same could hardly be said of me.

I parked the Beetle between a sloping-backed Cadillac Se-ville and a Daimler Sovereign, to be as near the great Tudor porch as possible. But a butler had anticipated our arrival and came hurrying out with a Technicolored umbrella under which we ran into the Manor. As I shook myself in the hall, I suddenly remembered what I had forgotten because of the downpour. I patted Arabella on the shoulder of her dinner jacket, as the butler was trying to assimilate the idea of her turning out to be a girl after all.

"Darling, would you mind making my apologies?"

"Why, what have you done?" she answered, smart as a whip, in a Groucho Marx voice.

"Nothing. It's what I haven't done. Remember I said I'd pick up the boxes for those Minics Gus brought me?"

"Do it on the way home."

"I can't," I whispered. "The old lady will be in bed by then. It won't take me more than five minutes or so. It's only round the corner and down the road to the sea."

The butler came to my rescue.

"I will look after Miss Trench, sir, if you have a problem."

Arabella looked at me and smiled. The butler looked at me and didn't smile. I looked away in embarrassment, and saw my reflection in the mirror. My sodden hair was raining drips down my nose. "Thank you," I said quickly, and with a split-second smile of my own, went back out into the rain.

Luckily, the little old lady in Osmington Mills did not take an age to find the boxes, although they did smell a little of the kinds of things you find in dustbins, and soon I was beetling back up the hill towards the main Weymouth road.

It was not long after I had turned right at the junction that I saw it. Or thought I saw it. There's a point where the change from unkempt wild hedgerow to well tonsured hedge plus stout wooden posts and laterals quite clearly marks the edge of the Lana-Lee property—it's about two hundred yards from the entrance to the main drive up to the Manor. My headlights suddenly seemed to pick out a kind of white apparition or shape that seemed to be materializing from the rails and the hedge just a few yards within the boundary of the grounds. I thought, at first, I was just seeing things, but as I proceeded, the whiteness seemed to hesitate, then start to disappear again, as if into the hedge—or else into the night air. The clacking windscreen wipers did not aid my concentration, let alone my vision, and by the time I reached what I thought was the section of the hedge from which it had materialized, there was not a dicky bird to be seen. I drove very slowly along that area, then reversed and drove past it again. But, beyond a certain raggedness in the hedge in that general area, I could see nothing untoward, and certainly nothing white. I was now rapidly deciding the whole experience was a figment of my over-excited imagination, but had to admit that, even in my more inebriated moments, I had never conjured up anything quite as disturbingly real. And I mean disturbing! As I drove on, I literally shivered, and it wasn't just because of the chill of my wet hair.

Once at the Manor, the butler did his Gene Kelly act again, and soon I was back in the dry, and being ushered into a vast drawing-room, that seemed big enough to play professional football in—but far too gracious to contemplate such an event. At the far end, logs almost the size of trunks spat and glowed in the Elizabethan open fireplace, painting a group of figures standing beside it with flickers of orange light from its flames. I ran my fingers through my hair to anticipate any further liquid fall-out, and hunted for Arabella amongst the DJs clustered around a figure I could not quite make out, but who I assumed was our famous photogenic hostess.

As I walked forward, a champagne glass appeared in my hand, and I took a lengthy draught for a modicum of Dutch (or, more accurately, French) courage. A DJ turned round, but it was much taller and more powerfully built than Arabella. And it had a coarsish face and a moustache.

"Ah, this must be your friend, my dear, come in from the storm."

He had an American accent too, from somewhere south of Washington DC, I guessed. He came up to me and grasped my hand. "Let me introduce myself. I'm Ben Maxwell."

"Peter Marklin," I smiled, and could feel another raindrop starting on its journey.

"My, you've got a mite wet, Peter. Would you like to use the bathroom?"

"No, no," I replied. "I'm not that bad. Just my hair, really. The fire should. . . ."

"Well, that's just great, Peter." He propelled me forward into the group he had left in order to greet me. Now, for the first time, I could see the centre of attraction, and knew instantly why she could never fail to be so. It was not just that Lana-Lee Claudell more than lived up to her screen image, it was something far deeper, and it was centred mainly in her bluest of blue eyes. They somehow spoke of scenarios that I felt no camera could ever film, no writer ever adequately convey. They were kind of streetwise, yet childlike, warm, yet with a flicker of fear, confident, yet sad. They fascinated me, and by the end of the evening, I had decided her eyes had to be her devastating equivalent of the Mona Lisa's smile.

But there was no enigma about the rest of her. I just could not believe she was only a year younger than myself. (I'm thirty-nine. Honest. But I won't be so honest next year.) Her figure was straight out of *Vogue*, as, indeed, was her dress— pure white, clinging closely to every delicious curve. It seemed to have been spun in some kind of silk, slightly more matt than usual, and was cut to leave one bare shoulder, then sweep in an elongated s-shape to an undulating hem, split at one side to reveal an elegant glimpse of leg. Coloured and plain diamanté were sewn on to the bodice and down the front to form the shape of a fabulous leaping panther, its out-stretched legs and paws seeming to embrace her body. It made the dresses in *Dynasty* look like yesterday's cast-offs.

"Honey, this is Peter Marklin. My wife, Lana-Lee." Maxwell introduced her with a slight note of hardness in what I now placed as a Texan drawl. In my impetuous way I took an instant dislike to him, safe in the knowledge that, according to Gus, I was probably not alone.

"I'm so pleased you could come," she said warmly, in that

20

voice that had sent cinema audiences into a quiver for nigh on twenty years. Her eyes moved off me, and I followed them. That's how I found Arabella. "You know, Arabella here has told me quite a bit about you."

"It's all untrue," I said, smirking. But before Lana-Lee could react, Arabella was by my side.

"No, I only told Lana-Lee the good things," she laughed, then stage whispered in my ear, "I didn't tell her you liked going swimming at Osmington Mills before parties at manor houses."

Lana-Lee laughed and ran her elegant fingers through her long, blond hair—sort of Lauren Bacallish.

"But I've heard about your antique toy collecting, Peter. Sounds fascinating."

I was just about to pick up her very welcome cue, when reenter husband stage left, with a big fat grin on his over-large face.

"Let me introduce Peter to the others. Arabella has already met them."

I looked at Arabella. Her expressive face gave me the split-second equivalent of a thumbs down. Whoever I was going to meet had not been awarded the Arabella Donna Trench seal of approval. I inwardly sighed, and glanced across at the figure to whom I was being introduced. It was female rather than feminine; willowy rather than full-bodied. And the face not, I suppose, without attraction, although I don't really go for the slightly sinister *femme fatale* type of look, outside Yvonne de Carlo in the countless reruns of *The Munsters*.

"This is Lavinia Saunders. Peter Marklin. I'll leave you two together for a moment." I saw Maxwell give her a knowing glance, then turn to a rather blue-faced man, who was now endeavouring to engage Arabella in conversation over near the fire.

"Peter. That's a gentle name," she said, huskily. "I have never known a violent Peter."

I didn't quite know how to respond to that comment, so I didn't try.

"Lavinia," I countered instead, "I've never ever met a Lavinia before." I was longing to add, "Can Lavinias be violent?" but thought I had better not.

"My mother's second name. But you're right, it is unusual." She fluttered her eyelashes just enough to invite a
compliment. I couldn't think of one.

"You here alone?" was all I could muster.

She looked across at the blue-faced man with Maxwell.
"No such luck," she grinned. "That's my husband over
there." She looked up at me through the mascara.

"You're not alone, are you?" she asked. "I gathered that
from the rather striking girl with the immaculate short hair
and dinner jacket. She your wife?"

"No. Not . . . er—"

"Going to be?" Lavinia was nothing if not direct.

"Oh, we'll see."

She ran her scarlet-tipped finger slowly around the top of
her champagne glass. I think, by her smile, she thought the
gesture was mildly suggestive. I was rather miffed, and
prayed the party was not going to prove to be one of those
that ends with car keys thrown into a bowl.

"If you'll pardon my curiosity, Peter, I would hazard a
guess, though, that you *have* been married? Am I right?"

I nodded.

"Didn't work out?" Her finger was on its fourth lap of her
glass.

I couldn't resist saying, "No, it worked so well, we di-
vorced so that we wouldn't go on hogging the benefit of our
magic all to ourselves. Share it around, you know."

Her green eyes double-took. Then she laughed. "You're
right to send me up, Peter. I shouldn't really have asked,
should I?" She struck a naughty little girl pose, and took a
sexual sip of her champagne. "I like you, you know, Peter. I
like a man with a sense of humour."

I glanced at her husband, who was now talking with
Maxwell in low tones at the other side of the room. His
Nixon-blue face looked as full of laughs as an income tax
inspector's. As I looked back at her, she leaned forward to

22

brush some minuscule something or other from the lower part of her black silk dress. I couldn't avoid seeing her breasts for the dress was low cut and she wasn't wearing a bra. I had a feeling her gesture was not so much intended to remove something as to attract something. Me. And I could not deny what I'd seen of her was a little disconcerting. I changed the subject.

"Know everyone here?"

She nodded. "Yes. I know most people around here." I bet she did. "I'll introduce you to the others if you'll promise to come back to me later." She took my hand (her fingers felt icy) and led me over to a grey-haired man who was stubbing his cigar out in a chunky glass ashtray. When he looked up, I was startled to see he was much younger than I thought—mid-thirties, I would guess—and really rather good-looking.

"Peter, may I introduce Jean-Paul Gautier?"

He gave a slight bow and shook my hand. His English accent was so precise, he obeyed the *My Fair Lady* line about over perfection of accent being proof of foreign origin.

"How d'you do, Peter? I saw you come in, looking a little damp from the English rain."

"That's why so many English people are short," I joked. "We shrink in our climate."

"Oh, the weather in Paris," he grinned, "is not much better. You English decry yourselves too much."

"Jean-Paul is a business colleague of my husband's. He heads up the export division of Reinhardt Cosmetics in Paris. My husband, John, as you probably know, is marketing director of the UK side of the company," Lavinia offered, as huskily as ever. I was starting now to see what kind of party it was—mainly a business one. I wondered what Arabella and I were doing there. Leavening the bread?

"The new Lana-Lee perfume, I guess you're excited by its prospects." I couldn't think of anything better to say. Still, Jean-Paul warmed to it.

"Yes, we are, Peter. Advance orders are being taken now—and first signs are extremely healthy. We're lucky to have such a famous name associated with our new perfumery

23

range. It's all due to the persuasive powers of your husband, Lavinia."

Lavinia's eyes flickered for a second. "Oh, John can be persuasive when he wants to be." Jean-Paul took the hint and turned back to me.

"And what do you do, Peter?"

I felt a trifle self-conscious in my reply, but, after all, it is what I actually do all day.

"I'm in toys."

"Manufacture them?" Jean-Paul asked.

"Play with them?" came languorously from you-know-who.

"I buy and sell antique toys. But I'm sort of thinking of going into some very esoteric and small scale manufacturing shortly—strictly for collectors, you understand."

I could see Lavinia's interest in me waning fast, but Jean-Paul soldiered on as if he genuinely wanted to know a bit more.

"Fascinating, Peter. May I ask how you first got into such a rare line of business?"

"I've collected old toys for almost as long as I can remember—anything that took my fancy that was in good condition. Used to be able to pick them up for almost nothing. It's different now."

"That's perhaps because of people like you who make a living from them," Lavinia observed. I could have done without that remark, even if it is the truth.

"But you haven't traded in them all your life?" Jean-Paul went on.

"Oh no. I used to be in advertising. Enjoyed it at first, until I found myself not being able to see the truth about things quite as clearly as I used to. Somehow, the hype over the years began clouding issues—even in my personal life. And the pace of that profession left little time for reflection as to how to cure the problem—or even to see it clearly."

"So you threw it all up?" he asked.

"Yes. Retired into my old toys. They seemed more genuine, somehow." I smiled. "Not regretted it."

"I envy you." Jean-Paul began lighting another cigar from an expensive leather case. Lavinia, needless to say, insisted on holding his match.

"Is that when your marriage broke up?" she husked.

I nodded. "She likes advertising. She's still in it."

"I take it your girlfriend is not in that business, then," she continued.

"No, she is not." And that wasn't me speaking. I spun round in surprise. It was Arabella. I could have kissed her. (It's a habit of mine.)

"This is Arabella. Arabella Trench. Jean-Paul Gautier," I explained.

"Beautiful name, Arabella." Jean-Paul kissed her hand. A gesture I would normally consider OTT, but from him it seemed rather charming. I think Arabella thought so too, by her expression.

"Trench isn't so good," she laughed. "And my middle name is worse."

"What is it?" he asked.

"Donna. God knows what my parents were thinking of."

Lavinia looked non-plussed, but Jean-Paul got the point instantly.

"I see. Ara-belladonna."

"Yes," Arabella grimaced. "Belladonna. That's what I was sometimes called at school."

"Anyway, what do you actually do, Arabella? Are you a model?" (Oooh! Paris must be the world's centre for charm.)

"You're Reinhardt, France, aren't you? John Saunders told me about you at the Lana-Lee perfume press party a little time ago. You see, I'm a reporter on a local paper, the *Western Gazette*. That's how I came to get invited. But thanks for pretending to think I was a model."

"No pretence, I assure you, Arabella."

It was at this point that Lavinia undulated away towards her husband. As I watched her, I saw a flash of white out of the corner of my eye. I spun around, but it was only Lana-Lee's scintillating dress. She had come up on my right and joined us. But it brought back with startling clarity the image I had seen in the dark on my drive back from picking up the boxes. And I made a mental note to tell Arabella about it at the first opportunity.

An hour and three glasses of champagne later, I'd met everybody. And my hair was dry enough not to cause further comment. But I'd still had no chance of a private word with Arabella, for I had become stuck with dear Lavinia's husband, well and truly stuck. Soon after Lana-Lee had introduced me to him, Maxwell had vamoosed to the other side of the room with Lavinia clinging like ivy to his arm. Saunders had obviously decided that I was a perfect audience for a tedious and lengthy lecture on the inadequacies of British marketing methods, and the lack of creativity in British advertising compared with the French. But, at least, it stopped him asking what I did for some sort of living. When I could, at last, get a word in edgewise, I innocently asked how the Lana-Lee perfume deal had come about.

"Luck, Peter. Pure luck. Lana-Lee came over to England to get away from Hollywood, at just the time Reinhardt were considering the development of a new perfume range. And the idea suddenly occurred to me. I got in touch with Jean-Paul in Paris, and the deal was done very quickly. She's a lovely lady to do business with. And so is her husband."

I expressed surprise. "I didn't know Ben Maxwell was involved at all."

Saunders looked a little uncertain for a second, but recovered instantly. There's your trained executive for you.

"He's not, in the way Lana-Lee is. You see, I've known Ben for some years. We met through motor racing. As you know, he was one of the few American drivers to be successful in European Formula One. I came across him first at the Monte Carlo Grand Prix. We found we had the same kinds of interests so we kept in touch over the years. After his retirement from actual competition, three years or so back, he took up motor racing commentating for an American network, and was often in Europe. When that contract terminated, I lost touch with him for a short time, until I signed up Lana-Lee for the new perfume range. It was pure coincidence he was her husband, you know."

"Remarkable," I managed to chip in. "But they were separated for quite a time, weren't they?" I continued, keeping my voice down.

"Yes. Amazing how they seem reconciled again."

"Amazing," I agreed. "Unbelievable" was my thought. I just could not conceive that Lana-Lee would go for such a character in the first place, let alone in the second place. But lo and behold, she had.

"Do you think they got together again for their daughter's sake?"

"For Tara-Lee? Could be. Whatever the reason, I'm glad they did. I use Ben as a kind of sounding board for new ideas. I like him around."

Even more unbelievable. Ben looked about as creative as the proverbial brick gentleman's room, but, I reckoned, he might have hidden shallows, who knew?

I took another caviare canapé from a silver tray, but this one exploded in my hand as I raised it to my mouth. Puff pastry and I have never got on particularly well. The butler came to my aid, as if his only purpose in life was just such a moment. Perhaps it was.

As I looked up from picking a crumb out of my cummerbund, I caught a glimpse of Lavinia and Maxwell over by the huge mullioned windows. She was so close to him, they looked like one black-draped figure. But her eyes spoke of anger, and her rather large mouth was set in that thin horizontal hold that always suggests the transmission of venom. I wondered what Maxwell had said to trigger such a change of mood. I glanced at Saunders, but his eyes were desiringly fixed on Lana-Lee, who was now with Arabella by the fireplace.

"Shall we join the ladies?" I said quickly.

Saunders' thin, blue face broke into a smile. "Why not?"

As we walked across to them, I felt a certain sympathy for the Reinhardt director, even though I couldn't say I was mad keen on him. For living with Lavinia was obviously no bed of roses (bed, yes; roses no), and I guessed that it didn't help that he was about ten years older than her seeming thirty or so summers.

"Ah, Peter, you can now tell me all about your interest in toys," Lana-Lee smiled. "I'd really like to know."

"How many hours can you spare?" Arabella asked. "You don't know what you're letting yourself in for."

I put my arm around Arabella's shoulders. "Don't worry, my sweet, I'll restrict myself to the Reader's Digest condensed version of my obsession."

Lana-Lee raised her glass to her generous mouth, as if in a toast.

"Here's to your story. I'm genuinely interested."

But, as she finished speaking, her expression froze, as I heard the sound of a door being thrust open, followed by the cacophony of voices raised in anger. I looked around to see the butler obviously attempting to stop someone bursting into the room. But that someone was a giant of a man compared to the frailty of the retainer, and quickly disengaged himself and shambled forward with that awkward gait that shouted many over the eight.

"Where's that bloody Maxwell?" the intruder yelled, his eyes scanning the assembled company as if through a haze. I guessed he must have come straight from some riotous party of his own, for he was dressed fairly formally, but his tie was loose and his shirt collar unbuttoned. He lumbered forward, then spotted his quarry. Lavinia moved away from Maxwell with the slinky speed of a rattler, and I didn't blame her. The newcomer had the build and the belligerence of someone who plays rugby in preference to chess, and referee-ruffling rugby at that.

I looked round at Lana-Lee, but she had moved. Arabella clung tightly to my arm.

"There you are, you bastard," the intruder bellowed, and I turned back in his direction. The white figure of Lana=Lee was moving rapidly towards him, but the Frenchman intervened.

"No, it's all right, Jean-Paul," the actress said quietly, in a surprisingly calm voice, and moved his arm aside. "I'll deal with this."

"No, it's not goddamned all right." I heard Maxwell's Texan drawl. "Get out of here, Longhurst. You're high as a kite. Go back to your cowsheds and sleep it off."

By now Lana-Lee was by the intruder's side. I made to move forward, but Arabella held me back.

"Don't," she whispered. "It's not our business."

"Ben, keep out of this." Lana-Lee took the big man's arm. "Adam, go home. Please go home. For Christ's sake, don't do anything we'll all regret."

He jerked his arm free, and began moving unsteadily towards Maxwell, who was standing his ground.

"Why the hell do you put up with him, Lana?" the big man countered, with sadness rather than anger in his voice. "He's a bum. He's always been a bum. A two-timing, three-timing, four-timing bum."

Jean-Paul and Saunders moved quickly between Maxwell and the man, who I now knew was called Adam Longhurst.

"Get out of here now, Longhurst, or I'll call the police," Maxwell shouted back.

"Not before I've finished with you, you won't," Longhurst bellowed, and tried to bulldoze his way between the Frenchman and Saunders.

"Who was that bloody woman you had in your car, when I saw you lunchtime, Maxwell?" he continued shouting, as he struggled so violently with the two men that Saunders was knocked sideways into an antique table, which shed its canapés and champagne glasses to disintegrate on the floor.

It was at that point that I ignored Arabella's advice and moved forward into the fray. For by now, Longhurst had managed to grab Maxwell by the neck, and the one thing I do dislike at parties is murder.

As I arrived, Jean-Paul jumped on to Longhurst's back, and clung like an ape to its mother. I pulled Saunders up from the broken glass that was like gravel under my feet, and indicated to him to go round Maxwell's side, to the right, whilst I went to the left. Meanwhile, Longhurst, amongst burps, was still bellowing.

"You take your lousy prick back to America, Maxwell, or I'll end up breaking every bone in your body. You're ruining everybody's life while you're here."

Gurgles were all his throttling hands were allowing by way of his adversary's reply. I tried prizing his left hand from around Maxwell's neck, whilst Saunders worked on the right. Suddenly, Longhurst relaxed his grip my side, and I was just about to congratulate myself, when something at least as rock solid as a sledge-hammer struck me in the face and I went reeling backwards into somebody's arms, my vision, for a few seconds, approximating a fairly exciting evening at a planetarium. By the time I had pulled what was left of me together, I found that I was lying on top of something soft, distinctly tremulous and silky. It was Lavinia. I mumbled something or other, and we helped each other to our feet. By the time I looked back at Longhurst, the crisis had mercifully passed its peak, as he was now piniomed from behind by Saunders and Jean-Paul, after Maxwell (as I was told later) had managed to knee him in the groin, whilst Longhurst was recovering from sledge-hammering me. Conquered physically, he may now have been, but his threats boomed on. Suffice it to say, all of them centred around Maxwell's parentage and the different kinds of gruesome ends he would come to if he did not get out of England and leave Lana-Lee alone.

Suddenly, Arabella came up to me leading Lana-Lee by the hand. I could see that out of my now only one good eye.

"My God, you need a raw steak," Arabella whispered, and inspected my rapidly closing left eye. I grinned weakly.

"No, I don't feel like eating right now, thanks."

"Shut up and listen," Arabella responded kindly. "Can you see well enough to drive? I'll see to your eye when you come back. Promise."

I could just spot Lana-Lee shaking her head and pulling at Arabella's hand. I squinted. It hurt.

"More or less. As long as it's not a rally, I guess. Why?"

I looked across at Longhurst, because suddenly the room seemed cathedral quiet as his bellowing died away. I wondered if Maxwell had bopped him one, but apparently, it proved to be just the drink winning its own fight.

"To save the whole world knowing what has happened here tonight, could you drive him quietly home?"

"Him?" I pointed, slightly incredulous.

"Him." Arabella whispered, "Lana-Lee was going to get a taxi, as she doesn't want to bother the boys from Reinhardt with a personal affair like this. And I'm afraid I offered your services just in case he started up all over again in front of the cab-driver."

I gazed at Longhurst who had been propped up in an armchair. He now looked more like an overgrown baby than a bull. But, notwithstanding, he would still tip the wicker basket at close on fifteen stone, and reach at least six feet two inches against the nursery door. And who knew when he'd pummel his little fists again?

"Supposing he starts up once more with me?" I asked, wincing from the pain in my steakless eye.

Lana-Lee came close. "He won't. I know him," she said quietly. "He's like a lamb, normally. I don't know what got into him tonight. But please, let me ring for a cab and. . . ."

Arabella gave me one of her looks.

"No, no. I won't hear of it. If you say he's normally like a lamb. . . ."

"You'll take him back to his farm," Arabella smiled, and gripped my arm gratefully. "Like me to come with you?"

"Did Longhurst come in a car?"

"I don't know. I'll see." Lana-Lee went to the window and drew back the curtains.

"His Range Rover is outside."

"Then if you tell me where he lives, I'll drive him home in that. And Arabella can follow behind in my Beetle."

"I'll be eternally grateful to you, Peter," Lana-Lee's voice was starting to break and I could see moisture welling in her eyes.

"His farm's not far. About two miles back towards Weymouth. Over on the right-hand side. There are two big, white five-bar gates, and a sign 'Maranello Farm.' His housekeeper, Maud Evans, should be there."

The penny suddenly dropped. "Strewth, he's not *the* Longhurst, is he? The famous flying farmer, the Ferrari enthusiast with the thousand acres?"

Lana-Lee nodded. "I'm afraid so. Does it make a difference?"

"No, no," I lied, "not a bit." I looked at Arabella. "We'd better be going."

We moved over to the now gently swaying figure of Longhurst. Through the moist and blurred vision of my bad eye, the white of Lana-Lee's dress seemed to flare and then fade. Instantly, my mind, yet again, went back to that rain-swept road and the apparition that had disturbed my return from the Minic lady's house.

Three

It wasn't until the next morning that the reality of the events of the night before came through to me. At the time, they seemed somehow dreamlike, or scenes from some film or other, especially the eerie flash of white I had spotted on the rainy road, which Arabella explained away as probably a sheet of old newspaper blowing about in the wind. Later, maybe it was the champagne or the magnificent setting of the Manor, or just being in the presence of a famous movie star, who knows? Even the drive up to Longhurst's laughingly-called farm seemed to add to the sense of fantasy, the headlights of the special six-wheeled Wood and Picket Range Rover picking out the statuary (I counted five Greek-style naked figures. Arabella counted six.) in the manicured grounds immediately surrounding a huge cream thirties-style house, that rambled in sweeping curves and Crittal windows from one wing to another. The whole juxtaposition of styles unnerved me, and I was glad to see a shaft of light emanating from an open front door, as I swung to a halt. The housekeeper had obviously heard the cornflake crunch of my tyres on the raked gravel of the drive. Before I could open the walnut-silled door to help Longhurst out of the back, she had done it for me.

"Thank God he's back. He worries me to death when he goes out again in that state. Shouldn't drive, he shouldn't, like that. . . ."

By this time, Arabella had joined us, and we three manoeuvred Longhurst out of the exotic Range Rover, and supported him into his even more exotic Art Deco palace, that looked as if it had escaped from Bournemouth. Certainly the frail figure of the housekeeper could never have managed on her own.

We offered to help him up to his bedroom, but both he and his housekeeper, Mrs Evans, maintained Arabella and I had done more than enough already. So we helped him into a drawing-room that really blew my and Arabella's minds. It was huge and pure Hollywood, circa 1936. You expected Fred Astaire and Ginger Rogers to waft in from the French windows at any second. Practically everything in the room was cream, when it wasn't heavily figured walnut, and even the latter was often inlaid with horizontal bands of creamish wood, like sycamore. Arabella, with her Beatrice Lillie short hair and black dinner jacket, seemed splendidly in period.

As we made to leave this unlikely farmer, he beckoned us back to his chair and said very quietly, now without trace of a slur, "Can't thank you now. Not properly. Bit under the weather, you understand. Do apologize."

I waved my hand in a "think nothing of it" way.

He held his own up. "No. Will thank you and your super lady one day. Sure Lana-Lee will too. You'll see."

As he mentioned her name, his face tightened, and I thought for a second, the lamb might be metamorphosising once more. But no. I think he'd had enough for one night.

"Sorry. Just that bum Maxwell, you see. Lana-Lee and I were going to"—his voice trailed away—"before he came back. Can't understand it. Ruined everything." He looked up and gave a weak smile. There was a tear in his eye. "Anyway, thanks again for helping an idiot like me."

I shook his proffered hand, and winced slightly. Drink had certainly not weakened his shake. He looked up at Arabella. She leaned over automatically, and kissed his cheek. A stranger he might be, but he was that kind of man.

Business, as usual, was slack so I sat back in my chair, and, whilst waiting for a customer or two, read, as well as one can with a severely swollen eye, the previous day's local paper that I had not managed to get around to before. I soon regretted it; the local news seemed to be amazingly down-beat. The worst horror was that yet another child had been abducted and molested; she'd been found wandering on Chesil Beach. This totted up to three such appalling cases in the last four months. The police admitted that they were, as yet, without any significant clues as to the maniac who, in Inspector Digby Whetstone's less than tactful words, was "not only terrorizing our children, but prejudicing the Dorset tourist trade into the bargain."

The lesser items of news were hardly of help. There were strong rumours of an escalation in the rates, fears that a proposed oil drilling exercise might destroy thousands of acres of nature reserve, and, even coming down to the itty-bitty of our own modest village of Studland, I read that the mother of one of the guys who sells tickets for the Sand-banks Ferry had been killed by a poisonous spider, which had been hiding in the loo of a house in Sydney, Australia, whither she had gone to visit her daughter.

However, I suppose the local news did help put the events of the previous evening into clearer perspective, for it made the trials, tribulations and jealousies of the ultra rich brigade seem definitely shallow and unimportant, like spoiled kids fighting over a toy, or nursing a grudge about something simply to add a little spice and pace to their indolent days. I decided, in the end, it was all too Scott Fitzgerald for me to worry over, although I was still peeved about my black and swollen eye. So I turned my attention to laboriously addressing eighty-seven envelopes for the photostatted information that Arabella will insist on calling my monthlies, which I send out each month to known collectors and previous customers, updating them on my current stock of vintage toys. I do quite a bit of business through mail order, as do, unfortunately, a lot of my competitors.

Then, as there was still neither hide nor hair of a customer, I sat back and brewed on my Flamingo project. Within minutes, I realized brewing was no substitute for action, so I let my fingers do the walking through the Yellow Pages until I came to a listing of local packaging firms. I started phoning, outlining my project but *not* revealing the actual aircraft I was to make. Two phone calls elicited two separate polite refusals on the grounds that my order for boxes would be too small and irregular for them to consider, but the third call seemed quite promising, as the managing director was ex-RAF, and constructed and flew petrol-driven model aircraft as a hobby. I made an appointment to see him on the following Monday. Just as I was congratulating myself on having found a likely source for my packaging, the doorbell dinged. Bing woke up. I looked towards the door, expecting (as was my wont) to see a customer who would buy everything in my shop, thus breaking my rather pathetic trading pattern of late. But no, it was not to be. I looked into the big eyes in the big head of that big man again—Adam Longhurst.

"Hope you don't mind. I rang Lana-Lee. Got your address." He gave a self-conscious smile, and stayed by the door, as if I were somebody of whom to be afraid.

"No, I don't mind, Mr Longhurst. Come on in and shut the door."

He did just that. I came out from behind the counter. In a curious way he seemed different from the night before. And I don't just mean because he was no longer drunk or that it was day rather than night. I don't know what it was quite. He sort of seemed like his own twin brother. I guess it had something to do with a certain schoolboy (public type) charm, that his bull-in-a-china-shop behaviour of the night before had totally obscured.

"I say, you've got an awful lot of stuff, haven't you?" He looked around the place. "Suppose it's no good having a shop, if you haven't." He grinned, and went over to a glass cabinet that housed some of the more precious of the old Dinky toys I had for sale, minimum price twenty-five pounds for something like an Austin Atlantic, mint and boxed, up to two hundred and more pounds for rare vans, both pre- and post-war, with near mint paintwork and transfers. He pointed at a Jaguar XK 120 coupé. "I had one of those when I was a kid."

"A toy or a real one?" I joked.

"Well, I've had both, actually. Toy when a kid, car when a teenager." (Teach me to joke with a stranger.) He turned back to me and cleared his throat.

"Didn't really come here to look at your wonderful shop, though. Came to thank you. You and your lovely friend, that is." He blushed. I could see it clearly, even though his face was a little florid.

"Forget it," I said. "It didn't take a minute. Wasn't really out of our way."

"No, I'm very grateful." He indicated my puffy eye. "And I'm very sorry. I gather I lashed out at you. Unforgivable. Been carousing in a pub and drunk far too much, far too quickly. Got to thinking. Next thing I knew I was at the Manor, and—well, you know the rest. I really am sorry. I'm truly ashamed of myself."

"Happens to all of us," I exaggerated.

"Nice of you to take it so well. Millions wouldn't have."

"Don't know them. Are they nice people?" I quipped to change the subject.

"Love Mrs Million, hate him," he smiled. And I could see what Lana-Lee must have seen in him—before Maxwell's return, that is. He was a little boy in a big man's suit. And a rich little boy to boot. I knew enough about him by reputation. I guess most people in Dorset did. He had inherited the thousand-acre farm from his father, who had been a breeder of the most pukkah Friesians (I think that was the breed) in the whole world. At the time, Adam, I believe, had still been in the army. On his father's death, he left military service, and took over the running of the farm. Well, I use that verb "running" a little loosely, as local gossip maintained Longhurst contributed little himself, leaving all farm affairs to his manager. He apparently preferred racing around the countryside in one or other of his collection of fancy cars—Maseratis and Lambos, that kind of self-effacing machinery. That's why he had renamed the farm Maranello—the home base of Ferrari. (The six-wheeled Range Rover, even with all the trimmings, was a bit of a disappointment to me that night for, once I had realized who Longhurst was, I expected to be driving him home in at least an Espada or, given four doors, the Italian Quattroporte variety. Hey-ho.) He had also lashed out on flying lessons, and had bought himself the very latest in light aircraft—the revolutionary American Rutan, one of the very few in this country, with its distinctive shape, sort of tail first and looks back to front. It was when he bought that, I first read about him in the *Western Gazette*. Locally, Longhurst was, as the media would have it, rather "high profile."

"Like a coffee?" I offered, as Bing stretched himself on a Chrysler box and immediately fell off both box and counter in a teeth-tingling cacophony of vainly clinging claws. The counter was covered in such scratch marks. Bing is no easy learner.

"Yes, thank you," Longhurst smiled. "That would be nice."

"Then I'll push back all the crowding customers and shut up shop for a while," I grinned back, and, after locking the shop door, led him into my back sitting-room. And so began a relationship with a man I was to come to know so desperately well over the next few weeks.

To cut a long story short, coffee soon led to the hair of the dog, I'm afraid. Not a whole coat, but quite a few hairs—enough for Longhurst to reveal quite a bit of his soul, or, certainly, that part that now belonged to the gorgeous Lana-Lee. After a while, all I needed to do was listen, and pull the odd tab on a Heineken. His story proved to be very much what you'd imagine from his conduct of the previous night. He claimed that soon after Lana-Lee had come over to England and bought the Manor, he had been introduced to her by a mutual friend. They had got on like a house on fire, and had eventually, I gathered, become intimate friends and then lovers. They had got to the point of discussing marriage, when Maxwell suddenly re-appeared out of the blue.

Longhurst had assumed she would send him packing instantly, but instead, Lana-Lee had allowed Maxwell to move in with her, an action that Longhurst not only found totally unacceptable but wholly inexplicable, for he was certain that she still hated her ex-husband, and had no wish at all to have him around, let alone living in the same house. He had tackled her constantly about her behaviour, and could get very little sense out of her. When he heard that Maxwell had begun fooling round with other women, he informed Lana-Lee, but she had shrugged it off as something Maxwell had indulged in for nearly the whole period of their marriage. So you can imagine, as the weeks dragged on, Longhurst had become more and more incensed about the whole rotten scene, until, triggered by seeing some unidentified woman in Maxwell's Cadillac at lunchtime that day, he had drunk himself into a raging bull in a pub near Wool, and . . . the rest you know.

"The hell is, Peter, I'm in no position to castigate Maxwell really. I was about as faithful in my short-lived marriage as a jack-rabbit. And I've got a bit of a reputation, I'm afraid, for changing partners at the drop of a hat. But all that has changed since Lana-Lee. I know she's what I need. I love her. I love her like I have never loved anyone before. Hell, I'm forty now; it's time for me to settle down a bit. And meeting Lana-Lee was the trigger I needed. Her timing was impeccable."

"The mark of a good actress," I said, then realized the remark could be taken the wrong way. "I don't mean she's acting with you, Adam. Far from it, from the sounds of things."

"But you're right. She might be, mightn't she?" He looked now like a little boy lost. "Playing being in love, rather than feeling it. Might explain things a bit."

"Don't think she is. From her concern for you last night, I think her feelings are genuine enough. She doesn't strike me as a twenty-four-hour actress type. Far from it."

"So can you explain her behaviour? Having such an odious man as Maxwell back?"

"No, I can't. But it sounds much more like a woman with problems we don't yet know about, than anything else."

"Such as? I've wracked my brains to think of something—anything."

"Lord knows. Something in her past, that happened in Hollywood, maybe. I know so little about her. All I've seen are her old films on television."

Longhurst drained the dregs of his beer, glanced at his watch, then looked at me apologetically.

"Look, it's almost lunchtime already. I've taken up all your morning, drinking your beer, and boring you with all my problems, when I only came just to thank you and your beautiful friend for last night."

"Don't apologize. I've enjoyed talking to you. It's a bit lonely, sometimes, this old toy business."

"I guess it must be. Everything, I guess, has its down side, its own problems."

"Toys don't have too many, luckily," I smiled. "And at the moment, my major problem is of my own making."

"What's that?" he asked, with seemingly genuine interest. So I told him, all about my Flamingo project, and that I had just put the phone down on a possible box manufacturer, when he'd called at the shop.

"So what's the problem?"

"Finding a first-rate model maker to make the original brass master. I'd rather not put an advert in the *Western Gazette*— don't want to alert potential competition."

Longhurst did not comment right away, and I thought, for a second, I was boring him and his mind had reverted to Lana-Lee. But no such thing.

"Think, curiously, I might know of such a fellow."

I looked up. "They're a bit thin on the ground, you know."

"I suppose they must be. But about two months ago, I advertised a cottage on my estate for letting on a three-year lease, renewable. Curiously, had few replies, probably because of the shortness of the lease, which I drafted in case I needed the cottage at any time for one of my workers. Anyway, in the end, I let it to a very quiet and respectable couple. The husband is ex-army on a pension. He was invalided out. They were quite happy with a short lease, as they were moving from Buckinghamshire or somewhere near London, and wanted to see if country life and the sea suited them before investing in a house of their own. Name of Muir. Mr and Mrs Muir."

"Is he the model maker or is it his wife?"

Longhurst laughed. "No, his wife's a rather dour lady. Full of good works, I gather, WI and so on, and a great church goer, but I don't see her whittling away at lumps of metal. No, he's the one. Used to do it in the army when he was off duty and bored. The cottage is now full of the stuff he's made. Mainly figures, soldiers, angels and the like. But there are also some tanks and military vehicles, Chieftains, Saracens, that kind of thing."

"Are they good?"

"Look that way to me. Not big on the angels and the religious stuff myself, but the other figures and the army items seem first-class."

"Natural ability, I suppose, aided and abetted by lots of time on his hands."

"Like prisoners make huge galleons out of matchsticks."

"Yeah," I smiled. "Suppose so."

"I gather his father used to work in some toy factory doing the same kind of thing. So I suppose the talent runs in the family."

I leant forward, and offered him another Heineken. If this Muir fellow turned out to be all he cracked him up to be, Longhurst was worth every beer I could offer. But he put up his hand.

"No more for me, thanks. I ought to be going." He unfolded his large frame from the chintz of my chair, and towered above me. The Heineken seemed to have added inches to his height. I got up myself, and stood by him. I am five feet ten inches, but, as the sports writers would phrase it, I was giving him at least five inches in height. (And about the same in chest measurement, I wouldn't wonder.)

"Anyway, would you like to meet him?" he asked. "Then

41

you could see if the quality of his work is up to the kind of standard you require."

"That would be a great help."

"Well, I'll have a word with him. Perhaps get him to ring you." He began walking back towards the shop.

"Have you got a card?"

I stopped by the counter and gave him a Toy Emporium one.

"Better warn you, though," he added. "Muir's not a million laughs. He's almost as quiet as his wife."

"Doesn't matter." I saw him to the door. "Does he have a regular job? I mean, I assume he has an army pension, but he probably works as well, doesn't he?"

Longhurst nodded. "Yes. But he's freelance and works from home."

"What's he do?"

"Like you. What was once his hobby has now become his business. That's why I suggested him. He makes brass masters and sometimes one-off finished models for firms who market all that polished brass stuff you see in shop windows and specialist brass shops. You know, bucking horses that get used as doorstops, fancy door knockers, brass models of dogs and animals, eagles alighting on eeries, eagles for pulpits, angels, Christ on the cross, and so on. Keeps pretty busy, I hear. Still, I dare say he might find your Flamingo project quite a welcome change. Let me know how you get on."

He shook my hand vigorously, and I winced once more. And soon he was gone, the six special wheels of his Range Rover flicking the loose gravel on the road outside. I went back and sat down behind the counter once again. Bing jumped up on to my lap to remind me it was lunchtime. But I didn't take his hint right away, but just sat contentedly there, toying with the odd thought that one man's problems can, on occasion, go to provide another man's solutions.

I stayed open until four o'clock that afternoon, but only had one customer. Still, he did at least buy something. (A lot of

42

old toy buffs just haunt shops like mine to gawp, touch and compare, but seldom shell out for a purchase.) And seemed thrilled with his seventy-pound find—one of Gus's Ford Minics, mint and boxed. As Arabella, I knew, would not be back until around 7.30 p.m., I decided to stroll round to Gus's cottage, and regale him with an account of the events of the night before. Gus loves a bit of gossip.

Bing seemed to sense where I was going, for he began swearing at me in downtown Siamese as I made for the front door. So there was nothing for it but to attach a lead to his collar and take him with me. He loves going to Gus's, I guess, for the extra variety of smells around the place, from today's fish to yesterday's goodness knows what.

But when I arrived at Gus's cottage, no amount of banging on his knocker would raise him. As I was about to leave, I heard a regular swishing noise start up in the garden. I use the word "garden" rather loosely. You remember Brer Rabbit and the briar patch? Well, forget the rabbit. Just conjure up a briar patch, add some long, straggly grass, some bits of old agricultural and marine equipment rusting out of banks of stinging nettles, and two dilapidated sheds—one of which houses my old 1966 Daimler v8 that I am always intending to restore, the other the remains of a clinker-built boat that hasn't felt the brine since Gus was eighteen—and you have the complete picture. Still, there's no place like home. And certainly no place like Gus's home.

"You're late," Gus grumbled, and stopped what he was doing, which was beating an armchair with a stick.

"What do you mean, I'm late?" I remonstrated. "I didn't say I was coming at all."

Gus gave the chair another enormous whack, and dust flew out like smoke from a fire. Gus has cleaning spells, when he washes up, sweeps what's left of his carpets, cleans the cottage windows so that you can just see out, and puts his three piece "Utility Mark" suite in the garden to beat it to death. I'd obviously interrupted one of these fits.

"Expected you hours ago, I did. Had the beers on the table."

"Don't talk to me of beers," I grimaced.

"Went ahead without me?" Gus grinned, as he resumed his furniture flagellation.

"Had an unexpected visitor," I coughed through the dust clouds. "Otherwise, I might have been over sooner."

"Been itching to hear all about your film star woman's do last night. Who was the visitor who delayed you? The same one who poked you in the eye?"

"Longhurst."

Gus scratched his head, then asked, "Which Longhurst? The pop-eyed verger over in Swanage, the one whose sister got arrested the other day for soliciting sailors down at Portland?"

I shook my head, and I'll swear dust came out of my hair.

"Can't mean the other one, can you? That show-off, who races round the place in fancy cars with unpronounceable names. And who, I've heard, has turned his poor old dad's house inside out, so that it now looks like a toff's brothel. Given it a poncey Italian name too—Muddy Yellow, or something."

"Maranello," I corrected him, "home of Ferrari cars."

"Silly bloody name. His dad's was much better— Wideacres Farm. Still, what do you expect from a guy who was cashiered from the army, and chases everything in or out of a skirt for a living?"

I sat down in one of Gus's armchairs, and Bing leapt on to my lap. Gus raised his arm once more.

"Hang on, Gus, put that stick down. Tell me a bit about Longhurst—and I don't mean the one with the jolly jack tar sister."

Gus subsided on to the settee. I don't know which gave out the most dust, he or the furniture.

"What's he been visiting the likes of you for?"

I ignored the put-down and told him the whole story of our stormy night adventures, and Longhurst's morning apologies.

Gus did not comment for a while, then turned to me. "Lavinia whowasit?" he asked.

44

"Saunders. Lavinia Saunders."

"Yeah." Gus subsided into silence, his left hand idly playing with a rampant stinging nettle as if it were a dock leaf.

After a while, I couldn't stand it any longer. "Come off it, Gus. You can't ask 'Lavinia whowasit?', get the answer and then say 'Yeah.' You know something, don't you?"

"Maybe I do. Maybe I don't. 'Tis only rumour, after all."

"Okay. What rumour?"

"Well, did you notice anything between Longhurst and that Lavinia whatsherface?"

"Hardly," I laughed. "He was flailing about, shouting the house down, and everyone else was trying to stop him murdering Maxwell. That's how I got my shiner. But why do you ask?"

"They do say that Longhurst had a girlfriend called Lavinia, once. Year or two back now, I suppose. Married woman, she was supposed to be. Remember her name because it's not an everyday one, is it? Would have forgotten a Maud or a Mabel, a Dulcie or a Doris, wouldn't I?"

I forbore reminding Gus that these were hardly everyday names nowadays. Sometimes I think to Gus time stopped somewhere around 1928.

"Likes married women, does Longhurst, by all accounts. Means he doesn't have to marry them. Must be their attraction."

I then suddenly remembered the other little germ of information Gus had let slip, when I'd first mentioned Longhurst's name.

"Never mind his women for a minute, Gus. What was that about him being *cashiered* from the army? I assumed he had resigned his commission when his father first became ill, and he was needed back on the farm."

"Don't you believe it," Gus retorted, and exchanged a stinging nettle for a thistle. His huge hands make saddle leather seem sensitive by comparison. "Cashiered, he was. Striking an officer. Something like that, so I heard at the time. All hushed up, of course. His dad's money saw to that.

I got the wink from a corporal I used to know at Bovington Camp. Swore me to secrecy, of course."

"Of course," I smiled. Gus broke off the thistle and began smelling the few fading purple blooms at its lethal tips. "Not much control over his temper, it would seem, our Adam Longhurst," I remarked, waiting for the scream.

"Not much control over his willie, either," Gus guffawed, "from the stories going round of his love-life. I wonder if that Lana-Lee, who he claims loves him, knows a ha'p'orth of his goings on. Or doesn't it matter in show-business, where they're probably all at it, anyway?"

"No, I don't think she is. I told you, Gus, she seems a genuinely nice person. Quiet, if anything. Not the brassy type you're thinking of at all."

"Her husband, that Maxwell, he's a bad lot, isn't he? Maybe she's one of those women who go for the smell of bad eggs. Wouldn't be the first time. Now remember that Lady Whatsit, who used to live the other side of Corfe—her whose husband got killed later in the War. . . ."

I leaned across and put a hand on Gus's shoulder.

"Gus. Before you go on, I'll tell you now, I don't."

"How d'you know yet? I haven't got to the bit. . . ."

"Gus, don't bother. I wasn't even born till after the War."

Gus looked at me hard, as if I were suddenly a stranger.

"Yeah. 'Course. Forgotten that," he said slowly, then sniffed. Bing looked up, ears cocked. Gus's sniffs are like that. You can't miss them, unless you're using a pneumatic drill at the time. "Well, anyway," he went on, "does no harm knowing someone like Longhurst, especially if he owes you one. Money talks, you know. Get him to buy something big and expensive from your shop, did you?"

I sat a little straighter in my armchair. "No, Gus, I did not. I don't expect returns for favours, however rich the person involved."

Gus pursed his lips like a doubting Thomas. "Like that beer now?" he asked.

I made a show of looking at my watch.

Gus laughed like a drain. "Sums you up, that little gesture does."

"What do you mean?" I asked, a mite tetchily.

"Sometimes, old dear, you just don't know the bloody time of day."

Four

As I rolled back to my modest Toy Emporium and my equally modest living accommodation above and beside it, I was in no fit state to really appreciate what met my eyes on arrival. For there seemed to be some kind of flower festival in progress outside my front door, with Arabella's head peeking out between banks of profligate blooms. I went up to her, as she bent down to forage amongst the stems.

"Hi," I said. "What are you doing?"

"Looking for a card," she mumbled.

"Needn't bother." I grinned to myself as my mind suddenly snapped back into crystal-clear focus. Arabella stood up, holding two of the huge cellophane-covered bouquets. (There were at least ten others.) Her beautiful face bore a puzzled and incredulous expression.

"Can't be from you. Tell me it can't be you. . . ."

"Nope," I replied, "ain't me."

"Then who is it? Maybe they've delivered to the wrong place. I just found all this here when I got back tonight."

"They're from the man you kissed last night."

"You said it wasn't you," she immediately countered.

"It was the other man you kissed. Cast your mind back."

"I didn't kiss any . . ." She stopped abruptly. "Oh yes I did. It's Longhurst, isn't it? But how did you know?"

"He called this morning to thank me. Obviously the flowers are to thank you."

She pointed to the banks of bouquets propped up against the shop window. "*This* much thanks?"

"He's that kind of fellow. Lives life oTT all the time. Gus

has been telling me some more about Dorset's raging bull." I bent down and began picking up more of the bouquets. "Let's get this Interflora benefit night stuff in and I'll tell you all about it."

She looked at me. "What are we going to do with all this indoors? We haven't got enough vases by a million miles."

I laughed. "Screw the vases, my darling. We haven't got enough rooms."

I could hardly sleep that night, the aroma was so compelling. Still, the flowers did provide an incredibly romantic setting for our love-making, although Arabella did remark self-consciously at one point that she felt the other visitors to Kew Gardens must be watching us. I said, "Let 'em. Flowers do it. Birds and bees do it . . . etcetera."

At breakfast, we had to put some of the smaller blooms in the sink, whilst we used the teapot for its original purpose. And, of course, all this time, we couldn't help talking about their provider, Longhurst.

"Do you think he really cares about Lana-Lee?" Arabella asked after a while.

I nodded. "Yes. I think he does. I don't think he hates Maxwell because he's Maxwell. It's only because Maxwell has come between him and her."

"Maybe Longhurst has got so much in life that the only thing that turns him on is something he can't get any more. Happens, you know."

"Could be. But I don't think so." I poured myself another cup of tea from the vase. "Anyway, one good thing has come out of it for us." Arabella laughed and pointed round the room. "I don't mean the flowers, you idiot. I mean the introduction to a possible model maker for the Flamingo."

"Mr Marklin?" Bony fingers extended towards me. I shook them rather carefully. "I saw you coming up the path on the very stroke of four. A man after my own heart," his reedy voice continued.

It was the following afternoon, and I had found Muir's

small cottage deep in Longhurst's estate without any trouble at all, his directions, when he'd rung me earlier, proving impeccable. I was ushered into a low, dark hall, then into a room on the right. I saw the low beam over the door just in time, and ducked my head.

"Oh, I'm so sorry. Should have warned you. I've grown so used to it, I forget." I looked up again and saw Muir clearly for the first time. He was a slight and wiry man, with a balding head that looked a little too large to be in scale. Had he not lived in the heart of the countryside, I would have put him down as the kind of man who ends his days as chief clerk of a small bank, but never the manager. Even his clothing added to that suburban impression: a self-effacing grey suit, white shirt a little worn round the collar, and the kind of tie you normally leave hanging on the wardrobe rack. His eyes were his only unusual feature, for not only were they rather startlingly close together, but seemed in a permanent state of intense concentration and inspection—the latter phenomenon becoming the more off-putting the longer one spent in his company.

"Please sit down, Mr Marklin." I saw I was in a modest but pleasant sitting-room, whose furniture echoed suburban gentility rather than rural simplicity or cottage charm. But everything smelt or shone, or both, from polish, and the very neatness of the room would, no doubt, be seen as a virtue by some. I felt a trifle self-conscious sitting down in case I rumpled anything.

"It's good of you to see me so quickly," I said. "I only mentioned this problem of mine to Mr Longhurst the day before yesterday."

Muir sat down opposite me on a small hardback chair. I wondered why he didn't choose the settee bang next to it.

"Not good of me at all, Mr Marklin; sensible of me." He smiled, but his eyes didn't. "It's my living, you see, making prototype models—masters, if you like—so directly Mr Longhurst acquainted me with your need, I naturally got in touch."

I sat corrected.

He continued, "Something to do with a brass master for simple die-cast construction, I believe. Is that not so, Mr Marklin?"

"That is indeed so," I replied, amazed at my stilted reply. Somehow, Muir brought out the formal in one. "I'm planning to make a 1/200th scale metal aircraft model. Pre-war air liner."

Muir leant forward in his chair, and rubbed his thin hands together.

"Haven't made many aircraft, I must admit, Mr Marklin. Only one, in fact, for an old man I once knew. A Puss Moth in 1/72nd scale, I remember. Had difficulty with the wing struts, where they joined the fuselage."

I smiled. "If you can make a Puss Moth, you can make a Flamingo. It's just a one-piece casting, other than the propellers and wheels, which I can buy finished."

Muir's gaze, thankfully, left me for a moment, as he reflected. "Flamingo—now the name rings a bell. De Havilland, wasn't it? Ah, it's coming back to me. I had an aunt who lived in Jersey until after the War. Years ago she showed me snapshots of a Flamingo. I'm sure she said it was a Flamingo. She flew to England in it once, that's why she had taken the picture. Does that sound feasible?"

"Totally," I replied. "It was used on the Channel Islands route immediately prior to the War. You must have a very retentive memory, Mr Muir."

His gaze returned with even greater intensity. "I have a habit of never forgetting anything, Mr Marklin. Almost never, that is." He smiled. "My wife would tell you otherwise, no doubt. I keep forgetting our wedding anniversary, you see." He cleared his throat. "Anyway, tell me all about what you would require of me, and then I will show you some of my past work to see if you think it is up to scratch."

So I took him through the details of the project, omitting the bit about the fifteen thousand pound offer for an original Dinky Flamingo, in case it gave him wrong ideas. I told him I had sufficiently good plans of the aircraft for him to work from, which I would let him have the moment we came to any arrangement.

"Well, there won't be any arrangement at all, if you don't like my work, will there, Mr Marklin?" He rose from his hard chair. "So if you don't mind coming into the other room . . . I've arranged some of my pieces on the dining-room table. Normally they're scattered all over the house."

His choice of verb amused me. "Positioned" they might be, "scattered" they certainly would never have been.

I followed him across the narrow hall into the room almost opposite. Muir switched on the light, though it was hardly yet necessary.

"There you are, Mr Marklin. Just a cross-section of the kind of thing I have done over the years. Most, of course, since my retirement from the army. I do larger pieces, on occasion, usually one-offs for churches, halls, presentations and so on. But I thought you would not really be interested in those, from what Mr Longhurst told me."

I walked towards the table, but I knew already the quality of Muir's work. It shone out instantly. The polished objects, mainly in brass, but some in aluminium and what looked like silver, were quite exquisite in their craftsmanship, and what was equally important to me, in their sheer accuracy where they were representing a mechanical object.

"I'll leave you to look at them at your leisure," Muir said quietly. "I'll be across in the sitting-room, if you have any questions."

By the time I looked round, he had gone. The assortment of objects displayed covered a broad spectrum, and were neatly arranged in categories. At the window end of the refectory table were those Muir had obviously considered to be of most interest to me—exquisitely detailed small models of motorized transport, mainly military in brass, reminders, no doubt, of his army days. I recognized a Saracen armoured car, a Chieftain tank with every link of its tracks picked out, a wartime Sherman tank, a contemporary tank transporter, a squat Austin commercial chassis ambulance, and Montgomery's famous Humber Super Snipe staff car.

In the next shiny rank was a selection of more common-place items, the kind of thing you can see in a thousand rather kitchy shops: horse brasses, figures of horses with and without riders, hunting dogs, sporting dogs, working dogs; the next rank, ornate door knockers carrying every kind of image from the world of animals. Then others, less cuddly, from other worlds beyond our own—heads of angels, devils, imps and demons, recalling mediaeval gargoyles and the art and times of Hieronymus Bosch. Following on down the table were somewhat larger objects, mainly animals again, that I took to be doorstops, fireplace furniture and the like. Then last, and quite obviously not least, was a collection of religious items that quite transcended the familiar interpretations of each theme, and over which I quite unexpectedly spent the most time. For here it was that Muir was seen most clearly, not just as a meticulous craftsman, but as a creative artist, an artist with a particular vision of his own. These were no comfy and comforting angels, and their pained and austere features recalled El Greco in their sadness, but more vengeful in their fixed gaze. The figures of the Virgin Mary, of which there were quite a number, were, curiously, all sculptured heavy with child with the beauty of her face marred by a look that seemed to tell of the agony of child-birth to come. And agony, again, cried out from the figures of Christ on the cross. For this was no Son of God transcending pain to pass into that passive tranquillity that precedes death and certain resurrection. Muir's was a vision of Christ suffering as any mortal slave condemned to crucifixion, desperately fighting the intensity of the agony, and clinging to every last breath of life, as if, after the allotted three days, there was to be no life thereafter—nothing but a rotting, racked carcass for the jackals.

I felt strangely affected by the figures, and stayed gazing back at them for much longer than I had intended. In fact their imagery was so powerful, I almost had to remind myself of why I had come to this small cottage on Longhurst's estate. Eventually I went back towards the window end of the table, picked up the model of Monty's wartime staff car, and joined Muir in the sitting-room.

"Ah," he said, "I thought that might be your favourite."

I put the Humber on a small coffee table beside my chair, and sat down again. "It's not my favourite, exactly. You have so many remarkable things."

"It's very kind of you to say so."

"Tell me," I asked hesitantly, "your religious objects— were they commissioned or . . . ?"

A thin smile relieved Muir's face.

"Oh dear no, Mr Marklin. My vision of Christianity, I'm afraid, is a little too severe for the present day clergy and congregation, or so I'm told. I think I must have been born out of my time."

"So they are one-offs?"

"Yes. I sell a few, mainly to older folk, who still believe more in the disciplines of religion than in the laxity of present day practices." He leant forward in his hard chair. "Anyway, Mr Marklin, let's get back to you and your Flamingo. Do you think I might be of some use to you for the master?"

"Yes, I'm sure you could. That is, if you would like to take it on. It seems rather humble after some of your creations. . . ."

"Not at all, I assure you. My interest will be in the challenge of it all, approaching as near possible to the ideal you have in mind. For instance, I seem to remember from my own childhood, Dinky aircraft had the name Dinky written underneath the wings, did they not? Lettering of that sort will be quite fascinating to reproduce."

"Correct. They normally had raised lettering 'Dinky Toys' with the name of the aeroplane underneath. And then, 'Made in England by Meccano Ltd.' But I wouldn't want you to reproduce that exactly. 'Dinky' is still a protected trademark."

"Have you an equivalent in mind?"

"Yes. It would simply be the name of the aeroplane, 'Flamingo,' underneath the left-hand wing, and 'Die-cast in Dorset by P.M.' underneath the right."

"Same type styles used by Dinky, I assume?"

I nodded. "Like to take it on, with all your other work?"

"Of course. I would be delighted. Er. . . ."

I saved him the embarrassment, for while Muir looked like someone who worked in a bank, I had the feeling that actually talking about the sordid business of earning money would be anathema to him.

"For the brass master, I sort of had the figure of three hundred pounds in mind. Does that er . . . ?"

A profound look of relief came over Muir's face. "That would be very reasonable, Mr Marklin. Let's talk no more of it." He rose from his chair. I followed suit. "When can you let me have those plans of yours?"

We walked out into the hall to the front door. I remembered to duck my head.

"I'll drop them by tomorrow."

His close-set eyes sparkled for a second. "Come to think of it, I have to deliver a figure over Bournemouth way tomorrow, so I'll go via Studland and take the ferry for a change. Is your place easy to find?"

"Bang on the only route through. On the left a couple of hundred yards before you get to the lanes down to the sea."

He opened the front door and extended a bony hand. "I'll see you sometime before lunch tomorrow, if that's all right. Goodbye, Mr Marklin. And good luck with your project. It's refreshing to meet a man who has sympathy with something as innocent and guileless as the playthings of the past."

I said goodbye and was surprised to feel how fresh the early autumn breeze was on my face. As I walked down the path to my Beetle, I saw a Morris Minor Traveller turn in to the garage to the cottage, which lay some hundred feet or so from the house. A small, slightly hunched, grey-haired lady, whom I assumed was Muir's wife, emerged from the car, holding a wicker basket full of what looked like groceries. She looked across at me for a split second, as I put the Beetle in gear and drove away. But her eyes expressed no interest, and she resumed her rather dead walk towards the house, no doubt, glad the visitor, whoever he was, had now gone.

Muir was as good as his word and picked up the plans. He surprised me by announcing he might have something very embryonic for me to see in about two weeks. I could not have wished for more prompt action. My meeting with the box manufacturer went well, and we did a deal on one hundred boxes as an initial order, purely because the MD was such an aviation nut. I wrote the copy I wanted on the lid, designed a small logotype for the P.M. lettering and despatched both to him. The final question of the actual making of the dies from the brass master, I was sure Muir would be able to help me with, as I remembered Longhurst had stated Muir's father had worked at some toy factory or other. I was really starting to feel pleased as Punch with the whole "Flamingo" operation.

Even the turnover at my Toy Emporium began looking up after its doldrum weeks. And the affairs of semi-retired film actresses, ex-husbands and ex-lovers soon seemed like some ridiculous episode from a current American TV soap-opera, and not, any more, part of reality, rural Dorset reality in particular.

Five

Needless to say, I heard about it first from Gus. It was about midday, and it was raining, as far as Bing was concerned, cats and dogs, but mainly dogs, for he had refused to go out in the downpour all morning. I didn't blame him. And I liked his company whilst I replied to my collectors' mail; otherwise, it was a pretty dreary job wrapping up toys they had seen in my "monthlies," or replying in the negative to requests for toys that were, nowadays, next to impossible to find.

Anyway, I'd just finished wrapping up a Solido Ford Thunderbird (original early sixties version, not the recent 'L'Age D'Or' variety) for a customer in Leeds, when I heard Gus's Ford Popular draw up outside. How did I know it was Gus's car? Easy. For, round our way, unless you work in a slaughterhouse, the ear-drum rending noise of a pig in terminal pain has to mean Gus has his foot hard down on what's left of his old upright Popular's brakes. This is always followed by a sharp detonation as Gus switches off what's left of the ignition.

Bing leapt off the counter, and fled into the house, although he has heard such a cacophony a thousand times. I could do nothing but look up into Gus's abnormally animated face.

"Heard the news?" he said breathlessly.

"No, but by your expression, it has to be something like Mrs Thatcher has turned out to be a man, or the Pope's eloped, or Archduke Ferdinand's been found alive. Am I right?" I grinned.

"Wrong," Gus retorted. "That bloody man has got his comeuppance."

"What bloody man?"

"Maxwell, of course. Found dead—murdered they think—down on the beach."

"Where?"

"Where d'you think? Osmington Mills. Nearest perishing beach to his place isn't it?"

I ushered Gus immediately into my sitting-room, without even bothering to lock up shop first. He lowered his craggy frame into an armchair.

"Who told you all this?"

"Mrs Blunt next door. Heard it on the local radio, she did. Came round and told me. So I. . . ."

". . . came round and told me. Well thanks. No doubt Arabella will ring me from her newspaper in a moment to repeat the information. And just when I was starting to forget all the myriad problems of the country house set."

"Wanna know what he died of?"

"You're going to tell me, even if I said 'No.' "

"Head injuries."

"Are they sure it's murder?"

"Seems like it. Opened a murder investigation, any old how, so Mrs Blunt says."

"When do they think it happened?"

"Sometime last night, they believe. Been dead some hours when they found him."

I then sat down myself, much to Gus's disappointment. I think he hoped I might have raided the fridge for a beer.

"Who found him, then?"

"A little girl, I understand. Must have scared her rigid. Mrs Blunt said she wandered along the beach to see what all the gulls were doing up that end. Pecking his eyes out for breakfast, I wouldn't wonder." Gus shivered at the thought. "Nasty as he seemed to be, I wouldn't want anybody to end that way," he muttered.

Neither of us spoke for a bit after that. It was Gus who eventually broke the silence.

"Wonder who did it, don't you? Could easily have been your new friend, Longhurst, couldn't it? Got the motive— Lana-Lee. Got the temper, you say. Got a record of violence, according to my mate at Bovington."

"Could be anybody, Gus. Don't go jumping to conclusions."

Though secretly I agreed with Gus, I did not dare voice my suspicion. I had suddenly realized I liked Longhurst too much to think of him as a murderer, even though I knew next to damn all about his real character.

"A man like Maxwell," I continued, "would have built up quite a load of enemies over the years. Could even be some guy he knew in America yonks ago."

"Or one of his cast-offs? Dare say there are enough of them around to murder him a hundred times."

My mind instantly went back to Lana-Lee's party, and the look in Lavinia Saunders' face as she seemed to be spitting venom at Maxwell for some reason or another—or was it my overheated imagination? After all, I'd seen a white ghost in the hedgerow only an hour or so before. The thought of Lavinia reminded me of her husband from Reinhardt.

"Or a business colleague, like the John Saunders I told you about. Or the Frenchman Jean-Paul Whatshisface?"

"What's the motive there?" Gus asked.

"Oh, some business chicanery or other. There must be countless reasons for murderous feelings in business. There were, even in my old advertising agency in Bournemouth!" I smiled. "Or maybe every man Jack is in love with the delectable Lana-Lee. Who knows?"

"Or . . ." began Gus, and then realized he was stuck. He obviously could not lay his mental hands on another "or." I came to his aid.

"Or, maybe, they're all in it together, Longhurst included," I laughed, "a kind of Orient Express train of thought all over again."

"What's the rotten railway got to do with anything?" asked Gus, and I could see I'd lost him. I think the last thing Gus ever read is *How to use your Gas Mask,* His Majesty's Stationery Office, 1939 or thereabouts. I got up to get him some inspiration—from the cool shelves of my Electrolux.

I suppose I should have prophesied the next little surprise, but I didn't. I guess it was because the mind (mine, anyway) tends to try to obliterate those eventualities that could lead to trouble, or tragedy, or just down-the-line unpleasantness. And this particular unlooked-for eventuality I knew could lead to any one of the three.

It happened on the day after Maxwell's body had been found. I was on my way back from a fruitless visit to a retired accountant in Blandford Forum, who rang my shop to say he had some old toys I might be interested in—mainly pre-war stuff. I beetled over just in case I hit upon some real treasure. We toy collectors, let alone traders, are perpetual optimists, and follow up almost any lead. But what he brought down from his attic, unfortunately, had seen better days, to say the least. The die-cast Dinky and Tootsietoy cars were all chipped and broken, the aircraft incredibly metal fatigued, and the few tinplate Wells and Schuco items were play damaged beyond reasonable repair. So I thanked him for thinking of me, and muttered under my breath all the way home.

And the muttering did not cease when I arrived. For parked outside my Toy Emporium was something, I guess, I had been subconsciously dreading, ever since the Randolph Treasure affair of quite a few months before. It was white and shiny, with a stripe along its side, but no blue lamp on top. It didn't need one. It shouted "Police" by its clinical cleanliness.

I quickly parked my car round the back of the shop beside Arabella's Golf, and walked round to the front. When I got up to the car, I made a point of peering inside the driver's window. My heart sank to rock and muddy bottom, for I saw what I had been dreading—a tiny black Budgie model of a Fifties police Wolseley Six Eighty car. It was mounted on one of those rubber sucker things, which children's darts and arrows have, to hold it on to any car's fascia panel. Any car, that is, driven by Inspector Trevor "Sexton" Blake.

I let myself into the shop, thankful that Arabella was home earlier than usual so I wouldn't be alone with him. I looked at myself in the mirror in the hallway. The same chump who had been conned into helping the Inspector over the Treasure affair looked back at me. Maybe he looked a year or so older, but certainly no wiser. I pulled my shoulders back and went into the sitting-room.

"Hello, Peter." He was a big man, all rugby player from the neck down, so it took him a moment to unfold from the chair. He held out his hand. What could I do? I shook it.

"I knew it was you," I said, with not an excess of welcome in my voice.

"My little Wolseley mascot?" he asked, with a smile.

I nodded and went over and kissed Arabella.

"We met at Lana-Lee's place, and he came back with me," Arabella tried by way of explanation. I sat down beside her on the settee.

"How long have you been back?"

"Only about five minutes," she replied, and I could hear the nerves in her voice.

I turned to the Inspector. He didn't even look a year and a bit older. And he had always looked wise, anyway, for, in contrast to his rugged and rugbied frame, his face was that of an Oxford don, finely chiselled, as they say, and delicate in its detail.

"So, Sexton, what brings you down here so quickly? I can't believe the Bournemouth CID have already called in Scotland Yard on this Maxwell murder. Or, maybe, you're down here on a completely different case."

Trevor Blake smiled. "I'm not in charge of the Maxwell murder case, you'll be glad to hear. Inspector Digby Whetstone is heading that up."

"I believe he's known as 'Digger,' isn't he?" Arabella chipped in.

"So they tell me." Blake's face wore a wry smile. "But who told you?"

"Local paper I work for—the *Western Gazette.*"

"Never mind this Digger fellow," I interrupted rather irritably. "What then are you doing so far from the Yard, Sexton? And why have you turned up at my door?"

"I didn't say I wasn't interested in Maxwell. I just stated that I wasn't involved directly in the murder enquiries."

"Ah. So that explains part one of my question. What about part two?"

"As I said, I met Arabella at Miss Claudell's, where I was making some enquiries, and we came back together for old times' sake."

I laughed out loud. "Don't believe a word of it. Pull the other leg, Sexton, while it's still in one piece. You're one of the most deliberate people I've come across."

"Can't I just drop by on occasion, when I'm in the neighbourhood—even if it's only to look at your stock in the shop?"

"I can't stop you. . . ."

"We wouldn't want to," Arabella interceded and left the room. And she was dead right, for I was letting my fear of being used again by the Inspector, as an intuitive aid to his now computer-dominated force, override my sense of civility, let alone hospitality.

I relaxed a smidgin. "Okay. I'll show you my current collection of toys in a moment. Don't think I've any great Schucos for you right now (Blake was strong on that great German manufacturer's products), but there might be something. First, I'd like to know what your interest in the late, and I gather, fairly unlamented, Ben Maxwell is."

"I can't tell you any details, I'm afraid, at the moment. Believe me, I'd like to, but I can't. It might prejudice any action I may have to take fairly shortly."

"Action against whom for what?" I asked, not really expecting a direct answer.

"Against certain people I believe have been smuggling undesirable goods into this country." He looked hard at me. "That's all I can say for now, Peter. And that's not for public consumption either. Just for your own ears."

"Like a drink?" I softened. "The sun's over the Scotland Yard arm."

Blake winced at the joke, but nodded at the same time.

"Scotch and soda, wasn't it?" I recalled and went to the drinks cabinet before he had time to agree. I poured myself a generous one too, and a G and T for Arabella, for when she came back from what I assumed was making herself even more beautiful for our visitor. When we were settled once more, I tried again.

"Do you think that Maxwell's murder has something to do with this suspected smuggling racket?"

Blake raised his glass. "Do you?"

I smiled. Sexton had not lost a whisker of his cunning. He'd got me going already, blast him.

"I don't know anything about him," I replied. "Well, that's not quite true. I have heard he's a bit of a philanderer."

"You've met him, I believe?"

I nodded. "Just the once. At a party over at their place."

"What did you think of him?"

"Nothing much. Just wondered why the hell someone as seemingly nice as Lana-Lee Claudell would take him back into her life."

"They have a daughter, Tara-Lee. She could be the reason." Blake made a steeple with his fingers.

"You don't believe that really, do you?"

"I don't know. And that's the truth. I think Miss Claudell is very fond of her daughter—from what I saw today, anyway." He made to rise from his chair as Arabella came back into the room looking—guess what—more beautiful than ever. She motioned him to remain seated.

"Yes, I think she is," she said. "I've seen them together too, and not just this morning."

"Don't you think Miss Claudell is taking her husband's murder very well?" Blake asked.

"She's very upset, though. Who wouldn't be?" Arabella replied. "Murder is a terrible thing. But I know what you mean. She's not actually over distraught, or at a point of collapse."

"What do you put that down to?"

"Purely that I don't think there was any love lost between them. . . ." Arabella's voice tailed away, as she realized the implication of what she had said.

"Yes, that's what I gather from Inspector Whetstone."

"But you don't think she . . . ?" I began.

"I don't think anything. It's not my case, the actual murder, remember," Blake said quickly.

I took a long draught of my scotch. The burn helped me.

"Look, Sexton. It's not mine either. And not going to be. I really am not going to get caught in this one, if that's why you dropped round. By you, by Digger Whetstone or by the Chief Commissioner of the whole of your shebang. Include me out, please."

"I'm not really surprised—after last time," Blake said quietly, and downed the last of his scotch. "Now can I see what treasures you've got for sale in your shop?"

Arabella and I took him through, and we watched him browse for over ten minutes, hardly speaking a word. He ended up not buying an actual toy, but one of my selection of books on collecting—David Pressland's splendid volume *The Art of the Tin Toy.*

"It will help to while away the odd hours in my hotel room," he observed.

My heart missed a beat. "So you're not going back to London just yet?"

"Not just yet. Think I should stay a little longer. A few loose ends to follow up."

"Where are you staying?" Arabella asked.

"Just a walk down the road from here. Knoll House Hotel. Prettier here than in Bournemouth, and, for Osmington, it's the right side of the ferry."

"You must come round to dinner one night, if you can spare the time," Arabella offered, ignoring my frowns.

"I'd love to," he rejoined, and held out his hand. "It's been nice seeing you both again."

I didn't let go of his hand until I had said very firmly, "It's been nice seeing you. And it would be fine if you came to dinner, really. But as far as the Maxwell murder is concerned, and all the loony goings-on of that set over at Osmington, don't call me as they say. I'll call you."

Hell, when I made that last remark, I had no idea how deadly accurate it was going to prove to be.

Blake's visit, brief as it was, nevertheless rather ruined the rest of our evening. I just had to tell Arabella what Blake had said about the smuggling while she was out of the room and we ended up spending the entire time discussing one aspect or the other of the Maxwell affair.

I had a debrief from Arabella on what she had been doing over at Lana-Lee's. Apparently, her editor had decided she was the most qualified of all his reporters to cover the murder investigations, a judgement solely based on the fact that we had been "privileged" to attend one of Lana-Lee's parties, and so she had been duly despatched to interview her. She learnt very little while she was there, as Longhurst arrived almost immediately, acting a new role of responsible family friend/protector, and Blake had turned up ten minutes after that, taking Lana-Lee into the study for a private conflab. So beyond registering that Lana-Lee seemed considerably upset rather than grief-stricken, Arabella gleaned little for the front page of the *Western Gazette*. For her private memory bank, she noted that Lana-Lee demonstrated yet again her fondness for Longhurst, and seemed to take great comfort out of his protective attitude towards her.

We both agreed that it was lucky Lana-Lee had such a close friend in England on whom she felt she could rely during this dramatic time. But the thought did nag us that their relationship could well have been the cause of the drama. It all seemed too neat somehow. And Arabella had the feeling while she was there that Blake thought so too.

"But he's not on the case officially. Just the smuggling investigation," Arabella reminded me. I smiled.

"He's on the case," I said.

She shrugged. "Never mind, darling. You've told him you won't get involved, so it doesn't matter." She snuggled up to me on the settee, and Bing gave us both a reproachful look. (He likes Arabella around, but I detect he reckons he'd get more of my time if she wasn't, or at least, wasn't so temptingly cuddly. He's probably right. But we've all got our own lives to lead. And I've only got one. He's got eight more to come.) I put my arm around her.

"You meant what you said to Blake, didn't you?" She looked up at me. "Because I don't want us to go through, ever again, what we did last time. You risking your neck."

I held her tightly to me. "We won't go through that again, I promise. Anyway, murder and smuggling are a bit out of my league. And I haven't had any toys stolen this time. So there's no need for me to get caught up in it."

She held her face up to mine and closed her eyes. I accepted the invitation. "Thank God," she breathed, when her tongue took a rest. Then after a delicious while, she sat up straight, much to my surprise. "Wow, I forgot. I got the new Clint Eastwood movie out of the video shop this morning, so that we had something to view tonight."

"I think I've got something else I'd rather view, my darling, if you don't mind." She chuckled. "Something a little softer than our Clint."

"Prettier?"

"Much prettier. And the whole show is much, much less violent."

"Oh, you disappoint me," she whispered in my ear.

"Sorry. Dorset right now seems to be violent enough without us. . . ."

"Or Clint. . . ."

"So no video?"

"No video . . . I'll take it back in the morning and say we loved every minute of it."

I rose and picked her up in my arms, a heroic gesture, as I'm not exactly a Clint or a Stallone. Trading in toys does little to tone the muscles, and I have no Green God to help.

"Let's forget the video and Fast Forward it upstairs," I suggested, croakily.

And so I tottered up the crooked flight to our bedroom. Unknown to us, it was to be our last carefree night for what seemed like an eternity.

Arabella phoned me from the *Western Gazette* the moment she heard. It was late the next afternoon, and she had just returned from a press conference held at the Bournemouth CID headquarters.

"Inspector Whetstone has made an arrest for Maxwell's murder," she said, breathlessly.

"Okay," I said, "let me guess. It's some drug pusher who wanted to muscle in on Maxwell's alleged smuggling operation."

"No. It's more obvious than that. And a clear cut case, from what they said. They've detained Adam Longhurst."

"Hell!" I exclaimed. "And you say they're sure they've got the right man?"

" 'Fraid so." Arabella sounded as crest-fallen as myself.

"What's the evidence?"

"His Range Rover was seen down in Osmington Mills late that same evening."

"But there are loads of Range Rovers round here."

"Not with six wheels, you idiot."

"Oh yes, I remember now. They found tyre tracks too?"

"Yes, apparently. An old man walking his dog says he passed the car twice, and admired it. He says there was no one in it at the time. His wife says she heard it drive away, shortly after her husband got home."

"Do the times match with the police's estimate of the time of Maxwell's death?"

"Yes, around 10.45 to 11 o'clock at night."

"Anything else?"

"Yes, unfortunately. I gather they've interviewed quite a lot of people who knew Longhurst, and they've got wind of the various threats he's made on Maxwell over the weeks. It seems that party night was only one of the many times he's stormed around various places, shouting what he would like to see happen to that man."

"And I don't suppose his previous record is going to help him there." I thought for a second. "Was Sexton Blake at the press conference?"

"Nowhere to be seen."

"Bet he was in the wings. However, be that as it may, Longhurst is in big trouble. He has a classic motive—a lover removing his inamorata's unloved husband. He has been heard issuing murderous threats, and he's been observed at the scene of the crime. . . ."

"Correction," Arabella interrupted, "he wasn't seen, I understand. Just his car."

"Well, it wasn't stolen, was it?"

"No."

"What does Longhurst say about it all? Or I guess they wouldn't say at this stage."

"Right. They didn't say. All I know is that he states he's not guilty."

"Poor Longhurst."

There was silence for a moment. Then Arabella asked, "You sound as if you think they've arrested the wrong man. Or is your sympathy solely because you sort of like him?"

"Both," I said, and even surprised myself with the certainty of my reply. "What do you think, Arabella?"

"Don't know yet. The terrible thing is none of us may ever know for sure whether he did it or not."

"Unless he ultimately confesses. Some of them do, after a spell in custody. They sort of grow tired of lying."

"I did quite like him," she said quietly. "I would hate him to turn out to be a murderer."

"There's nothing we can do, is there?" I asked, equally quietly.

"Guess not."

"I'm keeping right out of it. Told Blake so."

"That's right."

"None of our business."

"None of our business."

"Got our own lives to think of."

"Got a lot to do."

"My Flamingo, for instance. Take a deal of time."

"And we promised ourselves a late holiday. Paris, remember?"

"I remember."

"Mustn't keep you. Only rang to tell you. . . ."

"Thanks. Know when you'll be home?"

"About 7.30."

"I'll have a G and T in the oven waiting."

"That'll be nice. Anything on telly?"

"Some murder mystery or other. Miss Marple, I think."

"Oh." Then she said sadly, "We don't seem to be able to get away from amateur sleuthing, do we?"

You know something? There was just no answer to that.

I had hardly put the phone down, when it dringed again. I knew who it was immediately. I guess I had been half expecting it. The conversation was very short and to the point. I said I would come over right away. She sounded tremendously relieved.

I hardly remember the drive over. And it wasn't because my mind churned over what few facts I knew of the case and the people involved. That didn't take long. What did take time was a heap of Peter Marklin self inquisition, the whys and the wherefores of my own motives in saying yes to the lady on the phone. Lana-Lee met me at the door, and just behind her skirts was another figure, a little eight-year-old variety. I could see the sucker punch coming. After receiving effusive thanks for turning out, I was ushered into the huge drawing-room. A scotch and soda was in my hand in no time at all, and, instantly, I was looking into four big, blue, sad eyes. (Tara-Lee was almost the spitting image of her mother in miniature. It was uncanny—I began to believe I was behind a looking glass.)

"Peter," Lana-Lee began at the deep end, "please help me. I've got no one else in England to turn to. You see, Adam is just about the only real friend I've made in my time over here. And now he's. . . ."

She couldn't even bring herself to say "arrested," which made the strength of her feelings for him very clear.

"Don't worry," I said (those four eyes were really doing their stuff), "I'll do what I possibly can. But what made you think of me?"

"I've heard a bit about you. Adam knows some friends of a Mr Treasure, I believe his name was, and learned that you had been involved in some private investigations—in conjunction with the police, of course—that had led to the unravelling of the real facts behind the disappearance of his wife."

I swallowed a gulp of scotch. Well, I thought, the Dorset grape-vine certainly bears bonny fruit, blast it.

"Yes, well, I . . . er . . ." I staccatoed, ". . . er . . . only got involved with that case because some antique toys were stolen, and it was heavily in my financial interests to get them back, you see."

Lana-Lee leaned forward, and the musk of her perfume worked overtime. "Peter, I understand what you're saying. And I'd like to make provision for that. I have not had a chance to discuss it with Adam yet, naturally, but neither of us is exactly poor. . . ."

"I did not mean—" I interrupted, but she interrupted back.

"Whether you did or not, Peter, we couldn't expect you to help us without some financial reward. One of the reasons for coming to you is that I gather you were infinitely discreet over the Treasure affair at all times, a virtue that I might not be able to discover, and certainly not guarantee, in a professional investigator."

Tara-Lee watched me intently as I took another sip of my scotch. I found it rather disconcerting. I hoped she didn't think I was an alcoholic.

"So, Peter, if you will agree to help us, I will pay you five thousand pounds, and a further five thousand when the—" she hunted for a suitable word—"business is over."

I whistled inwardly. That kind of money would come in very useful after the slack trade in the summer and the cost of producing the Flamingo. But she knew already, really, that she had got me with those blue eyes. The smackeroos were just a mark of sincerity, I reckoned, or were they, perhaps, to help atone for a guilt—which brought me to my next question.

"I hate to say this, Miss Claudell. . . ."

She stopped me. "It's Lana-Lee, please."

"Lana-Lee, I repeat, I hate to say this but I must know whether *you* really think Adam Longhurst is totally innocent of your husband's murder."

"Totally." She leant forward and grasped my hand. "I promise you. I know men. And I know positively that Adam, short-tempered though he may be, could never ever kill a living soul."

I believed her. I mean I believed her belief. And it wasn't just because a famous film actress's hand was touching mine. Or was it? My other hand found refuge in raising scotch to my lips.

"Tell me, Peter, will you help us?"

"Please say yes," added Tara-Lee quietly. "Then perhaps I could come to your shop and see some of your toys."

"You can come over any time," I smiled. "But I promise I will help your mummy as well."

"Real honest injun, cross your heart and hope to die type promise?" she went on.

I crossed my heart and spilt a little of my scotch. Tara-Lee giggled, I searched for my handkerchief, and Lana-Lee let go of my hand.

"Now you go off and play, Tara. It will be bedtime soon. Peter and I have some boring talking to do, I'm afraid. Okay?"

Tara-Lee got off the settee and ran out of the room. Lana-Lee went over and shut the door.

"Now, where would you like me to begin, Peter?" she asked, again seating herself directly opposite me. This time she crossed her long elegant legs, and I caught a glimpse of svelte thigh. I did not complain, but it did make concentration that mite more difficult.

"From the beginning," I smiled. "Or actually, before the beginning of this particular tragedy."

"What do you mean, Peter?"

"Well, if I'm to help Adam Longhurst, I've got to know everything that might have a bearing on this case, however irrelevant it may seem now."

"Okay, fire away."

"Firstly, I'd like to know what your feelings towards your husband were. I gather you were planning a divorce when he returned to you."

"We were. I won't beat around the bush with you, Peter. Ben and I hadn't got on for years. In fact, towards the end, I began to actively hate him." She hesitated, then continued. "So I have to admit that I'm more heartbroken that Adam has been arrested than that Ben is dead."

I thought for a moment, then asked, "Can you tell me then, why you allowed him back into your life?"

She hesitated again, then said quietly but positively, "I had my reasons, Peter. I'm sorry I can't tell you what they were. But I can assure you they had nothing to do with what's happened now. Nothing at all."

"Sure?"

"Sure. Sorry, but I've got to keep a little of me private, away from the public eye."

"Okay," I said, reluctantly. "I'll pass on to question number two. Why do you think your husband was murdered?"

"I don't know." She smoothed an imaginary wrinkle from her stocking. "He wasn't a popular man either in private or in business."

"What was his business now?" I asked, looking Lana-Lee squarely in her beautiful eyes.

"It sounds silly, but I'm not quite sure what it was."

"Please, Lana-Lee, if I'm to help you, I must know it all. Don't hold back. You must have had some inkling of what he did recently to earn a living. Or did he exist on his savings from his motor racing days?"

She smiled. "Ben never saved anything. It went out, usually, even before it came in. I paid most of his bills myself."

"So what was he living on?" I remembered Blake's guarded words about smuggling. "He seemed to have something going with Saunders of Reinhardt perfumery."

"Nothing formal. I don't think he got paid. They were just buddies from the old motor racing times."

"So what kept him afloat? Was it—er—anything illegal, do you think?"

Lana-Lee looked more than a little disconcerted. "I don't know. I don't know."

I had a feeling she had a darn good idea what it had been, but was terrified of her public image being tarnished by disclosure—even to a tight mouth like myself. I took a deep breath and plunged in.

"Was he into smuggling? Drugs maybe?"

She sat up straight and uncrossed her legs. Her voice was sharper now. "Have you been talking to Inspector Blake? Or was it Arabella the other day?"

"A guess," I lied. "First thing you think of with the movie world nowadays, I'm afraid. It's all the tabloid coverage such activities get."

Lana-Lee reached for my hand again. I let her take it. "Peter, I'd better tell you what I told Inspector Blake. Yes, Ben used to be in drugs smuggling in a small way. It was easy, you see. His wasn't the only Grand Prix team that tried it, I'm sure."

"Smuggled drugs in the transporters or the cars?"

"The cars, I gather."

"Packed into the chassis tubes, into the tyres, or crannies in the monocoque shells?"

"That's right. No one suspected, Ben told me when I at last got wind of it. The team's transporter was waved through most Customs checks in Europe without much of a search in the old days. So it was an almost foolproof way of distributing drugs across the continent—*and* into England.

And for the American teams like my husband's, into the States as well."

"So he made a pile from his driving and another pile from his hobby?"

She nodded. "When I discovered what was going on, it was just another nail in our marriage's coffin. I begged him to stop for my sake, for Tara-Lee's, but he just wouldn't listen."

I didn't say anything for a moment, digesting what I had learnt. At least I now knew what had brought Blake to the West Country. Or did I?

"Your husband retired from motor racing some years ago," I eventually continued. "But I suppose he had the same opportunities with other teams when he was doing the circuits as a commentator."

"I suppose so. We had separated by then."

"Do you think he came to England to set up some other kind of drug dealing?"

"It has passed through my mind more than once. But I didn't see any sign of big money. He was getting me to support him."

"But then, he had not been here all that long, had he? Blake wouldn't be interested if he didn't think something irregular was still happening."

"I know. But I honestly have not seen any sign of it."

I finished my drink, and she made to freshen it. I waved my hand. "No thanks. I'd better keep a clear head. Now, can I ask you again why you had your husband back again? You knew he was crooked. . . ."

Her big eyes flashed annoyance; I'd seen just such an expression from her many times in her movies on television.

"Please, Peter, don't ask me that again. I've told you it can have nothing to do with Ben's murder."

"And you really *are* convinced Adam Longhurst is not involved in any way?" I persevered.

"Of course. He's incapable of killing—especially *that* way."

"Oh, it's easy enough in a flash of anger to pick up a rock and. . . ."

"I didn't mean that. I mean the *other* things."

"What other things? The police have been saying he was simply struck on the head with a rock of some sort. It could have been a deliberately planned murder or just a spontaneous act. There are plenty of rocks down at Osmington Mills without the need for the murderer to bring his own."

"Please, don't joke. It's too horrible." Her voice began to break for the first time. "Maybe the police wouldn't like me to have brought up the question of the other injuries."

"What other injuries?" I leaned forward in my chair.

"His lower jaw was so smashed, some teeth were broken and missing. And—" she stopped, and tears started to roll down her cheeks—"his right eye was gone."

My mind leapt back to Gus's comment when he had first heard about Maxwell's death.

"The seagulls," I said very softly, getting up and putting a hand on her shoulder. "It must have been the seagulls. I gather that's how the body was first spotted by the little girl. There were gulls flocking all over him. But it doesn't explain the jaw."

She shuddered, and I sat down beside her on the settee. She turned suddenly and buried herself in my arms.

"Oh God, God," she whimpered. "I can't go on any more tonight. I can't, I can't. . . ."

I rocked her gently to and fro, my arms now tightly around her. "That's all right," I whispered. "Don't worry. We've covered enough ground tonight." The softness and warmth of her body, combined with the aphrodisiacal properties of her musky perfume, were not exactly helping my mind to think straight and I could feel my body starting to react in a distinctly non-professional manner. I prayed my client noticed not.

I cleared my throat. "I'll try to see Mr Longhurst in the morning," I said very softly. "I'll make an appointment with Inspector Digby Whetstone. I believe he's heading the actual murder enquiry."

"Yes," she mumbled into my shirt, "thank you."

I stayed a further three minutes or so, not so much for her, but for me. I needed time to relax myself a little before walking out of the room. For who knows, otherwise I might have shocked the butler.

Six

"I'm only seeing you for one reason, Mr Marklin." Inspector Digby Whetstone sweated behind his desk, not through any excess heat in the room, but because of all the excess calories he'd absorbed over his forty or so years. He had all the weight and more of a prize-fighter but none of the muscle, and his chubby face had made his pencil slim, ginger moustache seem like he had borrowed it from someone a quarter his size.

"And what's that?" I asked rather irritably, as I had been kept waiting in a draughty corridor at Bournemouth CID headquarters for an hour and a half before Whetstone saw fit to see me.

"My colleague from Scotland Yard put in a good word for you."

I tipped my mental hat to Blake.

Whetstone sat creakily back in his tilting chair, and smiled —I tell a lie—his lips just curled up at the ends. "I can't imagine what I can do for you. Or you for me. I told you that on the phone."

I went straight to the point for I had only been granted ten minutes in the Inspector's diary.

"Two things: first, I want to know the extent of the case against Adam Longhurst; second, I want to see him."

Whetstone's chair creaked some more as he chuckled. "My dear Mr Marklin, what on earth can be your interest in such an open and shut case as this? Are you a friend of his?"

"Not particularly. I'm just kind of pally with a thing called justice and fair play and all that." I knew I shouldn't have said that the instant it issued from my mouth. But that hour and a half's wait had done nothing for my temper. Whetstone instantly leaned forward at his desk and the message in his tiny eyeballs said it all.

"Mr Marklin, don't try my patience. I repeat, I've only seen you because of Inspector Blake, and I've no time for insults. I'm up to my ears in work. Not just this Maxwell case, but you may have read there's a child molester about; there's been vandalism this morning on a ferry; there's a youth in a coma at Bournemouth general after a punch up outside a pub last night; we have a guy in custody concerning sabotage to the oil-drilling operation; I'm about to interrogate two men from a caravan site about the rape of a fourteen-year-old girl . . . Get the picture, Mr Marklin? If you're starting to, then add thirty-seven unsolved burglaries, three with grievous bodily harm, umpteen stolen cars, would you believe an aeroplane pirated from Christchurch, half a dozen missing persons, suspected arson at a wallpaper factory. . . ." He began to run out of breath.

"I've got the picture," I said quietly. "Believe me, I'm only here to help."

"Help whom? Certainly not me." He pointed a finger. "Someone has convinced you that Longhurst is innocent, haven't they, that we've got the wrong man?"

"I don't know whether he is or not. That's what I want to help discover."

"You've been put up to this by someone, haven't you? And it doesn't take a genius to guess who it is."

"It's no secret. I'm trying to help Lana-Lee Claudell."

Whetstone sat smugly back again in his chair.

"I thought as much. She phones here on the hour, every hour protesting his innocence. Now she's taken to employing outsiders. God, as if I haven't had enough trouble with Longhurst's lawyer."

I was relieved to hear the last bit. At least I wasn't alone.

"She'd better be careful, that lady," he went on. "Just because I have detained her lov—Mr Longhurst, it doesn't mean to say she is not needed for further lengthy questioning herself."

"You haven't charged him yet?"

"No. We're still questioning him. That's why the answer to your second question is 'no.' You can't see him until we have finished with him, one way or the other. At the moment, we are restricting access to his lawyer, Mr Lynch."

I made a note to get together with Mr Lynch at the very first opportunity for I had probably been naïve to think Whetstone would disclose anything about the case beyond what had already been said at the police press conferences—until they brought a charge in court, that is. It certainly made me miss someone I thought I never ever would—dear old Sexton Blake.

Whetstone removed his bulk from behind his desk. "Look, Mr Marklin, a word of advice. I'm newish down here in Dorset, but I did a bit of checking about you, while you were waiting and what I heard was not too pleasing. Like about a year or so ago, you were involved in another case, and my local chaps consider you got up to some pretty dubious tricks under the guise of getting back some stolen toys, is that right?" He did not wait for an answer, but propelled me towards the door. "And, what's more, there could have been a little matter of concealing evidence and so on. So I'd watch your step, Mr Marklin, if I were you. We wouldn't want that kind of thing happening on this case, now would we?" He opened the door. "Stick to toys, Mr Marklin. And leave investigations to grown-ups." His lips turned up again at the ends, and he didn't offer his podgy hand. But then I didn't offer my slimmer one.

Lynch was in when I called. I got his address by phoning Lana-Lee immediately after leaving the cuddly warmth of Whetstone. Lynch's office was, surprisingly, in Dorchester. I had expected Longhurst's lawyer at least to have his office in Bournemouth, if not in the great Metropolis itself. But the moment I arrived, my fears about his professional standing disappeared. The premises explained all—in stone and gargoyles, mullioned windows and spacious grounds. Mr Lynch did not have far to travel to his office. He just sallied forth to the west wing of his baronial home.

As I pulled at the ancient bell rope, I wondered who his other clients might be, who helped him live and work in such secluded splendour. One thing was for sure, they weren't antique toy traders.

Inside, I was greeted by a slim brunette with John Lennon glasses, who showed me through to a waiting-room, leaving me to the mercy of a dozen or so ancestors in portraits on the wall. I buried my head in a copy of *Zoom* from a pile of magazines on a round table, and had just turned over a page which revealed a luxurious nude lady in the most Hasselbladt of poses, when she returned. Blushing, I followed her up a lofty lavender coloured corridor to a large white door with an "enter" sign above it. She dutifully knocked, then ushered me in.

"Thank you, Lydia. How do you do, Mr Marklin? I'm so glad you've come."

Before I could really take him in, he had pumped my hand warmly, and led me over to a cosy grouping of armchairs to one side of his (compared to the waiting-room) fairly modestly sized office.

"Miss Claudell has told me you have, as you might say, joined our side."

I smiled and sat down opposite him. "Yes, something like that."

"Good, good." Lynch relaxed back into his chair, but his eyes remained on red alert. I could now take stock of him, and I liked what I saw. He was shortish, but perfectly proportioned, so that his lack of height did not sing out (like Paul Newman, so I'm told, in that respect), around my age, I guessed, but with prematurely grey hair that gave him a look of maturity beyond his years—no doubt, a great asset in legal circles. But the singular impression one retained of him was his almost electric stage presence. You could almost see a very blue chip personal computer working overtime behind those eyes of his. I decided I was even more glad he was on my side than he was that I was on his.

"You've been with Inspector Whetstone, I gather?"

I nodded. "I might as well not have bothered for all I got out of him."

"Oh, the police have to be very cagey at this early stage. After all, they haven't taken Longhurst to court yet."

"Do you think they will?"

He sighed. "It looks like it, I'm afraid. You see, my client really doesn't seem to be able to produce any evidence that he didn't do it."

"Tell me all you've learnt. Whetstone won't let me see Mr Longhurst. So you're my only source of information."

"All right. My client has instructed me to tell you everything. It's not very helpful, as I've said. But here goes. He has admitted to an affair with Miss Lana-Lee Claudell, which he states terminated more or less after her estranged husband's return—a new state of affairs which my client obviously did not welcome or relish. However, beyond pleading his case with Miss Claudell on quite a few occasions and one unfortunate time, arriving at her home somewhat inebriated, I gather, and threatening Mr Maxwell, he maintains that he was responsible for no other reactions whatsoever, beyond loose talk at social gatherings. Certainly, he seems genuinely horrified at Maxwell's murder and, obviously, even more shocked by his own arrest."

"Do you believe him? It's important, you know."

Lynch smiled. "I know. I'm in one of those fortunate positions now, Mr Marklin, when I can pick and choose my clients. Very early on in my career, I was asked to take on the defence of an up-and-coming pop star who had been accused, quite unjustly, of rape. He got off. I won't divulge his name, but he's now one of the most successful men behind the whole pop scene. The word spread around the pop world and then show business in general. In no time at all, though my role had only been that of instructing solicitor, of course, I found I had some of the richest clients in the world, from professions where litigation, criminal or civil, seems to be as everyday an occurrence as I'm told groupies are at every stage door." He looked down at his well manicured, strong hands. "So suddenly, I was the guy to see if you had a problem in show business. In the end, it was those clients who forced me to buy a place like this, away from it all, where they could come without too much fear of instant publicity."

"And Longhurst?" I asked.

"I drew up Lana-Lee's contract with Reinhardt perfumery. That's how I met her. And she remembered me directly poor Adam Longhurst was detained."

I looked at him with a wry sort of smile. "I wonder why Lana-Lee didn't appoint as high-powered a private eye? There must be quite a few of them on the ground."

"You were highly recommended."

"By some friends of a Mr Treasure, whom I. . . ."

"Did she tell you that?" He chuckled. "I suppose she was just being cautious and covering for the real source of the recommendation."

Suddenly the whole truth hit me, and I could have kicked myself for having been so blind.

"It was Inspector Blake, wasn't it?"

He didn't even blink.

"Tell me, when did he recommend me? Before or after Adam Longhurst was arrested?"

"Before, I think. Yes, I'm sure it was."

The bastard. Blake had already recommended me *before* he came back with Arabella that evening. But why? There could only be one reason. He knew how Digger Whetstone's mind would work or was working, and had already guessed the likely outcome—Longhurst's arrest. So did that mean Blake thought Longhurst was unlikely to have committed the murder or what? My mind seethed with questions, all of which I knew I would have to leave unanswered until I had finished getting the information I wanted out of Sebastian Lynch. So I got back to the point immediately.

"So Longhurst claims he's innocent. You and Lana-Lee, and perhaps myself, believe him. Whetstone obviously doesn't. So tell me what Longhurst says he was doing that night. His Range Rover was observed down by the beach at Osmington Mills at around the estimated time of the murder. Does he claim he wasn't in it?"

"No. He was in it." The lawyer paused, then went on, "Let's go back a bit. My client had spent most of that day in London on business, seeing some Americans about shipping some cattle out. He had flown himself up to Denham airfield in his small private aircraft, then flown back, earlier than he had expected, arriving at the strip behind his house at around 6.00 p.m. Because he had not anticipated being home at that hour, he'd given his housekeeper the evening off and she had gone to her brother's in Weymouth. There being, therefore, no evening meal prepared for him, he went out again, and I gather, drank somewhat, at the Green Pheasant over Wool way. I've checked on that, by the way, and I have quite a few witnesses who saw him there. Unfortunately, drink exacerbated his loathing of Maxwell once more, and he was none too cautious about his comments. They included threats, so my informants report."

"But you say, at the estimated time of the crime, he was in his car at the scene of the crime."

"That's right," the lawyer sighed. "He was home by 9.30 p.m., says he saw some of the ten o'clock news on ITV, then as he was about to go up to bed, the phone rang. And this is the crucial bit."

I leaned forward as if that would help me hear better.

"He states that a woman's voice told him he was wanted down at Osmington Mills urgently, because there had been some kind of an argument with Maxwell near the beach."

"Did he recognize the voice?"

"That's the problem, Mr Marklin. He says he didn't—that the woman was so hysterical it was even difficult to hear what she was saying."

"And he took off in his Range Rover to see what it was all about, without knowing who the woman was, or quite what she was saying?"

"I know. It doesn't sound too convincing to me either, let alone to twelve good men and women and true."

I thought for a moment. "You reckon he knew who the woman was, don't you?"

The lawyer shrugged. "I could be wrong."

"There's only one name that will spring instantly to the mind of the prosecution, and that's what you're afraid of. That's providing they believe there ever was a woman at all, which I doubt."

"Lana-Lee."

"Lana-Lee. And if it was her, I'm pretty certain Longhurst is the kind of man who would rather get convicted than come up with her name."

Neither of us spoke for a while, then Lynch got up from his chair, and went over to the window.

"So you see the terrible problem, Peter. Longhurst has no alibi for any of the crucial time period. And his Range Rover was at the scene of the crime."

"What did he say he did there? Why didn't he find the body?"

"He says he couldn't find anyone on the beach at all. He did not go the whole stretch each way, because it was dark, and he didn't have a torch. What's more, he, quite sensibly, explains that he didn't imagine there had been anything as gruesome as a murder, and therefore was looking for signs of activity, or at least someone, or a group of people standing up, rather than a body lying down and two-thirds hidden by rocks and stones. Don't forget the little girl in daylight only really spotted it because of the gulls."

"Those gulls. Don't remind me," I shuddered, then went one, "So what did he do then? Go back to his car and home?"

"He sat in it for a while. About ten minutes or so, he thought. Then turned around, motored home and went to bed. The first time he knew anything about a murder was next day."

"So we both have quite a task on our hands, don't we?" I stared into space. "Longhurst has a classic motive for killing

Maxwell: the beautiful *femme fatale*. He has a record of fairly violent behaviour, and of even more violent words. He has no real alibi. His cover story sounds too weak even to convince a doting mother, and he confesses to being at the scene of the crime around the estimated time of death. Not bad for a start, is it?" I grinned ruefully, "No wonder bloody Whetstone thinks he's on to a winner."

"He's not won yet," Lynch smiled, and all the confidence in the world was back in his face. He came over and patted me on the back. "Cheer up," he added, "worse things happen at sea."

"Really?" I sighed. "Then I'm relieved I'm not working for Cunard."

Two hours later found me seated on a rather haemorrhoidally cold rock on the beach at Osmington Mills. For in my amateur way, I was attempting to follow what I loosely imagined would be a professional's way of going about a murder investigation. I was absorbing the atmosphere (and some of the damp) at the scene of the crime.

My mind, however, was not at its crispest, for Sebastian Lynch had insisted that I stay for what he described as his office "canteen" lunch. Some canteen! Smoked salmon and a salad like mother used not to make, followed by a crème brulée that was tempting enough to quash the strictest of dietician's qualms. All washed down by a modest little Sauternes that had never seen an odd bin, and a half inch of brandy served in a glass almost large enough to swim in. For myself, I'd use Lynch as a solicitor solely on the basis of his culinary credit-rating.

The beach did little for me. I was sitting at the spot where a fisherman showed me the body had been found, but no real vibes were coming through. Just cold. The only shiver I suffered from was caused by the keen autumnal wind off the sea. And it wasn't through lack of trying. I imagined Maxwell swishing down in the luxury of his Cadillac, parking, then strolling along the water's edge until . . . I reckoned he must have been with someone, for Maxwell had not struck me as exactly the solitary stroller type, especially at dead of night. So, did he drive his companion down to the beach? If so, why a beach? Seclusion? A clandestine business meeting, or maybe it was a lover? Or did he meet his companion by arrangement on the beach? And was this person, or maybe persons, the murderer or murderers, or was some other party involved? From a brief chat to a couple of people I found walking in the tiny village, no other strange car had been seen. Just Maxwell's Cadillac and Longhurst's special Range Rover.

I very speedily realized my visit was raising a load of new questions, and supplying no answers to the old ones, let alone the new. I turned my mind to Longhurst. Saw him spot the Cadillac parked. No one in it. Walk around the village, maybe, then down on to the beach. In the dark, it would be hard to see any distance as there had been no natural aids that night—like a moon. He had drunk enough to cloud both his mind and his vision, anyway. If he, truthfully, had not recognized the woman's voice on the telephone, he would eventually, I assumed, have considered the whole matter some kind of elaborate hoax, or a mystery to be solved in the sober light of morning, and driven off home. But it would be very different if he really thought that woman was Lana-Lee. I made a mental note to check on the phone call the very next time I saw her.

And that's about as far as my tiny mind went that afternoon in the pleasant, but by no means sensational surroundings of that tiny village by the sea, a village that, had it not been for Maxwell's murder, would have remained as one of Dorset's little-known holiday spots. For, beyond a cluster or two of mobile homes that are never mobile, there are few places to stay at Osmington Mills. That is one of its charms.

I guess, too, my brain was still preoccupied with my long-into-the-night discussion with Arabella—a discussion that had left both of us not only extravagantly tired by morning, but rather non-plussed. For we had not tackled, really, the whys and wherefores of the murder mystery itself, but rather the whys and wherefores of our involvement with it, though we really knew the answer to the latter, and it wasn't just Lana-Lee's blue eyes that swung it, either. It was Adam Longhurst. We just couldn't see him as a murderer. Bully, yes; but killer, no. Nor did the prospect of ten thousand pounds influence our thoughts one iota. Arabella and I had decided we would accept no financial reward beyond the recovering of legitimate expenses, and the odd bob for any loss of trade from the Toy Emporium.

So, after about an hour on the beach waiting in vain for some kind of inspiration to strike, I walked rather stiffly back to my Beetle, and decided, whilst I was in the area, I might as well go visiting. I drove back to the main road, and stopped at the first phone box. By a miracle it still had some of its glass left, and the phone itself actually worked—which was just as well, as I could see what was left of the phone book lying like confetti from *Gulliver's Travels* along the ditch outside. Directory enquiries was coldly prompt, and I soon knew where I was going—physically, that is. It was no distance at all.

The house was very much what I had been expecting—post-war executive righteous. To describe it, as no doubt estate agents would, as neo-Georgian was wholesale flattery, and enough to make those poor old German-speaking kings of ours turn in their tombs. However, to some, no doubt, a highly desirable assembly of brick and breeze-block. Its saving grace was its setting—up a private road, and in an area liberally besprinkled with trees.

I pulled the Beetle up the salt-and-pepper-tarmacked drive, and stopped beside an all white Escort XR4 that flashed indiscreetly in the downing sun. I regretted not having brought my sunglasses. I reckoned by the look of the place, I might have a need for them indoors as well.

I rang the bell, and heard it Westminster chime away. I'd finished shuddering by the time she came to the door.

"I'm sorry, we make it a practice not to . . ." she began. Then the penny dropped. "Why, it's you, Mr er. . . ."

I had a feeling her puzzled expression wasn't just due to her hunt for my name. "Marklin."

"That's right. Peter, isn't it?" A veneer of a smile came over her face. "I mistook you for one of those awful door-to-door salesmen."

"Thanks," I grinned.

She hesitated, then stepped aside at the doorway.

"Oh, Peter, how rude of me. Do please come in."

I thanked her once more and entered. She went ahead of me, but looked back continually in case I got lost. The hall was as predictable in style as the house: discreet in its muted pastel colour scheme, loud in its furnishings and effects, especially the latter. I particularly hated the elephant's foot stool and the bull's horn dinner gong.

"Come into the sitting-room, Peter. I hope you will excuse the untidiness."

I went in and excused it immediately. There wasn't any. Everything was just where it should have been, that is, if some of the things had to be anywhere. In this room, I guess it was the curved copper hood over an open fire basket that scored lowest on my taste-ometer. It was shaped like the roof of a Chinese pagoda, and had little brass balls on its corners to boot. However, it was certainly a costly error.

"Do sit down." Her green eyes looked a little less nervous now, but they still said, "Why the hell are you here?"

I sat down on one of those G-Plan settees, where even the arms have separate cushions. She curled her willowy frame into a chair to match, but was careful to be careless with how much leg she showed.

"I'm sorry to burst in on you like this," I began, but she stopped me.

"Peter, burst in on me anytime. I'm delighted to see you. Our little chat that unfortunate evening wasn't half long enough for us to get to know each other, even just a teensy bit."

"Well, thank you," I stuttered, "but I'm afraid I'm not really here on a social visit."

"You're here on a social visit whether you like it or not,

Peter. I'll round up some tea in a moment, or would you prefer something stronger? I know some men do about this time of day." She smiled. "Like something stronger, I mean."

"Yes, maybe later. That would be nice." I was starting to regret I had arrived unchaperoned to see Mrs Lavinia Saunders. "But I've really come about Ben Maxwell's death."

She put on an expression of shock/horror and raised her hands in the air.

"Oh Peter, don't remind me. What a dreadful tragedy! Poor darling Lana-Lee. What on earth can have made Adam Longhurst do it? I mean—jealousy is one thing, but murder is quite another, quite another."

"Well, that's why I'm here, really," I explained. "I agree with Lana-Lee. I don't believe Adam Longhurst did kill Maxwell."

"You don't?" Lavinia adjusted her position slightly in the chair, and revealed yet more nylon. "But the police, from all accounts, think he did it. And everything seems to point to his guilt. He has constantly made threats against Ben. His car was seen down by. . . ."

"Yes, I know all about that. Things certainly look bad for him."

"So why don't you think he's guilty? Wishful thinking? Don't like someone you've met turn out to be a murderer? None of us, Peter, like to think of Adam being a killer, but the fact remains, he might well be."

"That's true, Lavinia, but, for the moment, let's give him the benefit of the doubt."

She swung her legs down to the floor, and leant towards me.

"So what are you being right now, Peter? An amateur sleuth? I thought you were just into—old toys, wasn't it?"

"I'm just trying to help Lana-Lee."

"Did she ask you?"

"In a way, but that's not why I'm here."

"So why are you here?" Her green eyes focused on mine.

"I want to hear everyone's views on the tragedy, in case there's something the police have overlooked."

"Something that might help Adam Longhurst and Lana-Lee, or something that will actually nail the killer?" She smiled again. "They're not the same objectives, you know."

"I know. Maybe I want to help the innocent rather more than track the guilty."

She smoothed a hand down her leg, thoughtfully. "My, Peter dear, you *are* an amateur, aren't you?" Then she laughed. "Not even as good as Inspector Plodder."

I recognized the name, but for a moment, could not place it.

"Inspector Plodder?"

"Oh Peter, don't tell me you don't know. It was only on television a few nights back. The night of poor Ben's murder, in fact."

I cast my mind back. Then it hit me. Arabella and I had decided not to watch, as, despite our love of Olivier and Caine, we had seen it twice already.

"I'm sorry. I'm slow today. *Sleuth*— the fake inspector in *Sleuth.*"

"Didn't you see it the other night? I did. Riveting. It's incredible how sexy Olivier is in it, considering his age. Twice as sexy as poor Michael Caine."

"Arabella and I had seen it a few times before."

"Oh, you must excuse my going on. It was the first time for me, you see. Wonderful film. . . ."

I was starting to become a trifle impatient. "Look, Lavinia, however good *Sleuth* may be, I really want to talk about Maxwell's death. Now can I start by asking you who you think might have done it?"

"I've told you. Adam Longhurst. Everything points to him, poor lad."

"But Ben must have had other enemies?"

"Of course. Everyone has enemies. Don't you?"

"Yes, I guess so." I smiled. "And no doubt I'll have more after my little investigations."

She rose languorously, crossed over to my settee and sat down.

"I doubt it, Peter. You're not the type to ruffle people into hatred, I would have thought. Anyway, who do you think killed Ben?" She put a hand on my knee. "Me?" she piped in a little girl voice.

"No. Why should I? I just don't know. All I think I know is that Longhurst didn't."

We were both silent for a moment, and I could hear her breathing. For some unknown reason, it sounded sexy. It certainly did not aid my thought processes.

"Did you know Ben well?" I came out with, at last.

She sighed. "You're getting personal now, aren't you?"

"No, I don't mean to, Lavinia, believe me. I'm just after background facts."

I could feel her turn towards me on the settee. I didn't dare look across.

"Well, all right, if you want to know, there's hardly a woman around here married or unmarried, Ben Maxwell did not make a pass at. All in such a short space of time, too."

"And he made a pass at you?"

"Of course. Am I that unattractive you thought he wouldn't?"

I didn't rise to it. "Did you like him?"

"You don't mean that, do you, Peter? You mean, did I fall for his pass?"

"Okay." I looked round at her. "I know it's an impertinent question, but did you?"

She laughed quietly. "Well, I suppose it's an open secret. My husband and I have this arrangement, you see. Have had since we first met. We allow each other certain freedoms. We believe it's the best way to prolong and cement a marriage—prevent one or other of us running off just for the novelty of a new lover or a new whim."

"And you . . . ?"

"Yes. Not often. Three times, in fact. He was a good lover. Rotten man, maybe, but good in bed."

For the first time, she sounded genuinely upset about his demise, and I started to feel sorry for her.

"Do you know of any other women who . . . ?"

"Peter, I don't need reminding of Ben's other lady friends

91

right now," she interrupted, rather icily. "No doubt there were many. I'm glad to say Ben was not one of those lovers who feed their egos and virility by describing past conquests."

I notched up one for Ben Maxwell. Just the one. And nought for myself for getting my timing wrong, a mistake that would now prevent me from proceeding on to my next risky line of enquiry—whether she still carried a torch for her ex-lover, Adam Longhurst, and, if she did, whether it was in remembrance, or to be used as a firebrand with which to burn him. I regretfully changed the subject.

"Did your husband enjoy *Sleuth?*"

She looked at me in surprise, then burst out laughing. "You have changed tack, haven't you, Peter? Did I frighten you? I wouldn't want to frighten you."

"No, I wasn't frightened. I was just being a little more tactful, that's all. You were right to admonish me."

She edged a little closer to me. Her perfume, now at point blank range, was difficult to ignore. However, I tried.

"Now, what was that about my husband?"

"Did he see *Sleuth* with you?"

"No. He flew to Paris that morning, and stayed overnight. He had a meeting with Jean-Paul. You met him, remember, at that strange party."

I remembered. "So he did not return until after Maxwell's body had been found?"

Lavinia smiled, and put her hand on my arm. "Sorry, Peter. I'm not helping you, am I? I was watching *Sleuth* that night, and John was in Paris. Neither of us was on the beach at Osmington Mills."

"I hope I did not sound as if I thought you were."

She sat round towards me on the settee, until her knee touched mine. "Of course you didn't. If you are to help Lana-Lee and, of course, Adam, you have to ask questions. I understand that. I'm just so sorry the finger still seems to point to Adam." She put her own red-tipped finger to her matching lips. "Unless—" she added, "unless he's covering for someone."

This time it was my turn to move round to face her.

"Who?" I asked, trying to conceal that I guessed the answer.

"Oh no, forgive me. It's too far-fetched." She looked demurely down at her lap. I have seen that expression many times before. It nearly always precedes a pretty massive indiscretion.

"Murder is far-fetched to begin with," I said quietly, and leaned forward. She looked up.

"Don't whisper it to a soul, will you?"

I shook my head.

"Well, there's more than one person who gained from Ben's death, isn't there?"

I pretended to look mystified.

"Oh, come on, Peter, just because she is employing you. . . ."

"Lana-Lee?"

"Precisely. No, I'm not saying she did it, you understand. But she no doubt had enough cause to, without the added motive of freeing herself for Adam Longhurst. Maybe, even, she killed him by accident—didn't really intend to. You know, had an argument on the beach or something. Told Adam immediately. He came down in his Range Rover, stayed long enough to be seen, then went home. Perhaps they both reckoned it would be easier for Adam to escape a murder charge than Lana-Lee and so. . . ."

"You mean they more or less fixed it that he would be arrested to cover for her . . . ?" I said, in a rather disbelieving way.

". . . then she gets you, and maybe there are others, to help get him off, and, supposedly, track down the real murderer. . . ."

". . . which helps throw suspicion even further away from her doorstep, for what murderer ever commissioned a sleuth to track down himself, or, in this case, herself?"

"Far-fetched, I know. But. . . ."

I suddenly realized she had been trying to seduce me into going along with her hypothesis.

93

"There are a thousand 'buts,' Lavinia. Not the least of which is the strong risk that Adam might end up being found guilty."

She took my hand in hers. "Maybe she thought of that too."

"You mean, it's better to lose a lover than to be arrested yourself?"

"Precisely. Lovers can be very cruel sometimes, Peter."

I felt the pressure on my hand increase. I decided I had learned all I wanted to that afternoon.

"I ought to go," I said, "before we have any more wild theories." I tried to rise from the settee, but her hand restrained me.

"I'm sorry if I've upset you."

"You haven't upset me. I have an open mind at the moment."

"Won't you stay for a drink?" her eyelashes asked.

"I ought to get back." I tried to rise once more and, to my relief and surprise, succeeded.

"Next time then," she smiled, and got up to stand beside me.

"Yes. Great. I'm sorry to have interrupted your afternoon."

"I like being interrupted," she almost winked. I didn't almost wink back. "Let me know how your investigations proceed." She continued lazily, "I still think the police are right, you know. Sorry and all that. But I wouldn't want our theorizing of a moment ago to be proven correct, would I?"

"No, I suppose not." She led me out past the elephant's foot and the bull's horn gong, the undulation of her lips matching their unashamed impudence. At the door, I extended my hand, to be met with proffered lips and a "Oh come, Peter, we know each other well enough now for a goodbye kiss, surely."

I had no ready come back to that, so I kept my mouth closed whilst I obliged.

Seven

As I drove away, raindrops started pearling on my windscreen, and I could hear their pitter-patter on the Beetle's soft top. For some reason, I guess preoccupation, I did not switch my wipers on right away. Soon the raindrops began joining together in wind-tortured rivulets, and vision became as blurred and full of stray images as my mind. I slowed, then pulled to a stop in the first convenient gateway to a field. A clap of thunder resounded around me the instant I switched off the engine. I smiled, as it reminded me of Gus's old Ford Popular, and the remembrance made me feel slightly better. I shook my head as if to clear my mind of all the trashy ideas and theories it had been accumulating ever since Ben Maxwell's death, for their continued presence would, I felt, eventually disease my mind if I wasn't careful —or at least foul my imagination, and thus my life. My quiet rural life. I laughed out loud at the thought.

A raindrop eventually slurped its way through the stitching in the rag top above my head, and plopped, icy cold, on to my forehead. I was grateful to it, and did nothing to hinder its dribble down my nose, and on to my top lip, for it woke me from my mental and physical paralysis. Didn't tell me what to do, just what not to do, which was get so worked up about the problems of an actress I hardly knew that I sat around in damp cars in muddy gateways, listening to the thunderclaps of Zeus reverberate around me. I half switched on the ignition and operated the windscreen wipers. Away in the distance, I saw a tiny rend of blue in the black backcloth of the thunderclouds (but not enough, as my mother would say, "to make a sailor a pair of pants"). Across the blue were the white contrails of a high flying jet winging its way above the dark troubles of this world. I envied it, then blessed it, for I now knew what I was going to do. I turned the ignition the whole way, and the motor rumbled to life. The wheels slithered in the mud and then I was back on the road—to sanity.

Luckily, he was in when I arrived. The sky had shrugged off the autumn storm, and now had enough blue to open a dozen sailors' outfitters. The Beetle's soft top steamed in the sun, as I got out and walked up to the front door. Mr Muir had seen me pull in, and was there in the porch to greet me.

"I thought you might not be able to wait, Mr Marklin," he smiled. "Do please come in."

"I'm not disturbing you, am I?" I said a bit sheepishly.

"Not at all. I'm actually working on your master at the moment. So all you are interrupting is your own work." He chuckled and I felt distinctly better.

I followed his short figure down the hall, and remembered to duck my head as we went into the so neat and tidy sitting-room.

"If you make yourself comfortable, I'll go and get it."

As I sat down in an armchair, I noticed quite a few of the items I had originally seen on his dining-room table were now back in what I assumed were their normal places: the brass Sherman tank and Montgomery's staff car on the front window ledge, the Saracen armoured car and the Chieftain tank on a small formica-topped coffee-table, two of the better dog models, bloodhounds, on a side window ledge. But it was the angel centred on the mantelshelf above the tiled fireplace that riveted my attention. And, at first, I did not really realize it was an angel, for the spread of its wings and its hovering attitude were more those of a merciless predator such as an eagle, than a merciful emissary of God. I did not remember it from my previous visit. It was hardly something to be easily forgotten.

I heard what I took to be the back door slam shut and a

moment later Muir returned with a small object wrapped in crumpled tissue paper in his hand. I felt genuinely excited, and inched around in my chair with anticipation. Muir leant forward, removed the tissue paper and handed me the small brass aeroplane. I turned it over carefully in my hands. Though certainly by no means finished, it was still quite recognizably the elusive Flamingo, all four-inch wing-span of it. Muir's sinewy finger pointed at one wing.

"You'll see the wings are still over thick, Mr Marklin. That is because I have, as yet, not started the lettering you wanted on the undersides." His finger moved across to the slim fuselage. "And, of course, I have not yet detailed the cockpit or cabin windows. But. . . ."

"No buts, Mr Muir. It's wonderful, even as it is." I turned it over in my hands, and the brass glinted in the light from a standard lamp. "I'm just surprised you've got so far already."

Muir pulled up the hard, upright chair he had used the first time I'd called, and leaned forward towards me, his close-set eyes alive with what I took to be enthusiasm.

"Every task one takes on in life should be started as soon as one can possibly manage it. Procrastination, Mr Marklin, profits no one—except perhaps. . . ."

". . . the devil." I had a sudden inexplicable compulsion to complete his sentence.

Muir sat back in his chair and clasped his hands together. "Precisely, Mr Marklin. If there was less procrastination in this world, if we all actually completed everything we state we wish to undertake, there would be more employment and far fewer idle hands to make mischief." He shook his head, and then pointed back at the aeroplane in my hands.

"But I digress, I'm afraid. You're happy with my work so far?"

"Very happy. Excited even." I handed the Flamingo back to him. "It's a satisfying feeling to see a dream one has had becoming a reality stage by stage, even a little dream, like a reproduction toy aircraft."

"Little dreams are often the best, aren't they? They so

often come closer to being realized." His tone was reflective now, and he transferred his gaze to something outside the windows. Way, way outside, I had the feeling.

"Anyway, thanks," I said quietly. "When do you think . . . ?"

"About another ten days, I'm afraid."

"That's fine. I can understand the lettering underneath the wings. . . ."

"It's not the lettering." Muir pointed to the mantelshelf. "You may have noticed my new angel. I was on the point of completing that, when you commissioned the Flamingo. It's a kind of prototype for a much larger brass figure that is to be fixed to the front of a pulpit in a place of worship, near where I used to live in Buckinghamshire. I have to go there and take measurements, devise how it is to be fastened to the pulpit and so forth, before I start work on the final full-size angel." He grinned. "Luckily, like yours, it's a commission. The cost of the brass alone would more than bankrupt me otherwise."

"Congratulations. You must be very pleased."

"I am. Especially as it's where my father used to worship, in his last years. We're all serious, you see, Mr Marklin, about religion. Belief is important to us."

His mention of his father reminded me of something Adam Longhurst had told me the morning after the eventful party.

"Wasn't your father, at one time, connected with toy manufacture, or so Mr Longhurst informed me?"

"Yes, he was. In Liverpool."

"Binns Road?"

"Yes. By a curious coincidence, it was the Meccano factory where they also made Dinkies."

"Did he work on Dinkies?"

"Originally. Later he went on to be a foreman on the other products."

"When he was on Dinkies, did he work on cars or aircraft?"

"Both. He used sometimes to make the wooden prototypes for the Meccano board to discuss. Pre-war, that is." He smiled. "But I don't think he had anything to do with the Flamingo, if that's what you're thinking. I would have told you if he had, I assure you."

I grinned. "It would have been too much to ask, wouldn't it?"

"Perhaps. Anyway, I learnt what little skill I have in model making from him, first in balsa wood, you know, then harder woods, then aluminium, and finally on to brass and so on. He passed on some fourteen years ago now, I'm afraid, before Dinkies became so very collectable. He would have been very gratified to see so much enthusiastic interest in the past."

I suddenly heard a door close somewhere above me. I looked up in surprise. Muir proffered a calming hand.

"Only my wife, Mr Marklin. She must have just got up from her nap. She's not in the best of health, you know."

I heard slow footfalls descend the uncarpeted stairs, and a moment later the grey-haired woman I had seen carrying her shopping from her Minor Traveller on my first visit, hesitantly entered the room.

"Oh, Malcolm, is it . . . ?"

"Come on in, my dear. This is the Mr Peter Marklin I've told you about. The Dinky aeroplane, remember?"

She extended a hand rather shakily. I took it. It felt icy cold and far too fragile to grip tightly.

"I'm sorry if I woke you, Mrs Muir."

"No, no, no, Mr Marklin. I should have been up half an hour or more ago. Life's far too short to sleep all of it away." Her voice was far stronger than her handshake, and had a curious drawl—a little like a very English Katie Hepburn. Her husband helped her to a chair, and she sat down with obvious relief.

"I get pains in my legs, I'm afraid, Mr Marklin. An aneurism, I think they call it."

"She should have the operation, but she won't," Muir commented, smiling sympathetically at his wife.

"I don't believe in interfering with the human body, Mr

Marklin, in any way. I believe that Mother Nature, with God's help, is the finest healer. Never taken a tablet in my life."

I nodded. I've found there's little point in discussion with blind faith. It works best if it's left intact.

"How did you hear of my husband, Mr Marklin?"

"Mr Longhurst," I said, hesitantly, afraid that the mention to her of his name might raise issues she would rather not discuss. For, I reckoned, if you didn't take to interfering with the human body with a tiny tablet, you wouldn't take to someone interfering with one with a bloody great rock.

"Ah, Mr Longhurst." She shook her grey head, and one hand traced the deep lines beside her eyes. "Did you know him well?"

"Hardly at all. Met him once at a party at Miss Claudell's, that's about it."

"Miss Claudell. Mrs Maxwell, you mean. She was not a miss, she was married," she said emphatically. "It was forgetting she was married that no doubt led Mr Longhurst to do what he did."

Muir went over to his wife's chair, and, sitting on the arm, held her hand.

"Now don't get upset again, my dear. He's not worth it."

"*They're* not worth it, you mean," she countered. "She's as guilty as he is."

There wasn't much point in asking them whether they thought Longhurst *was* actually guilty, because he had obviously been condemned for adultery, let alone murder, so I moved on.

"Ben Maxwell wasn't exactly the world's finest husband, I gather."

My remark obviously fell upon stony ground. Not a reaction of any kind blossomed—just silence. I decided my little bit of vintage toy therapy was now starting to be self-defeating, and I didn't want to drive away to another muddy gateway and be leaked upon, for outside the window I could now see the powers that be had turned on the heavenly tap again, bless them. I rose from my chair.

"I should go. It's getting late." Muir rose from the arm of his wife's chair.

"It was nice to see you, Mr Marklin. As I say, the Flamingo should be finished in about another ten days. I'll ring you if it's earlier."

"Thanks." I went across and gently held the hypothermic hand.

"It was nice to meet you, Mr Marklin," she smiled. "I'm afraid it's raining again. Would you like an umbrella?"

"Thanks, but no. I'll run to the car. I lose umbrellas."

Muir saw me to the door. A different me, a me with a rapidly rising bump on my forehead. Somehow, my short time with the Muirs had completely erased my memory of that sodding low sitting-room doorway. And as I drove back to my seaside worry blanket of Studland, the rain seemed to pick on that bump, as it seeped through the rotten seams of my rag top.

"It's not been your day." Arabella poured me a glowing glass of scotch, and I steadied her hand on the soda.

"You can say that again."

"It's not been your day," Arabella instantly came back, with a Cheshire cat grin. You can see why I love that girl, can't you?

"I don't think I'm cut out to be a sleuth," I said miserably.

"What about being an Inspector Plodder?" she grinned up at me.

"Don't talk to me about inspectors. Just before you came home tonight, I had rung bloody Blake at least three times. Same stupid answer from the same tinny voiced girl every time: 'Inspector Blake is in conference right now. Can anyone else help you?' "

I downed a nice long burn of my scotch to drown the swear words that I knew were just bubbling to surface. "The bloody man got me into this mess. He can get me out again."

Arabella made no comment and I knew why. Blake had certainly opened the door for me a little, but it was I, Peter Antrobus Marklin (there, you know my middle monica now

—my mother's maiden name. Initials didn't help me at school, either), who had walked straight in, all of his own little accord. That's what made it all worse.

Neither of us spoke for a moment, except my throat as it coped with the scotch. It was Arabella who broke the relative silence.

"You need a rest," she suggested, and suddenly sat cross-legged facing me on the settee. "I've got an idea, Peter. You go up to bed now. I'll rustle up the odd omelette or two with some chips courtesy of Birds Eye, and bring yours up to you. We'll both eat upstairs. And then we can watch some TV on the portable, or whatever." I liked the idea of "whatever," so agreed. "Take the dreaded portable phone with you and keep ringing Blake," she smiled.

Before the omelettes were being helped up the stairs, I actually caught Blake in his office on the second bedside call. For a moment I was speechless, which was just as well. Blake had been on the point of ringing me, and had all his words professionally prepared and ready.

"I got your previous messages, and about Lavinia. Thanks for ringing, Peter. I've only just managed to surface for the first time today. Things are marching, as they say."

"In the right direction?"

"Well, let's just leave it that they're on the march. A lot of things."

"There are a lot of things I want to talk to you about, Sexton."

"Are you on the march?"

"Not unless it's backwards, no. That's not what I really want to say."

"Well, let's meet and have a pow-wow."

"When we smoke pipe?" I mustered in my best Red Indian voice.

"I was thinking of tonight. Say, in three-quarters of an hour or so."

My heart sank. I (normally) hate dressing twice in one day.

"Perhaps I could take you up on your previous kind invitation to some supper. Or can I take you both out?"

"Well—we'd be happy to see you, but . . . er . . . couldn't it wait, like until tomorrow?"

There was silence for a moment, then Blake said quietly, "Adam Longhurst will be in court tomorrow."

I suddenly decided my bedtime omelette was hardly of earth-shattering importance.

"Expect you in three-quarters of an hour. Do you like omelettes?"

"They're those you have to smash eggs to get, aren't they?"

"I guess so," I said, and put down the receiver. He had an apt turn of phrase, when he wanted to, did our Inspector Trevor Blake.

He arrived dead on forty minutes later. Arabella was still changing upstairs.

"Ferry left the second I boarded it. Bit of luck." He smiled at me. "Except for you, I guess. Made me early."

I led him into the sitting-room. "Don't worry. It gives us more time to get business out of the way before supper." I poured him a scotch and soda, without being asked. His eyes looked tired enough to demand one on their own. We sat down opposite each other.

"So Digger Whetstone is convinced Longhurst is guilty?"

"Yes," Blake almost sighed.

"What's the evidence?"

"Nothing very new. But it's all pretty damning. Lover of famous actress hates returning husband. Car observed at the scene of the crime, at the time of the crime. Known to have threatened the husband on several occasions. The last straw, I would judge, was when Whetstone discovered that Longhurst had been cashiered from the army for assaulting a fellow officer. A big man with a short fuse. And a man with no alibi."

"What about a phone call I believe he claims was made to him that evening?"

Blake smiled. "You must have been talking to his solicitor."

"Of course. I haven't been able to talk to Longhurst yet."

Blake settled back in his chair. "Well, Whetstone reckons that's one of the weakest stories he's heard in a long time. A lady whose voice Longhurst claims he did not recognize, asking him to come down to Osmington Mills, because there was some trouble with Maxwell."

"What do you reckon?"

"I must say I tend to agree. It sounds like a story you think up on the spur of the moment, when you're in trouble. And what's more, if it were true, and a lady *did* ring, then who is the lady, and why does he say he didn't recognize the voice?"

"One of his old girlfriends? He's had plenty, I believe, and so had Maxwell."

Blake downed some scotch, then said, "Or his current girlfriend, perhaps. And he *did* actually recognize her voice, but realized the implications if he said so."

"Lana-Lee. I've thought of that." I got up from my chair, went over to the window and drew the curtains on sleepy old Studland.

"By the way, Blake, that's what I wanted to say to you." I came over and looked down on him. "Why the hell did you tell Lana-Lee about me? The amateur sleuthing bit, I mean. What did you actually say? 'If you're ever in trouble, call old Peter Marklin. He's even better than Lord Peter Wimsey, because he's not so bloody snobbish about the *nouveau riche*?'"

"First bit's more or less right. Second bit totally wrong."

I leaned forward, my hand on his chair arm.

"You knew what was likely to happen, didn't you? And you reckoned Whetstone was going to get it wrong. But the dear old conventions of the police force don't allow one inspector to quarrel publicly or argue with another, although it can all be achieved through a third party—a gullible third party, more commonly known as a prize sucker. You didn't even have to look around for him. He was literally on Lana-

Lee's doorstep. So you dropped the word in her lovely ear, and bingo, the sucker is sucked in." I broke off to refuel from my glass. "Thank you very much, Sexton bloody Blake. But this time, it's all different. It's not like the Treasure case. This time I feel totally out of my depth. I don't know what you're up to, for a start. And my first full day at this investigation lark, has marched, as you call it, nowhere. All I'm getting are precious few facts, but more and more fanciful theories. I'm up to here" (I pointed to the ceiling) "with theories, and I'm no professional. Any one of them could be true. How would I know? Maxwell seemed to have upset enough people to have been murdered countless times. Anyway, maybe Whetstone is right, and Longhurst did do it. Or even worse for me, Longhurst and Lana-Lee arranged it together in some convoluted plan or other. Don't you see, Blake, it's all too big for me. And that's totally ignoring your smuggling investigations."

Blake put down his glass. "I'm sorry, Peter. Maybe I was wrong and it would have been better to have kept it simply a police matter."

"Better for whom?" a much softer voice asked, and I looked round and saw Arabella. She went across and kissed Blake on the cheek. It was the first time I had ever seen him blush. He pointed at the chunky sweater she had just put on. It had countless pussy-cats all over it.

"Which one is Bing?"

"All of them," she smiled. "I daren't say anything else. He gets very jealous."

By the time I had poured Arabella a glass of white wine, my temperature had settled back to around the mid ninety-eights, and my brain was starting to separate reason from emotion once more. After a modicum of general tittle-tattle, we resumed more sanely where we had left off. Blake took the stage.

"Well, it was unfair of me to involve Peter, by proxy, as it were. And I suppose, even more ungentlemanly then to leave him out in the cold as far as imparting my information goes. But believe me, I had to. Until tonight, that is. Now I can, at least, tell you where I fit into the whole picture, and how it might affect the Maxwell murder case, if at all."

He downed the last of his scotch, then continued, "I'm investigating the importation of drugs. I needn't go into all the details, because they do not impinge upon Maxwell's death. Or I don't think they do. So I'll just tell you what I think may be relevant, on the understanding that this conversation is totally off the record."

I nodded. And by my nod, knew he knew Mr Sucker had been sucked in again.

"From information we have received from Paris, via a source, curiously, very similar in character to your own—in other words, someone working with the police, rather than for the police. . . ."

"Good heavens, it's international," I groaned. "I thought you were unique. Who is your double in France? Inspector Clouseau?"

"Inspector Chasseur, actually. Anyway, to continue. From this amateur source, we learnt that Maxwell might have been getting up to his old tricks again. Oh, I'm sorry, I haven't told you what those old tricks were, have I?"

"Don't bother. I know. Grand Prix cars stuffed to the steering wheel with anything you can sniff or smoke no doubt."

"Correct. Interpol could never nail Maxwell for those little transgressions. We learned about them too late. But, directly we heard Maxwell had come into this country, and we couldn't stop him because he had never been accused of anything, we decided to keep a watching brief on him. Nothing much seemed to happen for a bit; his only sins seemed to be sexual. And it wasn't until I had a brainwave about Reinhardt that things began adding up."

"Reinhardt?" Arabella queried. "What's the connection?"

"Quite literally, a French connection, I'm afraid. Drugs. Might have gone undetected for months, or even years, if Maxwell had not been involved. It was a neat plan, no doubt triggered by the contract Lana-Lee had signed for the new perfume range. Almost as neat as Grand Prix cars."

I finished my own scotch, in my mental hunt for how you smuggle drugs in a perfume range. Arabella got there in a trice.

"Talc?" she offered. "Drugs substituted, white powder for white powder?"

"Not quite," Blake smiled, "but congratulations, you're on the right track. I guessed maybe it was the talc, but it turned out to be something rather more clever. I don't know whether you know the Lana-Lee range . . . ?"

"I was given some at the press conference. I have them upstairs," Arabella said, as she took Blake's glass to refresh it.

"Well, then, you'll know that because of this current *brouhaha* about aerosols destroying our planet's ozone layer and so on, Reinhardt reintroduced the old rubber bulb horn type of cologne sprays, like I remember my mother used to have."

"Ditto mine," I added, remembering how irate my mother had once become after I had decided to mend my bicycle horn with the bulb borrowed (stolen, actually; I had no intention of putting it back) from her Yardley cologne.

"Well, instead of those bulbs being full of air. . . ."

"Snowballs," Arabella exploded, and slopped a little of Blake's refilled scotch onto his lap, in her excitement. "What a fabulous idea. Black rubber snowballs," she continued enthusiastically.

I thought I had better intervene. "Arabella, you're not supposed to get delirious about the activities of criminals, however creative you think they are. Sexton will get the wrong idea."

"No, she's right. It was clever. We intercepted the first shipment the day before yesterday, thanks to our amateur informant. You see how useful right-minded citizens can be, Peter?" He winked at me. I didn't wink back.

"And you believe it was all Maxwell's idea? How ironic he didn't grow even fatter on the profits."

"He had an accomplice, obviously—more than one—in Reinhardt. The French police are rounding up a couple of lesser figures now. But he needed one key figure who would, quite naturally, during the course of business, be constantly travelling from France to England."

"Let me guess. That suave Frenchman fellow, Jean-Paul whatshisface—you know, Arabella. He kissed your hand at Lana-Lee's unfortunate party. I thought he was too smooth to be true."

Arabella frowned. Blake laughed. "No, Peter, I'm afraid you're wrong. Jean-Paul Gautier, I think you mean, was certainly involved, but not in the way you think." Blake played with his glass. "You see, he is Inspector Clouseau's Peter Marklin. It's through him and his intuition, we learned most of what we know."

"Monsieur Sucker," I whispered to myself, but loudly enough for Blake to hear. He laughed.

"Maybe. No, Maxwell's accomplice was not Monsieur Sucker, but an Englishman you also, I believe, met at the same party."

"You can't mean Saunders? I was only with his wife this afternoon."

"We picked him up just as he was leaving work for home. Around 5.45. He's still at headquarters."

"Are you sure it was Saunders?" Arabella asked with some disbelief.

"As sure as I can be of anything in this convoluted mess, yes. You see, he was hardly a hard nut to crack, otherwise I would not have been able to come and see you tonight. As it is, I've still got a busy night ahead of me, after supper. I've left him making a full statement of his part in the affair."

"He confessed?" I asked.

"The instant we brought him to Bournemouth. I think Maxwell's death had unnerved him more than somewhat. Maybe he thought we would accuse him of something worse —his murder."

"Now, that's a thought," I mumbled, trying to absorb the ramifications of yet another theory being added to my collection. "Maybe he *did* arrange for his murder. And that would solve my problem, if not his, and I could go back to the tranquillity of selling the odd toy or two to peace-loving romantics."

"Such as yourself," Arabella teased, raising her already quite arched eyebrows. I lowered mine at her.

Blake looked at his watch. "It's okay," Arabella took the hint. "There's a cheese soufflé in the oven. I noted that you have to get back tonight."

"I'm sorry about that. I left the boys taking the statement, because it sounded as if it would go on hours. As I have to go to London tomorrow all day, I thought I had better see you tonight and catch up later with the full details of his confession, when he has finished it. Otherwise, it might have been some time before I could have explained things, let alone apologize. And, with Longhurst going to court tomorrow. . . ."

"Well, thanks for coming, anyway. I can imagine how busy you must be. But tell me, did Saunders blame Maxwell for the whole affair, or what? And, if he didn't murder him, does he have any idea as to who did?"

"Question one—yes, he did blame him more or less. Said Maxwell came to him with the idea and traded on their old friendship and a bit of blackmail."

"Blackmail? About what?"

"Something that happened years ago, he claimed, on the Grand Prix circuit. Some girl trouble or other. You know how the racing teams attract girls like long limbed flies. Story sounded pretty woolly to me. I think it was just a fabricated excuse for his own greed—we gather he owed money left, right and centre. So Maxwell's return with a lucrative, if illegal, idea was a happy and welcome break for him. As to question two, he claims he has no idea who murdered Maxwell. And certainly vehemently, almost hysterically, states he didn't.

"Business partners, especially criminal ones, have been known to include death in their negotiations with each other."

"True. I—er—reminded my colleague of that phenomenon."

"And dear Digger Whetstone, I assume, still maintains Longhurst is guilty, despite these new revelations about Saunders. I assume he knows of them."

"Of course," Blake said, with the smile of an angelic choirboy. "Would I ever conceal anything from a colleague on the force?"

"But you obviously don't share his opinion?"

"Everything points to Longhurst, I'm afraid. That's the problem."

"It's all just too obvious, you mean?"

"Something like that."

"And you're relying on me to prove otherwise?"

"No. Let's just call it enlisting your intuition—like last time. Don't forget, it's Lana-Lee who is asking for proof, I assume, not me. So what does your intuition say about Longhurst? Guilty or not guilty?"

"Open verdict," I truthfully answered.

Arabella got up and pointed kitchenwards. "Soufflé, anyone?"

"Wonderful," said Blake with relish. "I'm famished." As we reached the door, he turned to me. "Peter, just one more piece of information for your mental digestion, so I don't spoil your physical one by talking shop at supper."

"I'm not sure I can down any more, but I can't stop you trying to feed me."

"Saunders could have murdered Maxwell, you know."

"How? Hiring somebody to do it? He was in Paris that night."

"No. He wasn't. That's one of the first things he confessed. He flew back to London early the evening of the murder."

"So Lavinia was lying this afternoon?"

"Probably not. You see, he claims he has an air hostess girlfriend, who lives in Windsor, near the airport. He states that it's paying for her flat and expenses that has helped get him in financial queer street."

"He says he spent the night with her?"

"Yes. Our boys are checking on that now. Just thought you would like to know."

"What's her name?"

Blake reached into the side pocket of his jacket, and produced a well-worn diary. He quickly thumbed to the right page. "Elizabeth Sumner. Want the address?"

I nodded. "Just in case I want to run up debts, you understand."

"Thirty-eight, Verulam Avenue, Windsor."

"I heard that," Arabella sang out from the kitchen.

We both laughed, I guess, for the first time that day. You know something? It tasted even better than a Johnny Walker.

Eight

"Are you going to do what Sexton suggested?"

I was startled for a second, as I thought Arabella had dropped off at least an hour before. I looked across at her tousled head peeping above the bedclothes.

"Haven't got much alternative, have I? Unless you call going out of one's mind an alternative."

She sat up on one elbow, and there was just enough moonlight in the room to dust what sheets now revealed into distracting prominence.

"Sounded sensible though, take each day at a time, not rush things, let the impressions build up in your mind before trying to tie them all up into neat parcels, or making them form a pattern, let alone a solution."

"Easy enough to say."

She reached for my hand. "I thought his analogy was very good."

I looked at her with mock horror. "Really, madam. . . ."

She shook her lovely head. "No, seriously, Peter, you were expecting it all to pan out like it does in those old Hollywood private eye movies, with every interview or encounter being wonderfully productive and pushing the plot merrily along to a hugely successful climax. It's not like that in real life, as Blake said. It's ninety-five per cent work for five per cent progress, and that's if you're lucky. It can be a hundred per cent for nowt. And, to quote him, another unsolved crime joins the others gathering dust and cobwebs in the basement."

"I didn't like him calling me Sam Shovel, the poor man's Sam Spade."

"He was trying to cheer you up."

"He could have chosen a million better ways of doing so."

Arabella sat bolt upright. "You haven't really answered my question. Are you going to take it more sanely—let impressions build up on their own, without forcing them to . . . ?"

"You make me sound like a sponge," I chuckled.

"Yes," Arabella said delightedly, "that's exactly right. That's what Blake wants you to be, not Sam Shovel, but Sam Sponge. Soak it all up, and only squeeze yourself out at the end to see what you've got, if anything."

"But I have to squeeze myself before poor Longhurst is found guilty by twelve good men and true."

"And women."

"Twelve good jury persons and true. That better, Gloria Steinem?"

She squeezed my hand. "That's better." Then she snuggled down beside me, very beside me.

"Do you know something?" I whispered.

"What?" she mumbled into my cheek.

"It must be the only time in my adult life when I have totally undressed twice in one day, and not made love."

"Has to be a first time." Her mumble translated itself into some rather soft brushing of her lips on my neck. Tired as I was, I turned towards her, and then the phone rang. And rang and rang and rang and rang. At last, I couldn't stand it any longer. I freed a hand and answered it. It was Lavinia. Deep down in the hysterical "Help me's" I soon traced the slur of alcohol. Lots of it. After about ten minutes I had managed to calm her down sufficiently to discover she reckoned I was about the only friend in the world to whom she could turn—for what, I couldn't quite make out. Hardly to help her husband, as the trigger for her call (beyond alcohol) had been the police informing her of his arrest and total confession. Maybe it was just a shoulder to cry on. In the end, I left it that I wasn't at my best at 2.30 in the morning,

113

but would bring both shoulders around some time during the day's more civilized hours.

"Don't forget to see Gus first, will you?" Arabella reminded me, as I put the phone back under the pillow.

"No. Otherwise, I'll go bankrupt. And I ought to go and see my famous client too, Lana-Lee, like a good Sam. . . ."

". . . Sponge."

"Shut up," I explained. And a moment later, unchivalrously, I went out like a light—a burnt out forty-watt variety.

I didn't have to go *chez* Gus. He came to me—to pirate a breakfast, and catch up on whatever news was going. Arabella had left some minutes before to go to her paper and cajole her boss into letting her cover Adam Longhurst's appearance in court. So I fed Gus's maw with toast and Robertson's, coffee and my lack of progress on the Maxwell affair. To cheer me up, he praised Blake for his cleverness over the Reinhardt snowball drugs operation. Sometimes, I think Gus thinks tact is what a carpet is. Eventually I managed to bring the conversation round to what I wanted. Luckily, he gave me the lead.

"What's my role going to be in all this thing, then?" he asked between giant munches. "Like to help."

"Friend and confidant."

Gus looked non-plussed. "No, I mean what am I going to *do*?"

"Well, it's this way, Gus. I nearly got you killed the last time you helped me. And I'm not willing to risk your neck again."

"My neck."

"My risk. My guilt. My fault I took this case on. So it's my decision."

"So what the hell do I do?" he muttered.

"Something I can't right now. At least, not properly."

"Think straight?" he offered.

"No. That I'm doing. I—er—would like you to hold the fort."

"What fort? You bought Corfe Castle, then?" He shook with laughter and slopped some coffee onto Bing's tail. The meow was hardly one of affection.

"Mind the shop for me. You know, open up and sell toys now and again, when I can't."

To say his expression was one of disbelief was the understatement of the year.

"It's not difficult," I quickly added. "Every toy is marked with its price. Only discount for cash sales, and then by not more than ten per cent. I'll look after all the direct mail orders in the evenings and. . . ."

Gus interrupted by clearing his throat. Sounded like thunder. "Like me to Hoover round? Do a bit of dusting? Windows need a wipe?"

"Oh come on, Gus, it was just a thought. If you don't want to do it, forget it. I was going to mention you get ten per cent of everything you sell too."

"Don't want charity, I don't. If I do anything, I do it because I want to. Not because I'm being bribed. Got my OAP to keep me going nowadays, besides me boat."

"Okay, I won't mention it again."

Gus's eyes suddenly lit up, as he put down his coffee mug. "Tell you what, old son. Let's do a bit of bargaining."

"What have you got in mind, Gus?" I asked with some trepidation.

"Well, I'll open up shop for you once in a while, if sometimes you take me with you, or let me help, with this Longhurst thing. Only fair, that is."

I thought about it for a minute, then had an idea of my own. I extended my hand. "Okay, Gus, thanks. I appreciate it. Keeps the wolf from the door. And I've got something I'd like you to do, if you would." I grimaced as he shook my hand. (He had a grip like a vice. Can tighten nuts without a spanner. Seen him do it.)

"What's that then?"

"This weekend, Saturday, would you mind if Tara-Lee came and helped you in the shop? She must be pretty upset about her father's death, and all the commotion it has caused at the Manor, let alone her mother's anguish. Might get her mind off it all." I bit my lip, but needn't have bothered. Gus reacted with one of his broader smiles.

"Do more than that. How about if we kept open all morning, then I took her and her Mum out in me boat for the afternoon? Give 'em both a break, eh? Nothing like sea air for blowing away the miseries."

I breathed a sigh of relief. Gus had found a way of meeting the famous film star at last. "Okay, that sounds good. I'll ask Lana-Lee. I have to see her this morning, anyway. I'll let you know tonight."

Gus slurped the last of his coffee. "But I want a bit of the *real* action as well, you know," he grinned. "I'm not just your social secretary." He grinned with pleasure at knowing there was such a post.

"No, I know, Gus. But that boat trip isn't just social, is it, Gus?" I tried. And it worked.

"You mean—" he thought on, "you mean, keep my ears peeled and all that. Chat 'em up a bit, and you never know what they will let slip?"

"Something like that."

Gus sniffed. "Yeah. Makes sense. I'll—er—whatdoyercallit with you when I get back."

"Liaise."

"Yeah," said Gus, rubbing his head. "Leehaze." He looked at me, all innocence, then asked, "Like another piece of toast?"

"Only if you're having one," I laughed.

Gus double-took, then laughed himself. Some of my happiest times are with Gus.

The drive to Osmington proved to be far less of a chore than I'd imagined. Indeed, I thoroughly enjoyed extending my Beetle a little. (It's a bit naughty. It has a Porsche engine. But everything that shows looks normal Beetle. Tends to get boy racers rattled.) The autumn sun was even warm enough for the top to be down, to help blow the grey from my mind, if not from some of my hair. (I'm discreetly greying at the edges. "Like a cheese," Arabella so tactfully describes it.) Mind you, Gus had beaten the wind to it. His almost gross normality is a wonderful tonic sometimes—politicians should adopt him to ensure a little more objectivity and common sense enters their pontifications. Correction: delete the word "more."

So, by the time I reached the Manor, I was more like my old self. A trifle tired, but with some old fashioned romantic optimism seeping back into my . . . ah, I had to remember that, sponge.

Lana-Lee answered the door herself, and we were soon in her, rapidly becoming familiar, drawing-room.

"I'm so relieved to see you, Peter." She indicated I should sit next to her on the settee. I rather nervously obliged.

"You've heard the terrible news?"

"If you mean about Adam being charged, yes."

"I was going to attend, but Sebastian thought it better I didn't. It would attract far too much press attention, he felt. He wants to keep the whole affair as low key as possible."

I grimaced. "Going to be difficult, I'm afraid."

She sat forward, resting her head on her hands, her long blonde hair falling like a gilt veil over her pain. "And now all that about Ben and Saunders."

"You've heard?"

"Yes. Inspector Blake phoned me late last night. I almost phoned you then." She raised her head, and the haunted look in her eyes only added to her stunning beauty. I could see why Sebastian Lynch wanted to keep her out of the camera's eye. She looked quite sensational enough to murder for. "But almost immediately I received another call," she continued. "I was so tired after that. . . ."

"Let me guess who it was," I said quietly. "Lavinia?"

She nodded. "How did you know?"

"She rang me also."

"To tell you she believed I put Ben up to the drugs scheme with Reinhardt?"

I didn't hide my surprise. "No. Why, is that why she rang you?"

117

Lana-Lee sat around to face me. "Yes. She was horrible, horrible. She ranted and raved, and said I was behind the whole drugs racket, and that because of me, at least three men had been destroyed, her husband, poor Adam and . . . Ben." She suddenly grasped my hands. "Oh Peter, Peter, she can't really think I had anything to do with any of it, can she? Especially Ben's murder."

"*Did* you have anything to do with it?" Hell, there I was being Sam Shovel again. Think sponge. I kicked myself.

She withdrew her hands slowly, and sat back from me a little. "You as well?" I had just added shock to the pain in her eyes, and I felt two inches high.

"No, no. I didn't mean it. It was a stupid question," I stammered.

"No, it wasn't. Not really. You won't be the only person who will harbour a suspicion about me. It doesn't look good, I know. After all, I negotiated the Lana-Lee perfume contract with John Saunders. Then Ben came back. The two of them seem to have got the drugs scheme going. I could have been their mastermind, couldn't I? Once the scheme was in operation, it might be thought Ben was then disposable. Hey presto, I kill Ben, and go back to my lover. Or maybe they might think Adam and I killed Ben together, somehow. I enticed him to the beach, say, where Adam was waiting. . . ." Her voice began breaking, and this time I took hold of her hands.

"Look, you're getting morbid. You mustn't let Lavinia. . . ."

"Ever since her call I've thought of nothing else. Tara-Lee even came into my room, because she heard me crying."

"Remember, if the police really thought what you say, they would be here already."

She looked up at me and shook her head. "They've rung this morning. They want to come to see me at two o'clock, after the court hearing. I've told Sebastian. He's coming at around 1.30. I'm terrified, Peter."

"Don't be. They're probably only trying to tie up some of the loose ends. From what I gather, the French police knew more or less who was and wasn't involved in the drugs operation. They had an inside informant."

"You really think so?"

I lied a little. "I really think so."

I felt a tear dampen the top of my hand. I got out my red spotted handkerchief (one of Arabella's Christmas presents), and wiped away some others which were thinking of following suit. We did not say anything more for a minute or two. We let the sniffs work through. Then she asked softly, "I'm sorry, Peter, I should have asked how you have got on. Anything?"

"Not much, I'm afraid. It's early days. But I've seen your lawyer because Inspector Whetstone wouldn't let me see Adam. I like Mr Lynch. We'll get on well together. From him I learnt about that phone call."

Lana-Lee looked up, and I waited for a comment that didn't come. "The phone call," I continued, "which Adam says he received that evening. From a lady whose voice he said he didn't recognize. Telling him there was some trouble with your husband down on the beach. He says that's why he went. Didn't he tell you before he was arrested?"

She nodded but didn't look at me.

"Why didn't you tell me? I can't help you if you don't tell me everything."

"I know. I should have. But somehow, I found it hard to. . . ."

". . . believe?" I suggested. She nodded again.

"I know Adam is not a liar, but it all sounded so goddamned far-fetched. That some unknown woman would entice him to the beach, to what—frame him?"

I looked her in the eye, with the severest expression I could muster. "He might have been lying about a bit of it, mightn't he?"

Her big beautiful eyes hunted around for the motive behind my question. I came to her aid.

"The bit about not recognizing the voice."

"Why should he do that?" Her naïvety seemed genuine enough. Anyway, she didn't rise to my bait.

"Because he didn't want to incriminate or involve someone he knew, or maybe was fond of."

"I can't think who you can mean." She hesitated, then
went on, "But then, I haven't really known Adam all that
long." I couldn't bring myself to tell her what I was getting
towards, so I changed the subject.

"The terrible thing for Adam is that everyone seems to
have an alibi except him. That, I guess, is where I have to
begin."

"Well, don't begin with mine." She smiled weakly. "It's
hardly cast iron."

"You'd taken an early night, I gather from Sebastian
Lynch."

"Yes, I was very tired. Ben had gone out somewhere. I
never asked him where he was going. I didn't really care any
more. I tried to watch some television but there was nothing
much on except *Sleuth,* and I'd seen that before. So I went up
around ten, and was asleep almost as soon as my head hit
the pillow."

"And your butler and housekeeper?"

"The butler lives this side of Weymouth and goes home
each night. He had gone by then. And Mrs Eames, my
housekeeper, always goes up to her room after the evening
dishes are done. She is over in the west wing, miles from my
room. She watched *Sleuth* apparently, then went to sleep.
Tara-Lee had been asleep for hours by then."

"I see what you mean about your alibi hardly being concrete."

"Yes. Mrs Eames would not have heard me if I had gone
out—unless, perhaps, I'd taken the other car. Ben had the
Cadillac. Inspector Whetstone queried me endlessly about
the hours between ten and midnight, but, in the end, seemed
to take my word for it, I guess because. . . ."

". . . because Adam's alibi was non-existent, and his car
was seen at the beach. It's not hard to see Whetstone's reasoning."

Lana-Lee suddenly rose and went over to the window. I
wondered why until I heard the crackle in her voice. "Oh

120

Peter, what a mess I've made of my life. It would never have happened if. . . ." She could continue no longer, as tears started to drown her words. But I was too intrigued by her last comment to let it go there.

"If what?" I asked softly. There was a moment's pause, then she turned to me, dabbing at her beautiful, blue eyes with a ridiculously small handkerchief.

"If—er—I hadn't married Ben, that's all. Hadn't married Ben years ago." She cleared her throat, and squashed her handkerchief up into a ball in her hand.

"Oh," I said, pretty certain that the hiatus had changed what she had actually been going to say.

"And it wouldn't have happened," I commented, "if you had not let him return." She looked at me and there was a sudden flash of fear in those red-rimmed eyes. I wondered why, and reminded my sponge to absorb its passing. But she wouldn't rise to my hint, so I let it drop.

"What you need is to leave as much of the worrying as you can to me and Sebastian. You're going to get ill if you don't, and that's not fair on Tara-Lee."

She turned to the settee, and sat next to me once more. "I know. She's getting very tense. She shouted at Mrs Eames this morning about just nothing at all."

"Look, a great friend of mine, Gus Tribble—he's a retired fisherman—thought you and Tara-Lee might like to go out in his boat this weekend. Saturday afternoon, in fact. He's looking after my toy shop in the morning, but would love to take you two out in the afternoon. Fresh air would do you both good."

She thought for a second, then asked, "What will you be doing?"

"Oh, ferreting around. Catching up with things."

"And Arabella? Could she come with us?"

"Would you like her to?"

She nodded, and then, without warning, collapsed forward into my arms, and burst into floods of tears. We sat that way for I don't know how long, and I did not leave until I was certain she was, as they say, as well as could be expected in the circumstances. As I walked to my Beetle, I caught sight of the soaking wet patch on the front of my sweater. I shrugged my shoulders. It was a side of being a sponge to which I guessed I'd have to grow accustomed. I just hoped Lavinia would not turn on the tap too. I was not sure how shrink-proof I, or my sweater, was.

Luckily for me, Lavinia was still too shell-shocked to cry to any extent and too tired to rant or rave. But, unfortunately, she wasn't too shocked or tired to remember she was a woman. Don't get me wrong. I'm not particularly averse to vaguely attractive ladies (or even wildly attractive ones) practising their wiles on me, but I don't go for it when sex is just used as a stand-in for desperation. And Lavinia was desperate—for which condition I was truly sorry.

It began badly. She threw her arms around my neck directly I arrived. I had disentangled myself sufficiently by the time we'd reached the sitting-room to be able to commence and maintain for a while some kind of platonic conversation. But I could see by the look in her eyes that Plato would be lucky if he was given very long. I decided to race through my repertoire of questions before the bell rang for round one. I started with, "Did you know your husband was involved with Ben in drugs smuggling?"

"No." She wouldn't look at me. Just sat there, her slim legs drawn up in her chair to let the slit in her skirt pay for its keep.

"Are you sure?" I leaned forward to try to catch her eyes. For a flicker, I got them, a flicker that didn't exactly agree with her answer.

"I promise you, Peter, I didn't know. If I had, I would have tried to stop him."

"Why?" I said unkindly. "Because he might get caught?" I was expecting a "No. I hate drugs. Society's poison."—all that bit. But I was wrong. Lavinia was more honest than I had reckoned. She nodded.

"It may be hard for you to understand, Peter, but we have the perfect marriage. I love him. And I think he loves me.

My odd affair did not mean anything. He knows that. We are just more honest with each other than other married couples. Trading in drugs would have got him arrested at some point or other. Any fool could have seen that. John isn't cut out to be a criminal."

I noted she only mentioned her affairs. I wondered if John had been as honest with her, as she claimed to have been with him.

"Did you know about the air hostess?" I asked. She looked up, and the slight curl of her mouth gave me the answer.

"Of course," she lied. "I knew of all his little dalliances."

I tried harder. "Did you know he had flown back to England a night early?"

"Yes. Of course, I. . . ." She looked at me, but couldn't keep it up.

"Lavinia. I came here to see if I can be of any help in all this mess. If you don't tell me everything, I might as well leave." I wished I hadn't said that, as it triggered her to move across and kneel in front of me, like an overgrown child pleading for forgiveness—or something.

"Peter, I'm sorry. Please don't go. I'm so alone." She rested her head on my knee, and I felt a single tear wet the denim of my trousers. Just the one, luckily, my sweater still wasn't dry.

"You didn't know he had come back, did you?"

"No," she admitted, then quickly added, "But I knew about the girl."

"Okay," I said quietly, but was certain I'd got the picture right in my mind—that she hated her husband having affairs, whatever she said to the contrary. She would have liked to have been the only one eating the cake. A hand joined her head on my knees. I spun through my mental cassette of questions until I came to the next key one.

"Lavinia, tell me. You were very friendly with Adam Longhurst at one time, I believe, before your marriage."

She nodded on my knees—a most curious sensation. I kept up the questioning. "Did you have an affair with him?"

"Yes. We saw a lot of each other on his leaves from the army." She sat up and rested an elbow on my thigh. "He was a great lover, if you want to know. Impulsive. Never knew what he would suggest next."

My imagination worked overtime. "Who broke it off?"

"We—er—sort of both did." I guessed that meant he did. "Then I met and married John."

"Seen Adam since your marriage?"

She hesitated, then smiled. "Seen him—screwed him, you mean?"

This time I nodded.

"Very occasionally." Then she added by way of excuse, "He's hard to resist. He likes married women even better. There's less risk of it getting serious, I suppose." She bit an over-red lip. "But it all stopped when he met little Miss Movie Star. She must pack some tricks in those pants of hers to keep a stud like Adam from straying."

I sighed to myself. Lavinia was missing a lot in life imagining love starts and stops in the groin.

"Maybe he really loves her."

"Adam loves his prick, Peter, and don't you believe anything else."

I moved uncomfortably in my chair, but her elbow didn't take the hint. Quite the reverse. Her arms took to wandering up my thighs.

"Look, Lavinia, I came here because you were in trouble, to see if I could help."

One hand moved across to my zip. "You can. You can," she breathed. "I need you to make love to me. I can't go on not being loved."

I tried to get out of the chair, but she held on to my legs. "All right, Peter, I'm sorry. I'm very sorry. But I'm so afraid . . ." Her hand moved away, and I relaxed a little.

"What are you afraid of? That John will go to prison?"

"Yes."

"It may not be an over-long sentence, if he can prove that Maxwell was the mastermind." But even as I said it, I sort of knew that wasn't really what was worrying her. She rose to her feet, and smoothed the rumples out of her skirt.

"But what do you serve for murder, Peter?" Suddenly she was now totally calm and collected. The metamorphosis was amazing.

"But last time, you theorized to me that if it wasn't Adam, you thought it might be Lana-Lee."

"So it could have been. It's not what I think. It's what the police might put together."

"That your husband killed Maxwell? I don't think so. Inspector Whetstone has Adam Longhurst in court this morning. He is being formally charged with Maxwell's murder."

Before she had a chance to react, we both heard a car draw up outside the house. She went immediately to the window, then turned to me.

"I've been expecting them. They asked me to stay in."

I crossed over to the window myself. There it was, a shiny white Granada with a red stripe, out of which two plain clothed men (very plain) I'd never seen before were emerging.

She took my hand and drew me back from the window. "Pray for me, Peter." She suddenly hugged me, and her cheek obviously alighted on the damp patch. She looked up enquiringly.

"I got rained on." I smiled. "Do you want me to stay?"

She looked puzzled, but disentangled herself, and led me to the front door.

"No, but thanks. They're bound to want to interview me on my own." She held her face up to be kissed. I obliged out of genuine sorrow. "Anyway, I've got to get used to dealing with life on my own now, haven't I?" she added.

"Let me know what happens," I said, then let myself out of the front door—quite literally into the surprised arms of the law. The taller one of the two missed his footing and slipped off the front step and into a rose bush. I muttered, "Hello. Hello," then made my way swiftly past them to my Beetle, leaving the shorter one to pull out any thorns.

Nine

By the time I got back to my old Toy Emporium, the sun
(still out, surprisingly) was over the yard-arm, so I wandered
down to Gus's cottage to see if he would like to join me in a
ploughman's at the local hostelry, but, more importantly, to
join me in some brewing on the Maxwell affair. But, curses, I
couldn't raise him at his house, nor in his briar patch. I assumed he was out somewhere in his boat, or attending to
some middle-aged lady's shelves or whatever (probably
whatever), so I ambled over alone to the pub, kicking small
stones all the while.

I hadn't breathed second-hand beer fumes for more than a
few seconds, when I saw him. He'd beaten me to it, and was
standing over in the corner telling what looked like another
of his "fish that got away" stories to a regular old soak we
both normally tried to avoid, on religious grounds—he'd
never been known to buy a round.

I didn't want to get involved, so, as the barman drew my
pint, I asked him to catch Gus's eye. I grabbed the nearest
window seat and waited. But not for long.

"Been looking for you, old son." Gus sat down beside me
with a huge sigh, as if he had been on his feet for at least a
couple of days. "Came around to the shop but you weren't
in."

"I went to your place. Same thing." I raised my glass.

"Anyway, bloody relief you came when you did. Got
caught with the president of the 'Hook and Eye' club, I did."

(Gus and I call any spongers in a pub members of the

"Hook and Eye" club. Its derivation is simple: it's "who can I" get a drink off tonight?)

"I came round to say she has accepted your kind offer, Gus."

"The boat trip, you mean?" Gus raised his eyebrows with delight. Always fascinated me. They look too heavy to go up.

"Yes. She and Tara-Lee. And Arabella if you'll have her."

"She's welcome too." Gus rubbed his huge hands with anticipation, then suddenly sobered up. "Better give the old barge the once over. Not everyday I have glamorous ladies and film stars aboard, is it?"

I had to agree with that. "Doing anything this afternoon?" he smiled mischievously.

"I don't know," I replied honestly. "Depends on a lady coming down to earth."

Gus thought for a minute, then shattered me by getting my allusion.

"I got it. That air hostess. The one you told me Saunders claimed he was servicing that night."

"I'm going to ring her after we've downed the dreaded ploughman's. If she's in, I'll motor up this afternoon. If she isn't, I'll. . . ."

". . . be happy to help me." Gus raised his pint glass that looked quite puny in his hands. "Well, cheers. Thanks for the offer, old dear. Can't think of a better afternoon for it, can you?"

I didn't like to disillusion him.

Three hours later, and I knew why men had been press-ganged into serving with the navy. It wasn't the sea they disliked, it was the drudgery of the boats. And the merciless captains, like Gus, who kept them scrubbing and spitting and polishing until the sea-cows came home. Oh yes, Gus proved to be quite a Captain Bligh that afternoon. I'm not saying he didn't do his bit. But, somehow, I always ended up doing twice his bit, while he worked out exactly which of the million other chores we would tackle next, as Gus's boat was never the cleanest in Studland Bay. It couldn't be—it was just about the dirtiest. And yet he hadn't had it very long, for it was under two years since his other dirty boat had been blown apart by a bomb during the Treasure case. I came to the conclusion that Gus must attract grime like a magnet. Either that or he caught extremely dirty fish.

However, housemaid's knee or not, my turns of duty with the scrubbing brush and assorted oil rags did enable Gus and me, rather breathlessly, to mull over the Maxwell business. By quarter to five, I had taken him through every theory of mine, and a few of other people's, and refused to be lashed back to work until he'd given me a few of his own.

"Bit difficult, old son," he said laughing. "There can't be many left." He leaned back against the cabin roof. "Now let me recount. Number one suspect: Adam Longhurst. No alibi. Perfect bloody motive—Lana-Lee. Car seen near beach. Only excuse, rubbishy story about lady on the phone. Right?"

"Right, unfortunately."

"Suspect number two: John Saunders."

"It's your numbering, Gus."

"I know, old lad. Purely random, you understand. Well, Saunders could have done it, I suppose. Depends what his lady love says, don't it?"

"She could lie to protect him."

"True. Well. He could have a motive. Some argument over drugs. Maybe he wanted all the profit for himself. You say he was up to his whatsits in debt. Or he wanted out or something. Or he didn't really like Maxwell doing his wife a favour."

"Granted, he's got a few motives, Gus. But it still doesn't explain why Longhurst was down on the beach too."

"Wasn't Longhurst also doing his wife a favour?"

I hadn't thought of that. I nodded.

"Well then. Maybe Saunders got his air hostess girlfriend to ring Longhurst to get him down to the beach. Frame him, see?"

I saw. "Right," I said. "Next?"

"Suspect number three: Saunders' worse half. Lavinia. With a name like that she has to be guilty of something." Gus laughed—the cabin top creaked as if it were in a force nine. "Poor alibi—watching some old film or other. No one saw her do it. Now let's think of a motive. Ah, she could have had a lover's tiff with Maxwell."

"With a rock? And smash his skull, and then his mouth?"

"Well, isn't there a poncey French name for that kind of thing?"

"Crime passionnel," I tried, "but it doesn't quite qualify."

"Oh well, never mind. Or she wanted to frame Lana-Lee for murder, so that she could get Longhurst back."

"Not likely," I commented. "With Ben out of the way, there was nothing to stop Lana-Lee and Longhurst getting together."

"Except one or other of them being in prison."

"How would Longhurst's imprisonment help her?"

"Revenge. For him throwing her up for Lana-Lee."

I thought for a moment. "Somehow or other, Gus, I don't go for a woman rocking Maxwell to sleep. Not the way it was done. Feels like a man to me."

"You're too bloody sentimental about women," Gus retorted. "That's your trouble. Hard as nails some of them. I could tell you stories. . . ."

"Well, please don't, Gus. I'm confused enough as it is." I grinned at him. He grinned back.

"All right. So go on thinking it's a man. But this 'ere Lavinia woman—she's the one who's confusing you, not me. She fills your head with new theories every bloody time you see her. First time she led you to Longhurst. Then Lana-Lee. Then Lana-Lee and Longhurst. Now she's opened your mind to the thought it might be her rotten husband. Every bloody person but herself."

"Okay, Gus. Have it your way. What about suspect number four?"

"Well, that's easy. That's the little lady I'm taking out in my boat Saturday."

"Lana-Lee?"

"Who do you think I mean, Tara-Lee?" Not eliciting a reply, he continued, "You say Lana-Lee wasn't connected, as far as you know, with the drugs business. But that French guy could be wrong, couldn't he? He really only knows the French end, after all. She could have been the brains behind it. Then, once her husband had got the operation going, she thought she could dispense with him, and run off with her lover. Would explain why she suddenly had her husband back, wouldn't it?"

"To set it all up for her?"

"Hole in one, old son. But she played him for a sucker. Familiar story, that one."

"I can see she might have sneaked out of the house, walked down to the beach. But how would she know her husband would be there?"

"God only knows." Gus sniffed and began walking up and down on my newly scrubbed deck. Now I knew how housewives feel about their husband's dirty shoes on their clean kitchen floors. I grinned and bore it.

"Maybe she knew he would be there with one of his lady friends."

"And what has happened to that lady friend now? Why doesn't she come forward? Lana-Lee kill her too?"

"Don't scoff, old son. Only trying to help. Maybe she arranged for Longhurst to pick Maxwell up from somewhere and bring him to the beach. Then they both killed him. She with a rock to the head, he with a blow to the jaw. There," he said with satisfaction, "that would get your beloved male involvement in it."

I had to concede, I supposed it would.

"Why are you frowning? Don't like to think nasty thoughts about such beautiful ladies? Don't forget, old son, she's been an actress for donkey's years. Can never tell what an actress is really thinking."

I had to rise to that one. "Gus, you've never flaming known an actress in your life."

He held up a massive finger. "Not a professional one, I grant you. But loads of amateurs, old son, loads of amateurs.

There's an actress in almost every woman you meet, and you don't have to dig far."

"Oh, come on, Gus. I'm not in the mood for one of your homilies."

"One of my *what?*"

"Skip it, Gus. I just don't think Lana-Lee is capable of anything like that, that's all. Doesn't feel right. And it's not just because I'm sort of working for her."

"Won't dwell on it, seeing as how. . . .But she could have made that phone call to frame Longhurst, couldn't she?"

I couldn't agree with that bit, so I didn't.

"Any more suspects, Gus?"

"Not from the people you've talked about. But there must be loads of others, like people we've never heard of. In the drugs racket. Enemies of Maxwell's from way back—in America maybe. Old girlfriends of his—or Longhurst's, for that matter. Husbands of girlfriends. Both of them must have upset a few husbands along their horny way."

He chuckled at the thought, then grabbed a scrubbing brush off the cabin top. "Well, that's my ha'p'orth, old love. Now the boards in the cabin could do with a bit of a going over, whilst I just pop over to the village store to get some brass polish." He threw me the brush, and, with amazing agility for his age and size, disappeared over the side.

"Ta," I said and went below with my bucket. It was not until he had been gone an hour that the truth hit me. There wasn't a perishing piece of brass on the whole of his literally perishing boat.

It took me another twenty-four hours before I managed to raise the elusive air hostess. She claimed she had either been with the police or at her mother's place in Bagshot the whole time. She did not want to see me at first—not until I said I was on her lover's side, and might be able to save him from worse accusations than drug smuggling. We finally made a date to meet Saturday midday, as Gus was holding my toy fort, and looking after my client and my beautiful Arabella in the afternoon.

In the meantime, I had thought of ringing Blake for a pow-wow, then decided I'd almost nothing new to pow-wow about. The same went for Digger Whetstone. And I guessed they had nothing very new to tell me, either, as I had already heard what the latter had asked Lana-Lee that afternoon—basically, all the same questions as before. And Arabella had informed me of most of the rest, before the local radio had beamed it out. Adam Longhurst had been charged with Maxwell's murder, and remanded in custody for fourteen days. John Saunders had been charged with the illegal importation of drugs, and had been remanded for a similar period.

Things were certainly marching, but not in my direction. I just prayed the air hostess would land me some sort of lead, for I was starting to feel decidedly inadequate—even as a spineless sponge.

I was very relieved when Saturday dawned dry, and Radio Four promised it would remain that way, for Windsor is quite a trek from Dorset, and my soft top was really more ergonomic down than up, as well as being more pleasant. It also allowed Arabella to pat me on the head as I set off, with the farewell winked warning not to allow the air hostess to take off while I was there—like clothes. I gave my scout's salute in return, and then let the power of the Porsche engine propel me with satisfying speed eastwards, its unmistakable throb quite a tonic for my soul.

In the blue and blissful autumn air, Windsor came up on the signposts all too quickly, and soon I was ferreting around typically thirties streets trying to find Verulam Avenue. In the end, a little old lady on a bicycle, with half a dozen library books in her handlebar basket, set me on the right course, and I pulled up outside a large between-wars house, whose unloved garden instantly betrayed its division into flats.

I locked the Beetle, went up the weedy gravel drive, and studied the little slips of paper beside the four bell pushes. Miss E. Sumner was apparently on the top floor. I buzzed, and before I could say anything, an electrically distorted female voice emanated from a metal grill and bade me come up. I obeyed the instant I heard the front door lock disengage.

She met me at the door. The worried frown took not a jot away from why Saunders had shelled out so much on her behalf—like buying her flat for instance. She was certainly not like any stewardesses I had seen on my flights of recent years. She ushered me into what was obviously the sitting-room. Sixties uncomfy style, I would describe it. You know, matt black, metal-framed furniture, and lots of big basket-weave circular chairs with throw cushions to prevent your backside from carrying basket-weave patterns for life.

I sat down opposite her, and second impressions only clinched the first. I would have to go easy when I described her to Arabella. Her list of attributes, beside legs that seemed to end under her chin, included dusky olive skin, glistening ebony hair worn longish and loose to frame a face that was all wrong in individual features, but only too right when you added them all together. In a nutshell, she could give Raquel Welch's daughter a run for her considerable money.

After a few pleasantries, such as, would I like some coffee or something stronger after my long drive (I took the something stronger), and so on, we got down to business—or rather, she did. She wanted to know what was my connection with her lover. She said he had never mentioned me. I said I wasn't surprised, and then took her through an edited version of how I came to be caught up in the Maxwell affair. She didn't interrupt once, but listened intently. I was impressed. And as I rambled on, I came to the very definite conclusion she was not just a more than pretty face. When I had finished, and was putting a Teacher's to my lips, she asked, "And what do you think I can tell you that might help anybody? I've told everything I know to the police several times."

"I don't know," I admitted. "Would it be too much to tell a potted version of your story to me?"

"I can't go through it all again." She fiddled nervously

133

with her slender, red-tipped fingers. "You just ask questions."

"Okay. How long have you known John Saunders?"

"Off and on, nearly two years."

"Have you ever met his wife?"

She looked away from me, out of the window. "No."

"You knew he had one?"

"Of course." She smiled weakly. "That's the problem with attractive men."

"Did you know he was into a drugs operation with Ben Maxwell?"

"Of course not. God, won't any of you leave that subject alone?" She seemed particularly distressed, and got up and walked over to the big bay window.

"I'm sorry to upset you."

She turned back to me. "It's not you. It's the whole damn drugs business." She rubbed her eye. "My brother, you see, died last year of an overdose."

"I didn't know. If I had. . . ."

She moved quickly across the room towards the small table that held the drinks. "I think I'll join you now," she said quietly, and poured herself a neat scotch. Neither of us spoke for a while. I waited for her to break the silence.

"Okay. Fire away again," she said eventually, and resumed her basket-weave seat opposite me.

"If that's all right?" She nodded. "Did you ever meet Maxwell?"

"No."

"Did John ever speak of him?"

"Yes. Not often. Enough for me to know I don't think I would have liked him."

"What do you think John saw in him?"

"He was a stronger personality. John admired people like that. He used to tell me his best friend when he was young was the school bully."

"Did he ever mention Maxwell's past?"

"Once or twice."

"Anything about his Grand Prix days?"

The dark eyes suddenly flared with anger. "Okay, Mr Marklin. That's enough on drugs, thank you. I know what you're getting at. John used to tut-tut about Ben's murky past. Had me fooled every which way."

I changed tack. It was far too early to be thrown out into Verulam Avenue.

"All right, I'll be good. I'll stick to the night of Maxwell's death."

"What do you want to know? John wasn't involved with that. Can't you all see? John couldn't hurt a fly. Just couldn't."

I wondered if Eva Braun thought the same about Hitler, but made no comment.

"You flew back from Paris together that night?"

"Yes. We got back here, in the flat, around seven or so."

"And he stayed with you?"

"Yes, Mr Marklin," she said with a hardness in her tone, "he stayed with me. All night. All bloody night. Do you want to know what I cooked him for supper? It was a pizza out of the freezer. Followed by Neopolitan ice-cream and fresh fruit. And do you want to know how many times we made love that night? That's what seemed to turn on the frustrated boys in blue. No doubt, after I'd gone, they masturbated all over. . . ."

I held up my hand. "Miss Sumner. I'm not a boy in blue." I thought of saying I was a sponge, but modified it. "I'm just here to listen in case there's something all of us have missed so far."

Her mouth relaxed somewhat, for which I was greatly relieved. "Any more questions, Mr Marklin? I'm very tired."

"Only one or two more," I lied, as I had no idea really how many more I wanted to ask.

"Fire away."

"Did John make any phone calls that evening or that night —to anybody?"

I could see her mind working on my motives for that line of enquiry. I just prayed she would give me a truthful answer.

"None. None at all. He never used this place for phone calls, for obvious reasons."

"Okay. So nobody phoned out that night?"

"You mean, did I phone anybody?" She pursed her lips. "The answer to that, Mr Marklin, is the same big N for No. Hasn't anybody told you? Lovers tend to have better things to do of an evening than wrap their fingers round a receiver."

My sponge was picking up a forceful impression as to which of the two lovers was the strongest partner. I sipped at my scotch, trying to devise the best next question, for I had a feeling my time might be running out with Miss Sumner. In the end, I began phrasing it this way: "Look, I know all this questioning must be very distasteful to you, but the fact of the matter is I don't know what I'm looking for. Maybe Adam Longhurst is guilty. In which case, I'm on a hiding to nothing." She shrugged her lovely shoulders. I could imagine what they looked like in British Airways uniform—a damn sight better than even the First Class menu.

"I'm on that anyway, Mr Marklin. John's confession is going to put him away for a long time, isn't it?"

I didn't argue, but persevered. "But let's try and see that the police don't switch their attention."

"To John? For the murder?"

"If they can charge one wrong man, who knows, they could charge another," I tried, and could see her weakening a little. "So try and remember if there was anything about that night, or the days immediately before, that seemed a little odd, or unexpected, or . . . I don't know—not quite as usual."

She thought for a minute. "Nothing in the days up to that cursed night that I can remember. John was in a very buoyant mood. That came over clearly in our telephone conversations. I hadn't seen him for ten days before he flew back from Paris with me. We had planned it for nearly a month, you see. Getting together for a whole night, with my British Airways schedules, let alone his private and professional ones, was always tricky."

"I can imagine," I said with genuine sympathy. "What about the evening itself? You've only mentioned the run-up to it."

"Well. You see there was nothing you can actually put your finger on, but somehow, John seemed a little preoccupied that night, not quite his usual confident self."

"Did you ask him why?"

"No. I just put it down to the kind of let down you sometimes feel when you've looked forward to something too much and for too long."

"Did anything he said that night give a clue to what might be the trouble—if there really was anything worrying him?"

"Not really. I can't think of anything."

I was getting nowhere fast. I clutched at straws. "What kind of day did he have in Paris?"

"All right, I think. We never really talk business when we're together. There's too much else that's more important to say."

"So you gathered it was just another routine business day for him?"

"Yes," she said, then seemed to stop in mid thought.

"Remember something?" I asked.

"Not, not really. Only he told me on the flight back that he was thankful to be going somewhere where no one could reach him, for once."

"I guess he was. Businessmen often make their home numbers ex-directory to stop being pestered."

"No, I had the feeling at the time that someone must have called him during that day, and had annoyed or disturbed him in some way."

"Someone at Reinhardt UK, I expect."

"Maybe," she said thoughtfully.

"Maxwell, then?" I responded. She didn't reply immediately, then I got another "Maybe," but quieter this time.

"What have you suddenly thought of now?"

She looked at me and smiled for the first time. "It's not suddenly, really. I've just recalled what made me remember his remark in the first place. He used the word 'nag.'"

"What did he actually say?"

"I think it was, 'It's wonderful, darling, to be going where no one can reach me to nag at everything I do.' Something like that. It's just that word 'nag'—it's what a man says about a woman usually. Made me a bit jealous because it reminded me I wasn't the only woman in his life."

"You mean Lavinia?"

"Not necessarily. John's not exactly a one or *two* woman man, you know. I've always recognized that. However," she waved her hand, "I remember the impression I got was that someone had rung him that day to nag him about something or other. And I sort of assumed at the time it must be a woman."

"Men can nag, too," I grinned.

"Women do it better," she grinned back. "Like we do most things." I bowed my head.

"Anything else?" I asked.

She looked down at the big flower pattern in the carpet, as if the Chinese might have a solution for it all.

"Not really. Other than that funny feeling that something else was occupying John's mind other than myself that night, no. We actually had a super time, a super time . . ." Her voice trailed away, as I could see her realization grow that such a romantic idyll would probably never now be repeated—at least, not with that partner.

I rose to my feet, and cleared my throat.

"I'm sorry I haven't been able to help you, really," she said, almost in a whisper. "I have a feeling a lot of us are beyond help now."

I went over and rested my hand on her shoulder. "Don't think that, *ever*. I'll do what I can, believe me."

She looked up at me, tears now welling in her eyes. "You don't really think John had anything to do with Maxwell's death, do you?"

I shook my head. I hoped she would take that as a "no," and I could excuse the action to myself as simply shaking up my brains.

She came with me to the door. As she shook hands firmly

(a strong girl in every way), she asked, "When do you think they will let me see him?"

"Next week, I expect."

"I'm on the Frankfurt run next week. Hell, I can only make Thursday . . . and Sunday."

"I'll tell Whetstone, though I can't promise it will do much good. He's none too keen on my interference."

"Thanks, Mr Marklin. You know my number?"

"I know your number," I said, and made my way down the two flights of stairs, back out to my Beetle. But all the way home, I recognized I didn't know her number well enough to be sure she was telling the truth about her last night with John Saunders esquire.

I did not bother about lunch until I got back. Better very late than never, Bing and I shared some cold meat and bits of salad from the fridge. (For some reason Bing loves cold sliced mushrooms. Maybe they are a delicacy in Siam.) I was so preoccupied with running over in my mind my encounter with the belle of British Airways, that I had forgotten all about checking on what mayhem Gus might have caused in the shop. After lunch, with my heart in my mouth, I went through. Everything, at first sight, looked pretty normal, but as I walked around I noticed a few gaps in my stock, especially where I usually kept my mint boxed Japanese tinplate cars, and, near the window, where there was normally a small stock of mint Spot-On die-casts, also in their original boxes. (I bought them from a vicar who had hit hard Church times.)

I began cursing Gus for re-arranging my ordered disorder, before I noticed a note pinned to the wooden box that served in lieu of a cash register. I unfolded it with trepidation to see in Gus's large and rather childish scrawl, "Not bad morning. Cash under grill in cooker. (I assumed that piece of information was more for any burglar who might call by than for me.) Sold Mercedes £300, Bandai £140. Truck with 'Western' on it, Marusan £100. 1958 Lincoln, Bandai £200. Cadillac, Joustra £180. (These descriptions he'd laboriously copied off the boxes. From now on his patience had obviously run out, for he lumped all the Spot-Ons together.) Colecshion SPOT-ONS (7) = £310. P.S. Hope you don't mind. Aded a bit to prices to cover my comishion. See you when my boat comes home."

My hand shook as I took the note back into the kitchen and reached for the money from under the grill. It was all there—nine hundred and thirty pounds. I didn't believe it. Gus had sold more in one morning than I normally sell in a fortnight, or, if last summer was any guide, a month. And what's more, he had added about ten per cent or so to my normal prices.

For the rest of the day until Gus and Arabella sailed in, I caught up with my post and packed up a few toys that had been ordered from my monthly direct mail listings to be ready for mailing on the Monday. One of my correspondents actually enquired after Dinky's rare Avro Vulcan, and was willing to pay eight hundred pounds for one in good condition. I wrote back regretting I did not own such a rarity, and was almost tempted to mention my Flamingo project to lessen his disappointment.

Once I was reminded of the Flamingo, I couldn't resist phoning Muir to see how things were going, and see if he could set a date for my viewing the finished master.

He was courteous and dutiful as ever.

"I'm working on the very last piece of lettering now, Mr Marklin. The 'Die-cast in Dorset' piece. It's a little more tricky, as I assumed you would want that a good deal smaller than the rest."

I agreed. "Any idea when I might be able to see it? I'm sorry to act like an anxious kid, but, as you know, I'm very excited about my first venture into toy making."

"Midweek, possibly. I have one or two other things I must do, you understand. But I'll give you a ring, say Monday, to confirm, shall I?"

"Can't wait," I said jocularly, but I might have guessed Mr Muir would take the remark literally.

"Mr Marklin, waiting is what we must all do at one time

or another. It's not good for us to achieve everything we want at the touch of some magic button. That's what's wrong with today, don't you agree?" Before I could make any comment, Muir rolled on, "And anyway, Mr Marklin, don't you think that waiting really makes the event when it happens even more satisfying and rewarding?"

"Sometimes," I managed. "As long as something else doesn't intervene in the meantime to spoil the enjoyment." I laughed. "Like old age."

Needless to say, Muir did not join the glee-club.

"Ah yes, that's true, Mr Marklin. Very true. But then one must replace the old enthusiasm with a new one, don't you think? Perhaps one more fitting to the new circumstances."

I decided I had had enough home-spun philosophy for one telephone call, so I brought the conversation back to the particular.

"So, midweek, you reckon?"

"I'll phone you Monday without fail, Mr Marklin."

I was about to replace the receiver, when he added, "And how is your investigation going? I read all about poor Mr Longhurst being charged. And now I gather, there's some question of drugs being connected with that unfortunate film star family."

"Not with the family. Just with Maxwell."

"And a Mr Saunders, I think his name is."

"That's right. Well, I'm not making a great deal of progress." Then the thought suddenly hit me. "By the way, Mr Muir, how did you know I was doing any investigating into this affair?"

He answered immediately. "Ah, it's very simple you see, Mr Marklin. I phoned your shop this morning to tell you how I was getting on, and a Mr Tribble answered and said you were up London way doing a little detective work on the . . . er . . . whole business."

I cursed under my breath. He continued, "He seemed very excited about life, I must say, your Mr Tribble. He told me all about his plans for this afternoon. Taking film stars for boat trips, I believe. . . ."

Good old Gus. "Yes, he's not exactly a secretive man," I said with a chuckle.

"Openness can be a virtue, Mr Marklin." I raised my eyebrows, not that he could see them.

"Well, I wish you luck, Mr Marklin. We all need luck, as well as good guidance in this life."

I coughed a reply, and with a "See you midweek," was rather relieved to terminate Telecom's time. Talking to Muir was enough to make the most righteous feel a trifle guilty. To recover, I added to my own guilt level with a generous measure of Johnny Walker, and awaited the return of Arabella and Dorset's Mr Ten-per-cent, Bing soberly curled up on my lap.

Ten

I did not get the full unexpurgated account of the afternoon's odyssey until Gus had poured himself home. For Arabella, quite rightly, did not want to hurt his feelings, although alcohol must have anaesthetized them somewhat towards the end. Lana-Lee, in her generosity, had brought a few bottles of wine on board to repay Gus for his kindness and trouble. The two ladies consumed one of them between them, Gus consumed the other three between him and the ocean.

However, around 11.30 p.m., curled up with Arabella on my settee, the real story of the day's events began emerging, and, I must say, I was quite glad not to have heard it before. Right from the start, apparently, Gus had been a bit OTT, partly because of his luck in having a rich American on a late holiday, drop in to the shop and buy all those tinplate and Spot-On toys (Yes, they all went to one man. Happens on rare occasions, especially with vintage collectors new in the field. They want to have everything all at once to try to catch up with the old hands.), and partly because he was performing, for the first time, in front of a ravishing and famous lady. Suffice it to say, Gus had brought some of his own booze aboard, and, indeed, was fairly tanked up by the time Lana-Lee and Arabella arrived at his boat.

The captain's declared destination was Weymouth. Needless to say, they were late starting as Gus had remembered to get everything clean on the boat except the sparking plugs. This the adults did not find amusing, but Tara-Lee did. She seemed to revel in trying to get the motor started, and was quite disappointed, apparently, when it did. They set sail, or rather, chugged off out the bay, round Durlston Head, and eventually reached Lulworth Cove, by which time Gus was regaling Lana-Lee with some of the racier stories from his repertoire as if he'd known her for years. It was at this point, as Gus was tying up to get Tara-Lee and company ice-creams from the kiosk by the pebbly beach, that he first fell in—luckily, before he'd bought the ices. So now Gus was soaked pretty much inside *and* out, and had difficulty untying from the jetty.

However, he was still determined to get to Weymouth, which was starting to worry Arabella, as Gus had been known to run aground when he's sober. But as Ringstead Bay hove into sight, Lana-Lee suggested that, as the wind was getting up, it might be an idea for Tara-Lee to take a walk, as she was no great shakes as a sailor. Gus conceded, and brought the boat as near to the beach as he dared and dropped anchor. As the water level was still too high for any adult in clothes, let alone a child, to make it to the beach, Gus insisted on carrying everyone on his shoulders on to the shore. At points, it would appear, Gus's head was completely below water. Despite the discomfort of the porterage, Lana-Lee and her daughter seemed to be having a whale of a time, and Arabella was only too pleased the trip was proving a success as far as wound-healing was concerned.

Gus decided to play hide-and-seek for the first time, I guess, for fifty odd years—and I mean "odd." Tara-Lee, of course, was over the moon to have found an adult who was man enough to admit childish pranks still amused, and the walk up over the cliffs towards Osmington is alive with places to hide. Lana-Lee and Arabella brought up the rear in comparatively sober style, which gave my true-love time to engage her companion in more serious conversation.

Well, for the first quarter of an hour or so, all worked like a charm. Lana-Lee began talking about her life in Hollywood, and how hard it had been to start in Tinsel City, and that all the glamour was only a paper thin covering for some pretty shady dealing and tough grafting at the top. And hard, and sometimes downright unpleasant work for the actors struggling to rise from the bottom. Arabella received the strong impression that Lana-Lee's own climb to the top had been a damn sight steeper or more rock strewn than the cliff slope they were all now ascending.

Anyway, after a while, Lana-Lee remarked she hadn't seen Tara-Lee for a bit, but neither of them worried as disappearance is, after all, rather a key factor in hide-and-seek. It was not until Gus came perspiring up, his clothes still only half dry, and announced that he couldn't find Tara-Lee anywhere, that everyone began getting worried.

It was then that Arabella took charge, as Lana-Lee immediately began to get het up about all the child molesting and abduction that had been on the news in the area recently. Arabella could see all the good of the afternoon's trip being undone in a trice unless Tara-Lee was found but quickly. She organized a fan-like search of the area around the cliff walk, the three of them some fifty feet or so apart, peering behind and in every hedge, looking in every hollow and dip, and even retracing their steps almost back to their starting point. But no Tara-Lee was to be seen.

Lana-Lee, as you might imagine, was now near the point of collapse, and even Gus had sobered up enough to realize that Tara-Lee was unlikely still to be playing the same game they had initiated.

They had just started a sweep of the cliff, some hundreds of yards inland from their first search area, after which, if fruitless, Arabella had determined they must immediately call in the police, when over the brow of a hollow way ahead of them appeared the blonde head and then the petite body of their quarry, and behind her, a couple of hikers.

The tears and huggings went on seemingly for hours, according to Arabella, and eventually they wormed the story out of Tara-Lee on the boat ride home.

She had decided to hide in one of the old concrete World War II gun emplacements that still litter the Dorset coast and which she had espied some quarter of a mile or so ahead of where she had left Gus with his watering eyes closed.

"She said she was sure Gus wouldn't find her there," Arabella said.

"So that's where she'd stayed all the time, while all you lot were imagining the most lurid of fates?" I smiled, albeit with a certain note of sympathy in my actual voice.

"No. That's the point. She never got there."

"Why not?"

"Something distracted her."

"A cow?" I tried, knowing cattle sometimes stray around there.

"Not unless it was dressed in white." Arabella gave me one of her repertoire of knowing looks—"No, I'm serious" variety.

I didn't get the point at first. "Dressed in white?" I repeated as a question.

"Peter," Arabella grinned, "you must be still dreaming of your air hostess date not to get the significance."

"White. White," I intoned, then the penny (amazingly corroded) dropped. "White, like rainy night, fetch Minic boxes from little old lady before doom-ridden party."

Arabella patted me on the knee. Nice feeling, that.

"Clever boy," she said, then continued, "There may be no connection in this whole wide world, but as Tara-Lee described this sort of white sheet thing that seemed to beckon to her to come over to it some distance away, I suddenly remembered the ghost you said you saw that night, disappearing into or out of Lana-Lee's hedge."

"Tell me again, what did Tara-Lee say it looked like?"

"Like a ghost she had seen in an old Mickey Mouse cartoon on TV, a kind of Disney prototype of *Ghostbusters*, it sounded like. In other words, a sort of hooded figure in a white sheet."

"And she ran after it?"

"Seems so. At first she was scared, and then, when it disappeared behind a hedge, she became intrigued. She thought it might even be Gus playing a prank."

"Where would Gus get a white sheet? He hasn't even got

one on his bed—they're grey—let alone stashed away on a cliff."

"Children aren't logical. Maybe she thought it was an old sail from a locker on the boat. Who knows? Anyway, she followed over to the hedge, found nothing, then saw it again one field over, still beckoning."

"What did she do?"

"She went to the middle of the field and sat down and waited. She thought, if it was Gus, he'd get bored and come out and join her. She was a bit too scared to go right up to the hedge again."

"Then what happened?"

"Some hikers appeared after a while, and asked her what she was doing there. She explained. They then all went to look behind the hedge, and there was nothing to be seen. The hikers then advised her to go back to us, as we would, no doubt, be getting worried. So they saw her back to more or less where she had last seen us, and the rest you know. We thanked them, and then the hugging and kissing started, and Gus and I breathed just about the biggest sigh of relief Dorset has ever heard."

"I bet you did," I said, almost absent-mindedly. I was trying to recapture visually the details of my own fleeting ghostly encounter, but it had been all too fast to pull into any kind of focus.

"We mustn't go jumping to spectral conclusions," I said eventually. "Are you sure Tara-Lee wasn't lying?" I was in that kind of mood. That's the trouble with private eyeing, I guess. You get so that you don't believe anybody—even an eight-year-old.

"I don't know. Don't think so, especially if you put it together with what Lana-Lee admitted to me on the boat sailing back, whilst Tara-Lee was learning how to bait a hook with Gus up the sharp end."

"Prow," I said.

"Whilst Tara-Lee was learning to bait a prow up the sharp end." Arabella gave me an ear to ear smile. "I think she'd got so scared about Tara-Lee's disappearance that she felt she had to tell somebody."

"Tell somebody what?"

"For about the last six weeks before his death, Ben Maxwell had claimed he was starting to see things. Funny things. He began joking that he would have to give up alcohol and every other kind of stimulant if they continued."

"He saw sheets?"

"Apparitions—ghostly apparitions, he called them. White amorphous objects in the bushes, flitting across the lawns. And he'd say he heard tappings on the windows at night. And he claimed someone was constantly interfering with the cassette tapes in his Cadillac. He accused Tara-Lee and his wife of trying to drive him balmy so that he'd go away."

"Did Lana-Lee see any of all this?"

"No, or so she states. She put it all down to Ben's drug-ridden past catching up with him. She even toyed with the thought he might be getting some kind of brain tumour."

"Did she sound sympathetic?"

"No, not really. Why should she be? There was obviously no love lost between them."

"To hell with bed sheets," I almost shouted. "There's still that bloody great other mystery, isn't there?"

"Why Lana-Lee allowed him back?"

"Precisely. She claims the reason could have nothing to do with Maxwell's death, so she won't out with it. Or, at least, she won't tell me."

"She may be telling the truth."

"Everybody may be telling the truth. Then again, everybody may be lying."

Arabella smoothed my brow. "Been one of those days, hasn't it? Now tell me again about Elizabeth Sumner. I couldn't take it all in while Gus was gargling with the Sauternes."

"Do I have to?"

"Have to, or . . ." She made a "no" wiggle with her finger.

"In that case," I laughed, "here goes. Miss Elizabeth Sumner turned out to be a rather plain girl with greasy hair, in an extra long kaftan to hide all the scars and warts on her body caused by multiple mid-air collisions. . . ."

We got to bed very shortly after that.

I had fully absorbed Sexton Blake's advice, and was not trying to make four out of two plus two just yet, or even work out if I had any numbers to juggle with. Instead, I suggested to Arabella we take a few tenners out of Gus's sales of the previous morning, and treat ourselves to a sprauncy Sunday lunch somewhere over Lyme Regis way (Arabella had never visited the place). *En route,* we could stroll along Charmouth beach and catch a glimpse of Golden Cap—old childhood playgrounds of mine, of fond and loving memory.

So we stowed ourselves in her Golf, just in case it rained (of course, when you take precautions, it never does), and did just that. Dorset is great to explore at any time, but particularly now that the tourists had gone. Arabella loved Charmouth (bright girl) and was pretty enchanted with the little harbour town-cum-village of Lyme Regis, except for its precipitously steep hill, which we were silly enough to climb *after* we had absorbed the culinary (and alcoholic) delights of its highest-starred hostelry. Her only disappointment was that she didn't get to meet its most famous inhabitant, John Fowles, but I did take a photo of her on the cob, pretending to be a very short-haired Meryl Streep in *The French Lieutenant's Woman.*

The mental benefit of the day came when we had rolled home in the evening, had a bite of left-overs, and were relaxing in front of a non-turned on telly. For suddenly, in answer to a question from Arabella, I seemed to know what my next course of action must be without really, consciously that is, having thought about it. Her question was, what was I going to do this coming week? The answer, quick as a flash, was, "See Whetstone. Get to see Longhurst. See Lavinia again. Then, maybe, see Saunders . . ." And then I laughed.

"Why are you laughing?" Arabella asked, somewhat bemused.

"I sound so definite, don't I? As if I know what I'm doing."

"Perhaps you do."

"Maybe. Or maybe they're just the only people I know."

This time she grinned, and then reminded me, "You must leave time to see Mr Muir. Isn't it Flamingo time on Wednesday, or thereabouts?"

I nodded, but somehow I didn't feel like saying anything.

"Come on, Peter, why aren't you jumping up and down? Wednesday will be a great day, won't it? You shouldn't let the Maxwell affair ruin every private pleasure."

I put my arm round her shoulder, and gave a little hug. "I don't, do I?" I smiled weakly. "I suppose it's just because Muir is a bit of a self-righteous bore. Holier than thou, and certainly far holier than me. Seeing the Flamingo is exciting enough, but, unfortunately, I have to see him with it. And his wife, if anything, seems worse—or is it better?"

"Depends on where you're standing." She turned to face me. "Anyway, Mr Marklin, I feel like a spare wotsit at a wedding in all this business. Isn't there anything I can do?"

"Yes. Keep tabs on Lana-Lee. Filter what I'm doing through to her. You know, the odd phone call. . . ."

". . . And, on the odd visit . . ." She was one step ahead of me.

". . . keep digging away at why she allowed that bum Maxwell back. It may be irrelevant, or it may be key. Either which way, we ought to know."

Arabella saluted. "I'll do that, sir. Right away, sir." She rose from the settee, more's the pity.

"Where are you going?"

"To put myself in the hands of the receiver," she winked. And a moment later, I heard the "ding" as she began dialling. In the immediate short term, I regretted ever having opened my mouth.

"I don't know why you're still at it, Mr Marklin." Digby Whetstone's undersized moustache curled with amusement, and he lolled back in his creaking chair, the essence of a self-satisfied man. "The case against Longhurst is incontrovertible. Besides being observed at the scene of the crime. . . ."

"His car," I corrected.

"Okay. His Range Rover. Besides that, he had the perfect motive, Lana-Lee, and the most imperfect alibi in the world. Like he doesn't have one. He has a track record of violence. There was more than one example on his army records, for instance. The first one he got away with, because it was only against an NCO, I guess. The second one, he didn't. We have evidence from about twenty-five people that Longhurst has expressed his hatred of Maxwell on numerous occasions, and actual threats to his life on many."

"What about the phone call?"

"What phone call? You don't believe that story, do you? It's just about the weakest concoction I've ever heard."

"Maybe that's why it might be true." I countered.

Digby's chins rumbaed as he laughed. "You've been reading too much detective fiction, Mr Marklin. This is real life."

I decided to risk a googly. "Does Inspector Blake agree with you?"

Digby lolled forward again, and put his elbows on the worn plastic of his desk top. His moustache now curled the other way.

"Mr Marklin, I must warn you that you will get no cooperation from us whatsoever if you start getting impertinent."

"I thought it was pertinent," I couldn't resist saying. "For why can't Maxwell's murder be connected with his international drug smuggling rackets, past and present, rather than with this domestic triangle, which seems to be mesmerizing you?"

Digby Whetstone pursed his lips, and I knew I was about to receive a great truth.

"I get your point, Mr Marklin. You think that Inspector Blake disagrees with me because he has been investigating an international drug smuggling operation, and therefore, might like to link Maxwell's death with something larger than a lover/husband domestic triangle." He stopped for a second and looked at me. I didn't bother to point out his error. "Now let me inform you, Mr Amateur Detective, that when you've been dealing with crime as long as my colleague and I have, you know that most murders are unplanned, often unpremeditated, and overwhelmingly domestic. Great plots and intricate schemes belong to fiction, not to fact. And international scheming is even rarer, unless you're dealing with terrorism, which we are patently not." He lolled back again, and rubbed his chubby hands together. "Unless, of course, you're trying to prove that Maxwell was actually killed by Colonel Gaddafi." His burst of laughter made him cough, I'm glad to report.

When the spluttering had stopped, I said, "All right, I'll admit statistics may prove that most murders are for bad old domestic reasons, but you often need exceptions to prove a rule."

"Semantics," Whetstone beamed, then looked at his watch. "Anything more you want to know, Marklin? I've got more on my plate than this open and shut case. There's been another attempted child abduction."

I raised my eyebrows, then lowered them again. For I had been about to tell Whetstone about Tara-Lee and the ghost; then decided to hold it for Blake. In his present mood, Digby would probably equate ghosts with Colonel Gaddafi. So I went back to a question I had been about to ask before he mentioned the child abduction.

"Tell me, Inspector, about the injuries to Maxwell's head?"

"Why do you want to know?"

"Oh, it's just to help me sort out in my own mind whether the killer was a man or a woman."

Whetstone looked surprised, then smiled. "Oh—very professional of you, Mr Marklin. The first sensible thing I've heard you say. And I'm glad you asked, because in all our views, the murder is likely to have been committed by a man."

"Can you tell me why?"

"The nature of the injuries. If they had just been to the

back of the head, we might have guessed either sex because, though he was tall, he could have been sitting down or crouching when he was attacked, thus allowing quite a short person to bash his head with a rock."

"Found the rock?"

"No. It must have been thrown into the sea. We've combed the whole beach. But it's the facial injuries, mainly to the mouth, that make us think it must have been a man."

"Why?"

"Well, they were very violent. His whole mouth and jaw were smashed. We found some of his teeth in the back of his throat, for instance."

"And you don't think a woman would have been able to cause that kind of injury?"

"I didn't say that. It's a question of likelihood. In my experience, both direct and vicarious, women may kill but they tend not to beat up and batter their victims like the male of the species. They lash out and leave it at that."

"And you think Longhurst is a batterer?"

"Got the temper, and the strength for it. And a bit of track record, short of death—up to Maxwell, that is."

"What killed him, or can't you tell? The attack on the head, I assume?"

Whetstone nodded. "Your assumption is ours too. The blow on the back of the head would have been fatal—the facial injuries probably not."

"So whoever killed Maxwell . . ." Whetstone chuckled, but I continued, ". . . must have hated him with a vengeance."

"Probably."

"And you think that Longhurst hated him *that* much? I mean, he may have a reputation for violence and threatening behaviour, but it was all spur of the moment stuff, wasn't it? Flash of temper, regretted a second later."

"You forget one thing, Mr Marklin. Adam Longhurst had never fallen in love before in his life. He is forty. Lana-Lee Claudell is not only famous but rich, and, without question, one of the most sexually desirable women any man of his

age could contemplate as a mate. Put all those factors together, and you have a powerful set of triggers for
Longhurst's violent reaction to Maxwell's unexpected return. I can see him sitting in his Art Deco palace of a farm-
house, building up the grudge, stoking his ire, developing an
unbelievable level of resentment and hatred for Maxwell, as
he imagined his lover resuming her relationship with her ex-
husband, resuming it at *all* levels of intimacy, or so I'm sure
his fevered imagination would have had it. Don't get me
wrong, I'm not saying Longhurst plotted the murder for
weeks. I don't think he is that kind of person. But the hatred
built up over that period to a point where, maybe, he met
Maxwell by accident, say, then asked him to go somewhere
with him to thrash out the whole affair. They both motor
down to Osmington Mills beach; begin talking. The argument gets heated. Longhurst loses his temper, the pent up
hatred and resentment is released in a fury of blows with a
rock. All he knows is that he wants to obliterate every feature of the man who, so unexpectedly, came between him
and the love of his life. And what more satisfying features to
smash than the mouth that had lied, and made love to the
one who Longhurst now believed should be exclusively his
own."

There was no satisfactory answer I could make to Whetstone's reasoning. Unfortunately, I could already hear coun-
sel for the prosecution getting a persuasive mouth around
very similar arguments, with identical thought processes. So
I asked my last but one question.

"I heard tell Maxwell only had one eye when he was
found. Is that true?"

Whetstone nodded. "It happens when bodies lie around
for a bit. Haven't you seen those nature documentaries on
television? Vultures pecking out the juicier morsels. . . ."

I cut him short. Breakfast was still too recent. "Scavenging
gulls, you mean, in this case?"

"The little girl who found him said the body was sur-
rounded by them." Digby Whetstone rose from his reclining

chair, which creaked back upright. "Now, if that's all, Mr Marklin."

"Not quite," I said, also rising. "I'd like to be able to see Mr Longhurst now."

The Inspector consulted his Pulsar. "Right now?"

"If that's possible," I said most respectfully, for I realized creeping was now the order of the moment, if I were to succeed.

He thought for a moment, then went to the door, opened it and bawled out, "Sergeant!" He turned back to me. "All right, if it will keep you quiet. But you'll get no further than we have. There is one thing I'll say about him—he's consistent with his story."

"I'll let you know if he deviates," I smiled.

"Oh," Digger muttered, and I could see he wasn't quite sure what to make of my smile. It wasn't really surprising; he was only on a par with myself.

I don't think I've ever seen such a change in a man. When they brought Adam Longhurst in to the small interrogation room with the subtle bars on the single sky-high window, I hardly recognized him. It wasn't just the weight loss, either. There were grey hollows in his face where his confidence used to be, and emptiness in his eyes where boyish hope once shone. His frame was still that of a bull, but the picadors' darts had drained him long before the final lunge.

Greetings didn't take long; you don't waste time in a prison situation. What's more, the presence of the policeman in the corner didn't exactly encourage outpourings of an emotional kind.

"Sebastian said you'd try and come. Thanks."

"Forget it."

"No, I'll remember, believe me, if I ever get out of here." He looked round despairingly.

"Look," I said, leaning forward on the table that separated us, "don't let's waste time. Whetstone has only given me ten minutes."

"What do you want to know? I've told Sebastian everything I can think of."

"Yes, I've heard. Just a few questions, that's all."

"Okay." He folded his strong hands in front of him. I wondered if they had recently folded round a rock. I almost shivered at the thought.

"Tell me about that phone call, the one that got you to go to the beach."

"It was a woman, an hysterical woman. I could hardly hear what she was saying. What I gathered was that there had been some commotion with Maxwell down at Osmington Mills, and would I come quickly."

"That all she said?"

"Yes. But two or three times over."

"Did she say why you should come?"

"Not really, but I inferred someone might get hurt."

I didn't want to waste time, so I rattled on to my next question. "Are you sure you didn't recognize the voice?"

He shook his head. "She was so hysterical. It could have been—anybody. The voice wasn't familiar at all."

I jumped right in. "Are you sure it wasn't Lana-Lee?"

His eyes flickered for a moment, then he nodded. "It wasn't Lana-Lee."

I leaned further forward on the table and repeated, "Adam, was it Lana-Lee? Please admit it, if it was, for Christ's sake."

"It wasn't," he said quietly. "I'd have known, wouldn't I? She's American, after all."

"And this woman was English?"

"I—er, yes. Of course, she must have been. I'd have noticed otherwise."

I could hear the seconds ticking away, so reluctantly, I passed on.

"Tell me, Adam, can you think of anyone who would want to frame you for Maxwell's murder?"

He smiled weakly. "The murderer?"

"No, I mean someone who had it in for you for something else."

"Not really. No. I've thought a lot about it since my arrest. Murder is a hell of a thing to frame you for."

I decided time did not allow me to be diplomatic. "What about an old girlfriend? Or husband of an old girlfriend?"

He looked up. "No, I can't really imagine. . . ."

I guessed he couldn't, so I helped him. "You knew Lavinia pretty well, didn't you? Lavinia Saunders."

"Oh, you don't think . . . ?"

"Come on, Adam, we haven't got much time. I know you and Lavinia were lovers, and not just before her marriage to Saunders."

"But really. . . ."

I cut him off. "Don't be chivalrous, Adam. I know enough about her to know she really doesn't care a shit about anybody but herself. You know it too. And she was having an affair with Maxwell."

He didn't look surprised.

"But murder? *That* kind of murder?"

"No, I wasn't accusing her of Maxwell's murder. Just exploring whether she might have been the lady on the phone."

"No. No. No. She *wasn't* the lady on the phone," he said emphatically, and then, I think, realized what he'd implied.

"It was nobody I recognized, I told you."

"All right," I said and tried to catch his eye but he wouldn't let me.

He went on, "Lavinia's a tempestuous lady, a devious lady, a hot head—in fact, hot all over—and we had the most monumental rows, where we'd break most of the china in whatever room we were in. But I can't think she would frame me."

"You gave her up for Lana-Lee. She can't have been very pleased."

"She wasn't. That's how my Lalique vase went, and a load of Clarice Cliff . . . Got a black eye too. I did, I mean."

"Did you know her husband, John? You know he's been arrested?"

"Yes, Sebastian told me all about it."

157

"I have to ask you this. You weren't involved in the drug smuggling, were you?"

He looked horrified. "Why do you ask?"

"You've got an aeroplane, that's all. Look, don't get upset."

He shook his head in disbelief, as I saw the boy in blue in the corner consult his watch.

"Last question, Adam. You haven't seen any ghostly apparitions around your way recently, have you?"

"What the hell do you mean?" He looked dumbfounded.

"I mean sort of ghostly white-sheeted figures flitting about your gardens or your farmland."

"Don't be silly."

"I'm not being silly. Hasn't Lana-Lee told you? Ben claimed he used to see white apparitions. And on Saturday, Tara-Lee saw one too."

"At the Manor?"

"No, on the cliffs at Ringstead Bay. It's too long a story for now."

"Peter, what the hell's happening to us all? What have we all done?"

"That's what I'm trying to find out," I said quietly, as I saw the man in the corner starting his move to say, "Time, gentlemen, please."

Eleven

On my way home, on the Sandbanks-Studland ferry, my mind was, for once, not full of its usual nostalgic childhood memories of that primitive clanking conveyance, but of enigmatic thoughts of a much more recent origin: the look in Adam Longhurst's eyes when I popped the million dollar question about the lady on the phone that night. And another phone call about which Miss Elizabeth Sumner had some strange intuition. And white apparitions that flitted in and out of my mental vision, clouding rather than clarifying. I had a hell of a fight with myself not to start jumping to conclusions. But I knew the time must arrive shortly, when further delay would be counter-productive and just plain old-fashioned reluctance to face facts—like I wasn't getting anywhere worth a damn.

I was surprised to see the "Open" sign on the door of my Toy Emporium as I passed to park round the back, for Gus wasn't due to stand in for me until the next day. But, hey-ho, there he was sitting in the store, having let himself in with the key I had lent him.

"Thought I'd put in a few extra hours," he grinned. "Never know, might get another of those Yanks in, mightn't I?"

"You might, Gus, you might," I said, not wishing to dampen his enthusiasm, but the odds against were like a thousand to one.

"Well, how did you get on, then?" he asked, and I realized he had more than one motive for coming over.

"Let's put it this way, Gus, I'm well on the bloody road not only to being impressed with the strength of the police case against Longhurst, but also being dubious about the role of my perishing employer. Some private eye I am."

"Lana-Lee?" Gus looked most aggrieved. "Lovely lady, she is. Lovely daughter too. She can't have done anything. Your mind must be going, old son."

"That's as maybe, Gus. But listen to this. . . ."

Quarter of an hour later Gus had put some of his protestations away, but not all of them.

"Well, supposing then, it was her on the phone. Doesn't mean to say she murdered bloody Maxwell, does it? Nor that she intended to frame Longhurst, neither."

"No, it doesn't. But all the same, it's a neat solution."

"Neat for whom? You? The police? Use your loaf. If she had done what you say, she'd have hardly asked you to get old Longhurst off, now would she?"

I had to concede he had a point. It cheered me up just a smidgin. I told you Gus was good for one's health, mental, that is. It was then that the phone rang. I was hoping it was Arabella, but it turned out to be a house clearance and junk shop johnnie from Weymouth, whom I knew vaguely. He rang me from time to time, whenever he came across any old toys in his house clearance purchases. Normally they were hardly "eurekas," but this time they sounded more than promising. Apparently, the house he'd been clearing had belonged to an old man who had been a project engineer at a well known British maker of tinplate toys, Wells. And the attic turned out to be full of dusty pre-war tinplate cars, buses and commercial vehicles, not only of Wells manufacture, but also from German and American firms, who were Wells' competitors at the time. He said I'd better go over to Weymouth quickly, as he'd got a competitor of mine from Bournemouth viewing them in the evening. I said I'd be there immediately I'd grabbed some lunch. After all, I had a living to make, and luckily Lavinia's place was more or less *en route*, so that I could pop in on the way back. What's more, to be honest, if the toys matched my acquaintance's enthusiastic descriptions, they would fascinate me as a private collector, let alone as a dealer.

So, secretly glad of a break from the whole Maxwell mess, I trotted off with Gus to the local hostelry, downed a pint and ploughman's and, leaving Gus back in the shop, went to my faithful Beetle and turned the ignition key to be off to Weymouth. Not a dicky-bird. I turned the key again. Nothing. Six turns more and still zero. Cursing under my breath, I went round the back and took a look at my Porsche engine. Everything looked normal, but, for some reason, I wasn't getting a spark. Quarter of an hour later, I gave up and went back indoors to wash the grease off my hands.

"Won't start, old son?" Gus grinned. (He loved to see cars going wrong that were more modern than his old upright Ford Popular—which meant ninety-nine point nine per cent of vehicles on the road.) "Like to go in mine?"

Now normally, an invitation to go in Gus's old Popular was equivalent to a chance to spend a vacation in a Siberian salt mine, but this time I did not see how, short of hiring an expensive taxi, I could do otherwise than accept. So, with trepidation, I did. We locked up shop, trekked down to Gus's cottage, and picked up the laughingly-called Popular.

It's not all that far to Weymouth—unless you are riding with Gus. Then, it seems at least as far as Moscow—and Moscow over unpaved roads, what's more—for the Popular had hardly been famed for its springing when brand new in 1953, let alone some two hundred thousand hard miles later. And the piercing draughts where the doors didn't meet added to the whole Russian scenario, while Gus's driving style (I use the word "style" loosely) could make prunes obsolete.

However, we did get there—eventually—and pulled to a shrieking stop outside the pile of old furniture on the pavement that marked our destination, the shop lying somewhere behind it. Luckily, the toys were not on display, but packed in old supermarket boxes upstairs in what my friend

161

flattered by calling his office: a battered desk, a stack of papers and dust to match.

One look, and my cheque book was out, for what was left of Gus's cash from the American would certainly not cover this wondrous find. I was knocked out. All were pre-war. Ten of the items were in absolutely mint condition, three slightly chipped and rusting, and three semi-dismantled. Five I recognized as of Wells' own manufacture, ranging from a large blue and cream tinplate Rolls-Royce to a wonderful little Carter Paterson delivery van; then there was a motor cycle combination from Tipp of Germany, a racy looking Mercedes coupé from some unknown German maker, a huge "Inter-state" bus from Strauss of America— and more. Suffice it to say, I was willing to shell out for the lot. And I prayed the profit I could make from those I sold would cover the cost of the items I had already earmarked for my own private collection. It took a quarter of an hour's haggling to do a deal, and two seconds to alarm my bank manager with the size of the cheque I wrote, I guessed.

I felt so chipper by the time we left that even the return journey in Gus's Popular held no terrors for me. We packed as many of the toys as we could in the boot, and the rest we hid under a piece of old sacking on the floor behind the front seats.

"Pity the pubs are all shut," Gus observed with a sigh, as we pulled out with a lurch from the kerb, "otherwise we could have celebrated your find."

"Could have been a nice idea, couldn't it?" I smiled. Then a thought struck me. "Hey, know the Cutlass Club?"

"'eard of it," Gus said, narrowly avoiding a Morris Marina turning its rust down a side road. "Poncey theatrical place, isn't it? Actors hang out there, between their turns. That it?"

I nodded, "I used to be a member there in my old advertising days. I hated it, but clients liked it. Haven't paid my dues recently, but I'm sure they'd forgive me and pour us one or two for old times' sake. Worth a try."

"All right, old dear. Lead me there." So I did.

You couldn't actually miss her. She was propped up at the bar as if she owned the place, and there was no way of my arranging for a drink without her spotting me. So I thought, what the hell, and greeted her first.

"Hello, Lavinia."

She narrowed her eyes to look at me in that dim light that clubs seem to think is chic.

"Why, it's you, Peter." She reached for my shoulder with a wavering arm. "Lovely Peter. I didn't know you were a member."

"I'm not. I used to be."

"Doesn't matter," she slurred. "I'm a member. So I'll buy you one. That's legal."

Gus coughed and she looked round at him. He looked a trifle bizarre in the kitchy, pseudo Spanish decor of the club, like a fisherman out of water, so to speak.

"Who's your friend?" she asked, raising her perfectly plucked eyebrows.

"Oh, this is Gus. Gus Tribble." I propelled him forward. "Old friend of mine from Studland. Gus, Lavinia Saunders."

"Enchanted to meet you, Mr. Tribble."

I saw her wince as they shook hands. Gus didn't say, "Likewise," as was his wont, just glowered and stayed that way until she had bought him a pint, whereupon he grunted something, and wandered off to the far side of the somewhat claustrophobic room.

My surprise at seeing Lavinia was now starting to recede and allow my mind to function more normally, although my first question, "What brings you here?" was not exactly a world beater in the originality stakes. However, it did turn up an interesting stone.

"Oh, just had a costume fitting, that's all," she replied, insinuating her arm further around my shoulder. Through the almost overpowering pulse of her perfume, I managed to ask, disbelievingly, "Are you appearing at the theatre?"

"No, no, no," she laughed. "Only amateur theatricals in a municipal hall. Have done it for years now. I like acting."

She lolled her head towards mine. "In fact, my dear Peter, I'm rather good at it."

I guessed she would be. Most of her life was an act, after all. She continued, "I feared my husband's arrest might mean I couldn't continue in the play, but the cast insist I do continue."

I smiled. "The show must go on."

"Precisely, lovely Peter, precisely."

"What's the play?"

"The Man Who Came To Dinner."

"Ambitious for an English company."

She looked very taken aback. "Why? We're pretty good. We're not the WI, you know."

"I mean, all the American accents. Wouldn't it have been easier to choose an English play?"

"Jesus, Peter baby," she exploded, in what I took to be her best Stateside voice, which sounded like an unbelievable cross between John F. Kennedy's Boston, J.R. Ewing's Texan and Blanche du Bois's Southern drawl, "you just don't rightly know what little ol' me is capable of, now do you, honey?"

I agreed with her. I didn't rightly, but kept to myself that that was exactly what I was aiming to discover. I sank a little beer to give me time to consider my next question, by which time I could feel Lavinia's nose nuzzling my neck.

"Have you seen your husband?"

"Yes, lovely Peter." She nuzzled some more. "But don't let's talk of that bloody swine. He's got me into all this mess. He and his dead friend, Ben Maxwell."

Her voice had now taken on a tone that hardly mated up with the petting. I tried to move a little up the bar, but her arm was imitating a boa constrictor.

"Did you know, all men are the same, Peter? John, Ben, Adam. Doesn't matter what they're called—they're all bloody swine." She drained the last of what had looked like a Martini, then began sucking slowly on the olive. It did nothing for me, but then I don't go for the eating scene in the movie of *Tom Jones* either. I looked around for Gus, and he winked at me from the far side of the room. He was obviously having a great time watching me squirm, the sod.

"All except you, of course, Peter. You come over as different somehow. Are you different, Peter? Different from all those double-dealing jokers?"

"I doubt it," I said, and then instantly regretted it. For a thought had struck me that might well make it worth my while to play things Lavinia's way—at least for a bit. I turned to her. "We'll never know, will we?"

"Won't we?" she pouted.

"Not in here, we won't," I countered, for I knew that by teatime, the Cutlass Club would be filling up with bored businessmen with only two things on their mind.

She sniggered. "Where do you suggest?"

"Oh, somewhere a trifle more private."

"Very private?" she whispered, progressing to little wet kisses. I was relieved there was no one else actually seated at the bar.

"Sounds promising," I lied.

"My place or yours?"

"How about yours? It's nearer. And it hasn't got a shop," I smiled.

She sat up straight and looked over towards Gus. "What about your friend?"

"He hates three to a bed," It took her a time to double-take.

"Oh, lovely Peter, you're having me on, aren't you?"

I nodded. "Yes. But I think he really does hate three to a bed."

"I've never tried it," she breathed. "I haven't got tired of two yet. Have you?"

"No," I said, with all honesty.

"But I meant, Peter, we can't just go off and leave him here, can we? Or did he come in his own car?"

"He came in his own car." She looked relieved until I continued, "Trouble is, I came in it with him."

"But that's all right. I've got my car here. I'll drop you home—er—afterwards."

"No," I said quickly. "It will work better for me if I go home first, then come over to you, say, sometime this evening. Besides, I've got some things I must do this afternoon."

"What about your Arabella?"

"I'll dream up some story about some old toys I have to go and appraise. I'll think of something."

"You're as double-dealing as the others, after all, aren't you, lovely Peter?" Her long blood-tipped finger traced the outline of my mouth. I suffered for England—or rather, for America, I suppose.

"That's what we're aiming to discover this evening, aren't we?" I smiled, in as Burt Reynolds a way as I could muster.

"What time?"

"About nine."

"About nine." She looked more sad than sensual in the half light, as I felt her arm relax its grip to allow me to move from the bar. "I'll put my kettle on," she winked.

"You do that," I smiled, and with a half wave, moved over to where I'd last seen Gus. But he'd gone, out to the car, as I subsequently discovered.

"Hate to watch anyone being eaten alive," he grinned, as he grated around with the long lever for what was left of his gears.

When Gus, at last, dropped me home, shaken and shivering but all in one piece, I unpacked the precious toys and arranged them in immensely satisfying ranks on my small dining-room table to await later evaluation as to which I could afford to keep, and which I had to sell to do so. I was longing to get down to the task right away, but had too much on my mind to do justice to the pleasure. I made a note on the telephone pad reminding me to phone the bank manager in the morning to warn him about the cheque, and maybe my Volkswagen agent, then tried to get hold of Inspector Blake. He was out. I then phoned the Knoll House Hotel, but they reported likewise. I left a message with the desk for him to contact me, then fed Bing, who insisted on only toying with his Whiskas, instead of wolfing it down. I knew why, too. He often went on hunger strike when he thought I was out too much, or not giving him enough attention. I stroked him until I received massive shocks from static electricity, but to no purpose. I promised to make it up to him when the whole Maxwell affair was over. He didn't look too convinced.

Blake still had not rung by the time Arabella came back from her journalistic forays. I recounted my day, and explained (rather judiciously) my plan of action to her, and, after a moment's thought, she stated that I shouldn't really have rung Blake until I was more certain of my slender theories.

"You could be wrong, you know. And Blake can't really help us until you've got rather more than just hunches."

I had to agree, but even so, felt a talk with the law might not have come amiss before venturing into what might be rather hazardous waters.

"Do you want me to come with you, and wait outside in the car?" Arabella smirked. "Just in case . . ."

"I wouldn't mind, actually," I laughed, "but I think I'll cope. It's your car I'll have to use anyway, if you don't mind. Anyway, I have somewhere I'd like you to go at the same time, if you're not too bushed."

"Lana-Lee's?"

I nodded. "Yes."

"How will I get there? Don't answer that," she grinned.

"That's right. I've already asked Gus. He'll run you over there and wait. Sorry about that."

"That's okay. I'll survive. And you think Gus will be around as some kind of protection if I need it?"

I nodded again. "When you get there, probe about that call. I'm sure Adam Longhurst is certain she made it, whatever he says to protect her."

"But the police have been through all that with her before."

"You're not the police. You're a sweet generous attractive lady trying to help, an arm to lean on . . ."

". . . a shoulder to cry on . . ."

". . . a pleasure to do business with."

"Like you'll be with dear innocent little Lavinia? Only instead of arms and shoulders, I suspect she'll require parts of the anatomy that are more below the equator."

"Now, now, Arabella." I gave the clean version of the scout's salute. "I promise I won't let it get too tropical."

"A man's gotta do what a man's gotta do," she intoned in her best John Wayne voice. I kissed her long and hard. I love that girl, and I needed a spanking new reminder that the feeling was mutual, before I ventured into the night. I got it.

As I left, Muir rang to say Wednesday evening would be fine to see the finished Flamingo. That made a nice sanity clause, too.

At least she was dressed when I arrived. I'd half been expecting a negligéd Barbara Stanwyck act straight out of *Double Indemnity*— but, maybe, that only happens with insurance salesmen who look like Fred McMurray. But what she was dressed in was certainly not the old virginal Laura Ashley stuff, but tight, black leather trousers and white silk wrap-over blouse, not too tightly wrapped.

I was ushered past the bull's horns and elephant's foot into the awful room I've described before, and took my place dutifully on the settee next to her.

"You haven't asked me about my kettle," she smiled languorously.

I had to remind myself. "Oh—er, yeah, kettle. Oh yes, has it boiled yet?"

"Getting warmer all the time, Peter. Isn't that what kettles should do?" She put her long white fingers on my brown cords. Things were moving far too fast for me, as obviously, unlike her, I wanted my chance at conversation before I got into hot water, not after.

I tried a ploy. "You haven't asked me how my Inspector Plodder investigation is going."

She looked a trifle miffed. "Oh all right, I'll ask. How is Inspector Plodder?"

"Not too good, I'm afraid," I replied. "He's got a few nasty problems."

She moved a little closer to me. "What nasty little problems? Anything I could help with?" she breathed.

I perked up. "Well, yes, actually."

She suddenly put her arm around my shoulder, and drew me to her. She had changed perfumes. This one was three parts musk to one part subtlety. I suddenly wished Arabella had been outside in the car, available at the first scream for help.

"Come to Mama, and tell me all about it."

"Well, it's about phone calls really. Inspector Plodder has Telecom trouble."

I waited for a reaction. There was nothing, unless you call a snuzzling of the neck a reaction. So I was disappointed on two counts, but persevered.

"He thinks Adam Longhurst did receive a call the night of the murder."

"Oh," she murmured.

"And he thinks it was a lady with an American accent."

She moved her face upwards towards mine, and smiled. "So, if he's right, we know who that lady was, don't we?"

I nodded. She sat up a little straighter.

"I wonder what Lana-Lee's motive was in making that call —just to frame Longhurst? Then why . . . ?"

I cut her speculation short. "Inspector Plodder has a gut feeling it wasn't Lana-Lee."

Her eyes flickered. "But you said she was an American."

"No, I didn't. I said Inspector Plodder thinks it was some lady with an American accent."

She suddenly turned on the settee to face me directly. "Another American, maybe? Old girlfriend of Maxwell's, perhaps? That is, if Inspector Plodder is on the right track in the first place."

"Or someone pretending to be an American," I said, quietly, "pretending to be Lana-Lee."

Her undeniably attractive mouth quivered as she hunted

for the right words. "Who—who would want to pass themselves off as Lana-Lee?"

"The murderer. Or someone who knew about the murder, and wanted to frame Adam Longhurst."

"She would have to have been a good actress to fool him."

"Much better than the WI," I said and braced myself for an explosion.

"You can't mean you think I had anything . . ."

"I don't know. Did you?"

Her long fingers reached for my cheek, and softly rested there. "Oh, lovely Peter, you don't think I murdered Ben, do you? Oh, tell me you don't think I am capable of . . ." She broke off, and her hand slid gently down my face. I waited patiently. At last she resumed, and her voice was calm and collected. "I have to confess, Peter, I haven't been exactly truthful with you. But I *didn't* make that call and I *didn't* kill Ben, although, I must say, I felt like it after I found out about Ben and John's scheme to smuggle drugs into the country. You see, I *did* know before John was arrested. I had an anonymous phone call."

Hell, I thought, here we go again.

"Man or woman?"

"Man. I didn't recognize the voice."

"What did he say?"

"That Ben and John were up to their necks in a drug smuggling operation, and he thought he ought to tell me, just in case I didn't know."

"And you didn't know until then?"

"No, I swear, Peter, I didn't. I was absolutely horrified." I took her, for the moment, at her word.

"What day was the call?"

"The morning of the day Ben was killed."

Things, suddenly, began coming together in my mind, as I thought of Elizabeth Sumner.

"You then rang your husband in Paris, didn't you?"

She looked at me in surprise. "How did you know?"

"Inspector Plodder told me," I grinned weakly.

She took my hand. "Oh, Peter, I didn't know what to do,

when I learnt. I thought, if I rang John right away, I might somehow stop the whole thing there and then."

"Weren't you afraid someone at Reinhardt might be listening to your call?"

"I spoke in riddles, so that only John would understand what I was getting at."

"What was your husband's reaction?"

"He couldn't say much, obviously. He just said for me to keep my mouth shut and he would be home next day to deal with the whole problem."

"Did he know who the anonymous phone call might have been from?"

"He implied he thought it was probably someone at Reinhardt, who was making some wild guesses in the hope of blackmail, and he'd take care of it on his return."

She put her arm back around me, and snuggled her face up against mine. "Oh, I'm so sorry, lovely Peter, not to have told you all of this before. But I thought, if I kept quiet about knowing about the drugs business, I'd not get involved. But that's all I've kept from you, I promise."

Her mouth reached for mine, and I felt the probing of her tongue. I pulled back sufficiently to say, "Did you ring Maxwell, too?"

She nodded. "I tried, but was told by the housekeeper he'd been out most of the day."

"And you didn't try to see him later?"

"No."

"What about that night?"

"No. No. I've told you. I've told everybody. I stayed in all evening, with your Inspector Plodder and *Sleuth*." She returned to exploring my mouth, and tried to take my hand on a journey inside her blouse. I resisted, then remembered I still had a few questions left to ask. Her breast felt surprisingly cold, the nipple small and almost buried in the curves. I intended to let her relax for a few minutes in the hope my next question might take her off guard. But she was very soon not content with just a hand in her blouse, and as I felt her own hand tip-toe towards my zipper, I had to come out with it prematurely (so to speak).

"Lavinia, do you think John killed Maxwell? Flew back, and because of your call, drove down from Windsor, had a row with Maxwell over lapses in security or whatever, killed him, then drove back to Windsor to spend the rest of the night with his alibi, Elizabeth Sumner?"

"I don't know," she whispered, rubbing her hand firmly against my groin. "Why don't we talk about it all afterwards . . . in bed?"

I stayed her hand for a second, but couldn't disguise a growing hardness that I had been fighting ever since her first advances.

"Look," I cleared my throat, "before we—er—just one more question."

"What's that? It had better be quick."

"If John did murder Maxwell, then it might well be that he forced you to imitate Lana-Lee on the phone, to get Longhurst down to the beach to frame him."

I could see from her eyes that she was having difficulty deciding what her response should be, and, luckily, the delay stayed her zipper hand.

"I . . . er, no—Plodder's wrong, Inspector Whetstone's right. It was nothing to do with us. It must have been Adam . . . Adam." I felt her hand move back to its task, and I was about to intervene, when I was saved by a doorbell equivalent of the US cavalry.

She instantly raised her head, and rearranged her blouse. "Who the hell can that be?" she muttered with considerable venom. The serpent was never very far below the smooth skin of Lavinia Saunders.

I rose from the settee and did my own readjustments.

"Shall I peep through the curtains?" I offered.

"No. You stay here. I'll just dab some lipstick on, and see who it is."

She went out into the hall, and a few moments later, I heard her open the front door. I moved across the room to the sitting-room door, so that I could make an instant get-away the moment the visitor had gone.

"I'm so glad to catch you in, Mrs Saunders." It was a woman's voice, of the older, Women's Institute type. "I hate to bother you at a time like this, when you have so many other problems, but, if you remember, you did promise us some little items for our annual jumble sale. I called some time ago, but you weren't in. Or at least, I couldn't make anybody hear."

"Oh, that's all right, Mrs Olsen," I heard Lavinia reply. "But I'm a bit busy right now."

"Oh, that's a pity. I was so hoping, Mrs Saunders, you might have something."

Lavinia did little to hide her impatience. "I'm not sure I can lay my hands on anything just this second."

"But if you could, Mrs Saunders, it would be such a great help. We haven't had quite the response this year as last, and the vicar . . ."

Lavinia obviously decided that her own desires would be quicker satisfied by capitulating to her visitor than resisting. She popped her head around the door and blew me a kiss. "I won't be a minute. Bloody woman." And then she was gone, and I heard her footfalls on the stairs.

I took the opportunity to go out into the hall, and to the front door. Mrs Olsen turned out to be a personification of her voice, about sixty, prim, proper, and a pillar, I am sure, of her church—just the lady for saving me from a fate worse than (but rather different from) death. It was such a pity I couldn't tell her of her bell-push salvation.

"Oh," she said, rather startled. "I don't think we've met. I'm Mrs Olsen."

I shook her hand. "Peter Marklin. I'm just a friend of the family. Flying visit, was just off."

"Don't let me interrupt anything."

I almost laughed. "No, I had to go now, anyway."

She did not seem to be listening, somehow, but rambled on, "Collecting jumble can be quite embarrassing sometimes, especially in the evenings. But that's when everybody is most likely to be in, isn't it? One knows one is intruding and interrupting things, television often, these days, but, there we go. It's all in a good cause."

Her mention of television prompted me to try a long shot. "You said you called before? Do you remember what day it was?"

"Now, let me see, it was an evening. That I do remember. And it was late, very dark. I had to use my torch to see my way. Sometimes I can't begin collecting until quite late, meetings, you know, and . . ."

"But can you remember what day it was?" I interrupted, fearful Lavinia would return downstairs before I'd received the answer and made my get-away.

"Now, let me think. It was quite a few days ago now, and one's memory does not improve with age, Mr—er . . ."

"Marklin."

"Marklin. No, I can't quite place the day. It'll come to me, no doubt." She looked up at me. "Why, is it important in some way? I can't see how it could be."

Before I could reply, I heard Lavinia's footsteps on the stairs.

"Sorry, Mrs Olsen. Can't explain now. Must run." And run I did, out the door to Arabella's Golf in the drive. And, Lord be praised, Mrs Olsen had had the sense not to block my exit with her Hillman Avenger. Otherwise, who knows how the evening might have ended.

Twelve

It was well after midnight before Arabella and I could, at last, be alone. For Gus, as was his right, insisted on staying not only to hear my evening's exploits, but also Arabella's all over again, though he'd heard hers *ad infinitum* on the drive back from Lana-Lee's. However, there was one sugar plum in his staying; he told me where he thought Mrs Olsen lived—Broadmayne; her cleaning lady was an old lady friend of his.

After we'd dragged ourselves up to bed and had switched on the bedside lamp, Arabella gave an uncharacteristically deep sigh.

"It's not that bad," I laughed. "We did learn something on our travels."

"That both Lana-Lee and dear rapacious Lavinia vigorously deny making the phone call. Hardly sensational, is it?"

"No. But Lana-Lee did agree that it was quite possible that Adam Longhurst thought it was her, and Lavinia's confession about that other phone call ties in with our air hostess's feeling about her night of idyll with John Saunders. It's no wonder his mind seemed to be elsewhere. He was wondering who the hell had phoned his wife about the drugs."

"Doesn't help us much, though. Saunders could still have slipped down to Osmington, had a quarrel with Maxwell, murdered him and slipped back up again, getting his wife to do her American bit and lure Longhurst to the beach."

"True. I put that to Lavinia, as you know, but eventually, she went back on the 'Longhurst must have done it' line."

"Eventually?"

I sat up on one elbow. I can't think straight, somehow, flat on my back. Useful for other purposes, though, including sleeping.

"Well, I sort of felt she was working out what was best for her to say. Don't forget she's blamed just about everybody for Maxwell's murder already."

"Except herself."

"*And* her husband. But I think she'd shop him as soon as look at him now, if it suited her. Her only aim in life is what's good for Lavinia Saunders, so she'll throw suspicion just about anywhere, so long as she remains whiter than white."

"Murderers tend to do that," Arabella said quietly. "And murderesses."

"I know. I've thought long and hard about it. But venomous and hot-tempered though Lavinia is, I can't see her being so vicious as to beat Maxwell's head and face about the way it was. Kill him, almost accidently, in a sudden fit of jealousy, pique, sheer temper or frustration, maybe, but not then beat him around the face and knock half his teeth down his throat, surely?"

"I don't know. But what we do know about tonight is that Lavinia was mighty upset that day, after discovering about the drug smuggling."

"I'd love to know who phoned her."

"So would I. That is, if her phone ever rang . . ."

I silenced Arabella with a kiss. "Don't add any more 'ifs' to the argument tonight. I'm overflowing with them already."

"You don't want me to squeeze?" she teased.

"No," I smiled, and luckily, she didn't take me totally at my word.

Next morning, after I had phoned my bank manager about the toy purchase (he was surprisingly affable, as bank managers go—just like the ones in the adverts), I set to work on my Beetle, as I resented running up a garage bill if it wasn't necessary. What's more, I didn't want to be without the car, for reasons that are not hard to define. They come in the shape of a Ford Popular. The trouble turned out to be a loose lead to the coil, which, as often happens, took far longer to trace than to cure.

It was while I was indoors getting the grease and grime off my hands prior to ringing Inspector Blake, that Blake rang me. I took him quickly through my findings, but not quickly enough for their thinness not to show, even to me. At the end, I had to apologize for my lack of real progress.

"Don't apologize. I'm not employing you."

I'm afraid I sniggered. "Oh yes you are. By a proxy doxy. Lana-Lee."

He did not comment, and his silence made me feel a little cheap. "Okay. Have it your way," I said. "I'll apologize to Lana-Lee."

"Don't apologize to anyone. You may have done better than you think."

"How so?"

"Well, think of it this way: we've interviewed Lavinia Saunders and not uncovered her phone call to her husband in Paris. Nor did we know that Lavinia knew of the drug smuggling before we arrested Saunders. Whetstone and his boys have interrogated Longhurst countless times and not ever believed his story about that other phone call. You obviously do believe him, and by believing him, have disclosed another possibility—that he did actually recognize the voice, or think he did, as that of Lana-Lee."

It sounded better the way Blake was telling it, so I let him continue.

"What's more, you haven't just assumed, therefore, that it must have been Lana-Lee, because, I guess, your intuition baulked against it, but have taken a quantum leap to it being someone who wanted Longhurst to think it was Lana-Lee. And you've been clever enough to discover a person who might fit the bill."

"Oh shucks," I said, "it's only because of *The Man Who Came To Dinner.*"

"And a load of old toys. I must come and see them some time."

"You're very welcome. And I'm sure Arabella would say you must be the man who comes to a second dinner."

"That would be nice, but it's my turn next. We'll have to make it soon, for I'm only here on odd days now. My drugs dossier is almost complete."

"And you're going to leave me with Whetstone?"

"Maxwell's murder is his case."

"I know. I know."

"But Scotland Yard has a telephone number, if you really need to talk."

"Okay. Thanks."

"Now, before we hang up, do me a favour, Sam."

"What's that?" I laughed.

"Does your intuition tell you anything about what you've absorbed. I'd be interested to know, but don't force it. I'm not going back on what I said the other night."

"Good. Arabella's called me Sam Sponge ever since."

He laughed. "Well, does it?" he repeated.

I thought for a minute, then answered, "I think I've got some more investigating to do yet."

"Rain check?"

"Rain check."

"Don't forget to keep Whetstone informed too."

"I won't. When do you leave?"

"At the weekend. Maybe before."

"I'll be in touch—if only about dinner."

"Don't forget, it's my treat, or rather, Scotland Yard's."

"As if I'd forget."

It wasn't until I had replaced the receiver that I realized what I had totally forgotten was to tell him anything about the ghostly white apparitions and Tara-Lee's alleged experience at Ringstead Bay. I was about to ring back, then thought better of it. I didn't want to appear a bigger idiot than I had already, with such improbable stories. Anyway, I reckoned it could wait until I had seen Mrs Olsen once more.

She was out when I called at her small, neat, thatched cottage that was straight out of Disney, Dorset style. I banged the knocker until I was even bluer in the face than the cold autumn air had already made me, and was about to leave down the rose-lined path, when I heard a shout from somewhere nearby. "Just gone out. Only missed her by a hair's breadth, you have."

I looked across the hedge into the immaculate little garden of the cottage next door. An elderly lady was creaking up from her knees, wielding a small trowel with which she had obviously been tending a flower-bed.

"Oh, thanks. Which direction did she take? I could catch her up."

"Doubt it," she smiled. "She wasn't walking. A lady picked her up in a car. Went off with the speed of light, they did."

"What did the lady look like?" I said with some alarm.

"Tallish. Good-looking woman, elegant, if you know what I mean. More your age than mine," she chuckled.

"What was the car?"

"How do I know? All look the same to me nowadays, they do. Now, when I was young, you could always tell an Austin from a Wolseley, and a . . ."

"Was it white?" I interrupted sharply.

"Yes, I think so. Not big, mind you. Didn't half go, though, down that way."

She pointed to the right, but by that time, I was sprinting back to the Beetle, and praying its Porsche power, if not my driving, could find and overhaul the white Ford Escort xr3 of Mrs Lavinia Saunders, before it was too late.

Broadmayne is on the main a352 which runs, pleasantly enough, from Dorchester through to Wareham and then on to Poole and Bournemouth, a road pretty full of tourist traffic in summer, but on this brisk autumn morning, other than the odd lorry, it was not too crowded. As I accelerated away, I thanked the Lord I was not in Gus's Ford Popular, which I could so easily have been, had the trouble with my Beetle been more extensive than the lead to the coil.

At first, every car on the road was any colour but the one I was after, but at the Warmwell junction with the A353 Weymouth road, I thought I spotted a flash of white ahead of a giant car transporter. I took a chance and followed it on the long stretch towards Wool, but it was past the Owermoigne turn off before I managed to get past that damned transporter, as, sod's law, the opposite lane had filled with a procession of cars following its own transporter—an army one trundling a huge tank. And once I'd done so, there wasn't a white car in sight.

I kept the speedometer at around eighty-five, and prayed I wouldn't be spotted by another kind of white car—one with a red stripe and a blue lamp. By the time I had reached the Winfrith atomic establishment and there was still no sign of Lavinia's car (if it was Lavinia's car), I started to worry that I'd taken the wrong turning at Warmwell junction, or Lavinia had spotted me in hot pursuit and had high tailed it down one of the side roads. I thought of turning back, but then realized too much time had passed, and that I would be unlikely to find her now, unless she had taken Mrs Olsen back to her own house. And if she had done the latter, it would be unlikely that she intended any harm to the old lady. So Mrs Olsen wouldn't need rescuing, anyway. I pressed on.

By the time I had got to Wool, and had to slow to pass through the tiny town, I had more or less given up hope, and to salve my conscience, tried to play down the whole idea of Lavinia harming Mrs Olsen as just pure hysteria on my part. After all, I was only acting on the wildest of hunches, I told myself, and clutching at straws because no bloody bricks seemed to be available. Quite quickly I convinced myself I should turn around by the level crossing, and retrace my steps to the Warmwell junction, take the road to Osmington and Lavinia's house, in the hope that she was back.

But it was as I approached the level crossing that I saw it. A white Ford Escort XR3 ahead of a queue of traffic stopped at the barrier to await a train. I swung to the left, pulled up at the back of the queue, got out and sprinted to the Escort. Just as I came up to the driver's door, the figure at the wheel turned round, no doubt at the sound of my pounding feet, and I looked into Lavinia's startled eyes. She lowered the window.

"Why, Peter, what a surprise! What are you doing here?"

I shot a glance across the car to the passenger seat. There was dear old Mrs Olsen safely seat-belted and rosy with health, though somewhat amazed to see me. She waved a trembly hand.

"Mr Marklin, wasn't it?" she remarked, and I could do nothing but nod like an idiot as I heard a train approaching in the distance.

"You haven't answered me yet, Peter? You're such a funny man. First you run away from me. Now you run to me." I could see Lavinia was now starting to enjoy my discomfort.

"I—er, wanted a word with Mrs Olsen," was all I could think of to say. A flash of anger flitted across Lavinia's face, to be replaced by a Cheshire cat's smile.

"I can guess what that word is, dear Peter. Mrs Olsen told me all about your questions yesterday, after you had run off like a jack rabbit."

She turned to her companion. "We've laughed about it on the way this morning, haven't we, Mrs Olsen? Mr Marklin's funny fascination for the exact date of your first call on me."

Mrs Olsen waved at me again and smiled. "We weren't really laughing at you, Mr Marklin," she said kindly. "We were joking more about my terrible memory. These days I forget almost everything unless I jot it down on a scrap of paper."

I smiled back. "So you still can't remember the day you called?"

Mrs Olsen shook her head, and Lavinia jumped in and answered for her. "No, Peter, Mrs Olsen cannot remember when she called . . ."

Mrs Olsen chipped in, "I probably never will now."

". . . and probably never will now," Lavinia repeated.

"And anyway, I don't see what possible significance the date of her call can have. I think you should take a rest, Peter. Your mind is getting overloaded with wild ideas." She pursed her lips slightly. "Could be bad for your health, you know."

The train by now was lumbering and clanking past us, and conversation became virtually impossible. It gave me a little time to ponder my next move. I obviously could not detain them any longer, as it was plain as a pikestaff that Mrs Olsen did not feel she had been abducted or was under any threat whatsoever. But I was still fascinated as to why the totally self-centred Lavinia had bothered to call on Mrs Olsen at all, let alone take her for a ride, especially as she had presumably given her any jumble she had the previous evening.

As the train pulled away, I caught Mrs Olsen's eye. "Have a nice time where you're going," I tried. It worked.

"Bournemouth, Mr Marklin. I so rarely get to Bournemouth. It's so kind of Mrs Saunders to drop by unexpectedly and ask if I would like to keep her company on her shopping trip, isn't it?"

"Very kind," I replied and looked hard at Lavinia.

"I can be kinder than you think," Lavinia smiled. "Now can we go? The barrier is about to go up."

"Going all day?" I asked as Lavinia restarted the Escort's engine.

"Be back this evening, Peter. Why don't you drop by and check, and perhaps we can pick up where we left off last night?"

Mrs Olsen looked a trifle embarrassed, so I said quickly, "I'm helping Mr Saunders in his present difficulties."

Mrs Olsen nodded. "That's kind of you, Mr Marklin."

"Yes, it is, isn't it?" Lavinia smirked, as she put up her window, and with a little wave of the hand, drove across the railway tracks, and accelerated away towards Wareham. I stood watching the white car disappear, until a cacophony of horns reminded me my own car was now effectively blocking the eastward lane of the A352.

"Look, Mr Marklin, I only agreed to see you now because you claimed on the phone you had uncovered new evidence that might have a material bearing on the Maxwell case." Digby Whetstone's puffy hand pointed to a hard, unpuffy chair. I duly sat down on it. "Now, if I find out you have no such evidence, I'll not only kick you out of this office so fast you won't know what hit you, but also see you are never ever let in again. That understood?"

I didn't see much point in nodding, so just waited until his bulky frame had sweated back into his creaking recliner. He folded his hands carefully on the hump of his waistcoat. "Now, Mr Marklin, let me partake of these fruits of your amateur investigations."

I felt like tipping him, chair and all, out the window, but reckoned it would hardly help my case, so I began, "I think you should interrogate Lavinia Saunders again—at some length."

"And why, pray, should we do that? The lady has enough problems, I would have thought, without our repeating a procedure we have already carried out," he then mimicked me, "at some length."

"Because I believe she's afraid her alibi might come unstuck."

"That she was indoors all that night watching some television programme or other, as I recall."

"Sleuth," I said.

"Ah yes, that's right. That's where I handed the interrogation over to one of my sergeants. He's a great film buff. He should be on that programme, answering questions on old films. Anyway, I had him ask her about almost every foot of *Sleuth* to be certain she had actually seen it. And at the end, he was sure she had."

"She could have seen it before. It's been on the box several times, in fact. She could have seen it more than once."

"Maybe. And maybe not." He creaked his chair upright. "Now, Mr Marklin, get to your point. What are you trying to prove about Mrs Saunders? That she killed Maxwell?" He chuckled. "You'll have a hard time of it. That murder bears all the signs of a male hand, in my judgement. I've told you that before. And what the hell would be her motive anyway?"

"I didn't say she was the murderer—or is it murderess? I just said I was pretty sure she was concerned that her alibi might be about to be blown."

Whetstone looked at his watch. "Okay, I give you five minutes to explain yourself. If, by that time, you haven't . . ."

I interrupted him by starting. I knew I would need every second to get Digger to see things my oh so conjectural way.

A quarter of an hour later I finished. I was somewhat amazed I was still in his office. For a full minute Whetstone didn't say a dicky-bird, then a smile slowly raised the tips of his undersized moustache. I breathed a silent sigh of relief.

"Well, well, well, Mr Marklin. You have been a busy bee, haven't you? I'm amazed at your tenacity, if nothing else. No, that's unfair. To be honest, you have uncovered one or two little facts that we missed. Like the phone call to Paris, for instance. And the anonymous call Mrs Saunders claims she received about what her husband was up to. So well done on those points, but they are irrelevant to the actual murder, and all the rest is purely conjectural, I'm afraid. Not a shred of evidence or proof of any kind, especially connected with that other phone call Longhurst claims he received on the night of the killing. As you know, I doubt such a call was made, so as to your theory that someone imitated Lana-Lee to lure him to the beach—really, Mr Marklin, you should pull my other leg, it's got bells on."

"Concentrate on that call, when you get Lavinia Saunders in. I think she will . . ."

Whetstone raised his eyebrows sky high. "Mr Marklin, I am not willing to drag Mrs Saunders in here just because you've seen her take little old ladies on shopping trips to Bournemouth. Really, I'd be . . ."

". . . being very bright," I interrupted. "I'm sure she is terrified that Mrs Olsen will remember she first called for her jumble on the night of the murder, and found she was out."

"But, you say, Mrs Olsen has told you to your face that she can't remember which day it was. So Lavinia has no worries, even if what you say is true."

"But she can never be sure Mrs Olsen won't remember, at some time or other in the future, can she? For that reason, I believe until you interrogate Lavinia Saunders further, that little old lady may be in considerable danger."

"What would you like me to do—ring her cottage with armed guards, and put a tail on Mrs Saunders everywhere she goes? Come now, Mr Marklin, it's a thousand to one all she was doing with that old dear in the car was being kind to her. After all, you don't know they didn't discuss such a shopping expedition the evening before, after you had gone."

I scoffed. "You're kidding. Lavinia Saunders has about as much sympathy for her fellow beings, as—as Lucretia Borgia had for her dinner guests. That's why I'm so certain, don't you see?"

Whetstone glanced at his watch once more. "All I see, I'm afraid, is an amateur detective dying on his feet, or rather, on my chair, and wasting too much of my goddamned time." He rose creakily to his feet. "Now, don't try to see me again unless . . ."

I too rose, but in anger. "What the hell will it take, Whetstone, to get you to unblinker your bloody mind, and, at least, get Lavinia Saunders in here for further interrogation? Mrs Olsen's dead body?"

"Something like that, Mr Marklin, something like that." He went over to the door and opened it. I took his hint and joined him.

"I'll save you the bloody trouble," I shouted. "Sergeant!"

I don't remember much of the drive back to Studland as anger joined worry in clouding my mind. And the clouds did not lift when I finally got indoors and was greeted by Gus who was holding my toy fort once again.

"Phone's never stopped since I've been here," he claimed, which, upon examination, turned out to be just two calls, one from Sebastian Lynch, apparently to check on any progress I might have made (Gus said he'd brought him roughly up to date, minus, of course, my adventures of the morning), the other from Lana-Lee with an urgent message for me to ring back. I did just that, and needed her news like a hole in the head.

"I've seen it now," she said, and her voice was shaky.

"Seen what?"

"The white shape. You know like Ben and Tara-Lee said they saw."

"Where did you see it?"

"From the drawing-room windows. It seemed to flit between those two great rhododendron bushes, just before the steps down to the lower lawns."

"What did it look like?"

"I only saw it for a second, Peter, and then it was gone. It was like a ghost."

I had to get her to be more precise. "The proportions and size of a human figure, or bigger or smaller?"

"Yes. I guess it was about the size of a human figure. I can't remember the head, though. Seemed to be all white."

"Could it have been a hooded figure of some sort?"

"I suppose so. But I don't know. Honestly, Peter, if it hadn't been for Tara-Lee, and Ben, claiming to have seen something of the sort, I would have thought it was a figment of my imagination."

"It obviously isn't. Four people have seen it now."

"Three, surely. Ben, me and Tara-Lee."

"And me."

I heard her draw in her breath. *"You?"*

"Yes. I saw something of the sort going through a gap in your hedge the very first night I met you—at your party that Adam interrupted."

"You didn't tell me."

"It didn't seem significant at the time but now it is."

"What does it all mean? Have you any idea?"

"Not really. I should advise you to be careful until we do know. Keep doors and windows locked and I think it's time you informed the police."

"Do I have to? I'm terrified to have anything more to do with them than I need."

"Then let me ring Sebastian Lynch, and get him to come round to you. He'll ring them when he arrives, so that you won't be alone."

"That would be a great relief. Thanks. And Peter, have you made any more headway in your investigations? When I last saw Adam, he was very down. I think he's very near giving up hope."

"Tell him not to. I have a lead at last that may get us somewhere. I'll let you know as soon as I've checked it out a bit further."

"Oh let's pray it leads to Adam's release."

"Meantime, don't forget: be careful until I discover what all this apparition business means."

"I promise."

If you've never sat for over three hours in a cold Beetle convertible, whilst the heavens opened, then you're not SAS material. After the first hour, I was more than damp; after the second, more than half-way to hypothermia; and during the third, numbness began paralyzing my nether end, for my Beetle seats are in the winter of their days. (Certainly there is precious little spring left in them.) Even all that might have been vaguely bearable had not my brain been in angst and turmoil as to why Mrs Olsen had not yet returned to her cottage, just up from which I was parked, partly concealed by a hedge in a muddy farm track.

After three hours and a quarter, the time then being after seven o'clock, I started to feel what an idiot I had been not to have rung Blake instead of going to see Whetstone, but I reasoned that the man on the ground could move faster. I'd just about decided to move off and find a public phone box to try and remedy my mistake, when I at last saw the flare of a pair of headlights slowing down in front of the cottage.

The lights were dipped, and, a moment later, the fragile silhouette of the old lady emerged from the passenger side. I saw her wave, and then the headlights resumed full beam, and the white shape of Lavinia's Escort splashed away past me and out of sight. I waited about five minutes, just in case, and then, damp and stiff, knocked at the door.

Mrs Olsen, needless to say, was not only surprised, but somewhat alarmed to see me once more, especially in my rather wet state, and didn't invite me in. So what little conversation we had was of the doorstep variety, but sufficient for me to gather she still had not remembered which night she had called on Lavinia.

"I was out quite a few evenings collecting, as you may imagine, Mr Marklin, and which night I went round to Mrs Saunders, I still can't recall. But I can't see why you are so very interested in knowing. How can this help poor Mr Saunders?"

"It's a long story, Mrs Olsen, and it may not be relevant to his case at all," I replied, truthfully, "but I'd still like to know."

She smiled, patiently. "Well, to save you keep calling on me, Mr Marklin, I promise to get in touch with you if it ever does come back to me. Now if you'd just give me your address or telephone number . . ."

I gave her both. "Now, please, Mrs Olsen, if you do remember, be sure to ring me before you ring Mrs Saunders. That's very important. I don't want her getting worried about things unnecessarily, you understand. She is naturally upset enough, as it is, and the date may, as I say, turn out to be of no help to any of us."

She promised, and I left. But I wouldn't have taken bets on my hopes.

That evening, Arabella triggered the idea. I don't know why I hadn't thought of it. Maybe because I could no longer see the wood for the trees, let alone for the ghosts that seem to flit between them. We'd discussed our own certainty that Lavinia had been out the evening of the murder, was desperate to conceal the fact, and knew, in all probability, far more about Maxwell's death than she had admitted to anyone. Our problem, quite clearly, was proving it, if Mrs Olsen's memory remained true to form.

"And I feel if we don't get at Lavinia very soon," I remarked, "while she is still obviously rattled, then she'll have time to regain her composure, and we could be back at square one."

Arabella thought for a moment, running her fingers through her deliciously cropped hair. "Then don't let's wait for Mrs Olsen. Let's accelerate the process somehow."

"Oh great," I laughed. "Wouldn't I love to, but how, pray?"

"I don't know. It's a pity Lavinia knows you, me and Gus, otherwise you could have pretended to blackmail her or something."

"What about?"

"Seeing her at Osmington Mills that night. You know, something that would expose whether she had actually been there."

"But nobody reported seeing her. Just Longhurst's car. Her white Escort would have shone out in the dark, wouldn't it?"

"Supposing she didn't take her car. She could have walked. You say her house is only a couple of miles away."

"Lavinia, I don't think, would walk anywhere, unless she had to."

"So, perhaps, Maxwell picked her up and took her down in his car."

"Possible, but how did she get back?"

"Walked, because she had to, like you said."

I looked at Arabella hard. "You think she killed him, then?"

"I didn't say that. I just said, if she turns out to be desperate to hide the fact she was out the night of the murder, then she probably was somehow or other connected with it in some way."

"Like making the telephone call to get Longhurst down there, maybe to save her husband."

"Something like that. Lord knows exactly what."

I poured us both another glass of Pouilly-Fuissé in the hope that grapes would miraculously solve our dilemma, or, at least, make us feel better about having failed.

"I could disguise my voice and phone her," I offered with a wink.

"She knows you too well. And I reckon she's a better actress than you're an actor. Can't you get some mate of yours to ring her?"

"Do you know the penalty for blackmail?"

"No," she laughed. "You'll have to ask a lawyer."

"My God," I exploded, and leant over and kissed her. "I think you have found us the linchpin we were looking for!"

Thirteen

Next morning Gus arrived, full of the joys of the wrong season, chipper as anything, because he'd managed to sell the previous day four pre-war Dinky aircraft, including a mint boxed Mayo Composite (a marvellous sea-plane atop a flying boat), for a grand total of a hundred and twenty pounds. I asked him where he had put the money, and he fished in his sweater and presented me with it, minus fifteen pounds.

"My commission, old son. Know it isn't quite ten per cent, but I'll make it up next time."

I said, "Think nothing of it. Wrap your brains round this little thought instead." And I told him our plan. Before I could glean any comments, the doorbell interrupted us. As I went through the shop, I saw the whites of his car—it was a policeman I'd never seen before.

I guessed what he had come about. He wanted my description of the white apparition Lana-Lee had reported I had seen on the night of the party. What I could tell him certainly hardly caused him to need a new notebook, and, as he left, I asked him to give my love to Inspector Whetstone.

It wasn't until I was making a fresh cup of coffee to keep Gus quiet, that something the constable had said rang a bell. He had asked whether I agreed with Lana-Lee's description of the phenomenon as a "ghost or an angel." Somehow, the mention of the word "angel" disturbed me, and I couldn't quite think why until, suddenly, I had a vision of Muir's dining-room table that day, and its disturbing ranks of brass angels, none of whom could really be described as benevolently angelic in the conventional sense. I tried to dismiss the thought as ludicrously irrelevant, but it would go on nagging me.

Gus's comments on my plan of action, provided I could persuade Lynch to go along with it, were not really of vintage Tribble quality, ranging from "Bloody let me go and scare the living daylights out of the woman instead," to "Force old Mrs Olsen to pretend she has remembered she came round on the murder night." The comments in between were even less intellectual. However, he did insist that he should be written in to my own scheme, if it were at all possible. I thanked him and said I'd let him know soonest.

I rang Sebastian Lynch about 11.30, and I was with him in time for another of his lavish "canteen" lunches, served, on this occasion, in the privacy of his office.

"You're asking me," he smiled, fingering the stem of his wine glass, "to be a kind of Perry Mason, aren't you? Half legal beagle, half soft shoe? Doesn't happen in England."

I nodded. "I suppose not." I looked across at him quizzically. "But I thought you were different. Maybe I was fooled by your pop star clientele and your manor house offices."

He laughed. "Forget all that. I'm still a solicitor."

I thought for a moment. "Lavinia Saunders doesn't know you, as far as I'm aware."

"Very possibly not. But I'm supposed to practise the law, not break it."

"The police are supposed not to arrest innocent people," I countered, and Lynch licked his finger and marked one up for me.

"Are you really convinced about what you're saying?"

"Yes. If my guts are any guide. How are your guts?"

"I'll bust them to get Adam off. And, to be honest, not only for his sake."

"Your reputation?"

"Precisely."

I suddenly twigged what he was getting at. "Thinking of doing a deal with me?" I asked.

192

His face broke into a broad smile.

"Outline one," he said.

So I did, and an hour later I was still with him when he made the telephone call.

"Did you tell that lawyer fella I was coming?" Gus muttered, as he clambered awkwardly out of my car.

"No, Gus, I didn't."

"Why not?"

"I didn't bloody know you were," I grinned.

Gus tried to smooth a few of the rucks out of his sweater, as always, without success.

"Couldn't let you go alone. Never know what she'll do, woman like that."

"Keep your voice down, Gus. We don't want to advertise to the whole ruddy neighbourhood that we're around."

I locked the car, and led Gus cautiously out of the clearing, and up the private road that would eventually lead to the house. I cursed the fact it was still light, for, the way God had made Gus, even if you sprayed him in alternate streaks of green and brown, he would still have been about as conspicuous as a zebra crossing.

We made our way slowly, dodging in and out of the small bushes that lined the road, until we came to the bend, beyond which the house lay. I cautioned Gus to stay where he was, whilst I did a recce. He gave the scout's salute and crouching, I ran from cover to cover to where I could just see the house. As I expected, the Ford Escort was in the drive, but, luckily, no other cars, so I prayed she was alone. I looked at my watch. It was 5.30. Quarter of an hour to kill.

I crept back to Gus.

"Come on, crouch down. Don't say a word and do exactly as I do." Amazingly he did, and a moment later, we were both lying on the damp grass across the road from her driveway, hidden pretty much from sight by a rather sick looking rhododendron.

"Now we've got to wait," I breathed.

"Now we've got to wait," Gus breathed.

"Shut up," I said, but couldn't help grinning.

"Shut up," he said, and winked.

So we both did for about ten minutes, until we heard the sound of a car. It parked about fifty yards from us, a black and gold Lotus Esprit. (I heard later it was Lynch's wife's shopping car.) We watched as the solicitor looked around, then walked slowly up towards us and the house. As he passed, I hissed and he looked around. I was pleased he did not stop when he heard the signal. He turned into the drive, and soon we heard the front doorbell. We hardly saw Lavinia, for the door seemed to be shut almost as soon as it was opened. Lynch must have been lucky not to have had his heels clipped.

I looked at Gus and held up my crossed fingers. He undid them for me and grinned.

"Lawyers like him don't need crossed fingers," he grunted, "just crossed cheques," and he wheezed with chuckles. I was too nervous even to dig him in the ribs.

Though it seemed an age before Sebastian Lynch re-emerged it was actually under a quarter of an hour by the watch. I was just relieved to see him still all in one piece and as self-possessed as ever; he did not even glance our way as he passed us.

I looked quickly back at the house, and could just see a figure standing by the front room curtains. It stayed there for quite some time after Lynch had passed—indeed, until he had turned his car and driven off—then it vanished. It was then that Gus and I took the opportunity to do likewise.

We all met again, as pre-arranged, at the Warmwell junction. Lynch came over and sat in the back of my car.

"Well?" I asked, my heart, as they say, in my mouth.

He looked at Gus. I nodded. "This is Gus Tribble. He's on our side." He shook hands.

"Well," he grinned, "thank God for Mrs Olsen."

I leaned round and grasped him by the hand. "Thank God for Perry Mason."

"And for you and Mr Tribble, for keeping a watching brief on the house just now. It made me feel much more secure." He took a small tape recorder out of his pocket. "I should have it all here." He rewound it, then played the first few seconds. Lavinia's voice came over, slightly muffled, but very recognizable.

"Well done," I said.

"Not for court use," Lynch reminded me. "Just for our private satisfaction. I'll play it to you once, then destroy it."

"When have you arranged the next meeting?"

"Tomorrow morning. The International Conference Centre in Bournemouth. The foyer. It was her choice. She said her bank wasn't far from there."

"Did she admit anything?"

"No. She doesn't need to, does she? The thousand pounds in fivers should do the confessing for her in the morning— when the police take over. The money is apparently the last of a legacy her mother had left her."

"Even though I will say it was all my idea and that we only did it because Whetstone wouldn't listen, and we were afraid Mrs Olsen's life might be at stake, you'll get plenty of flack, won't you, from your profession?"

"Probably, but nothing fatal. When you hear the tape, you will realize I was very careful and chose my words with infinite care."

"How d'you mean?" asked Gus. "It was still blackmail, wasn't it?"

Lynch smiled. "Not really. You see I put the whole proposition in the third person."

"What third person?" asked Gus. "I thought there was only you and her there."

"What I meant was that I put it to her as a hypothetical question: what would she do if someone had seen her getting out of Maxwell's car at Osmington Mills, etcetera? If such a witness demanded a thousand pounds for his silence, would she be willing to pay, and so on. When she had got the money, where would she like to meet such a person? She naturally assumed such a person was myself or someone for whom I was working, but she was too frightened to ask which. In a way, this third person talk made me sound even more sinister, like I might be a hit man for the drugs mafia."

"So she was really frightened?" I asked.

"Out of her mind," he replied. "I almost felt sorry for her."

"I wonder what she is actually trying to hide," I mused.

"We'll know in the morning, I think, when the police empty her handbag. I felt she was very near blurting it all out tonight instead of paying. Kind of appeal to my mercy."

"Let's hope whatever it is, it helps clear Longhurst. Now, who's going to tell the police about getting their butts down to the Bournemouth Conference Centre?"

I made the call from Lana-Lee's, as it was then after 6.30, and I had promised to be with Muir to see the finished master of the Flamingo at 8.15, so unless I'd gone by helicopter, I could not have made the journey to Studland and back in time. Besides, I felt Blake should be informed at the earliest possible moment in case Lavinia tried any little tricks between then and the morning. He was still at the Knoll House Hotel.

I took him through the events that led up to our ploy, and the results of said ploy, and made it quite plain that the whole operation had been really forced on us by Digger Whetstone's intransigent attitude, an intransigence that could well have endangered Mrs Olsen's life.

"Don't go on your knees, Peter, please," was Blake's initial response. "You've done very well. Takes quite a sleuth to break a *Sleuth* alibi. Congratulations. I think my colleague might even change his mind about you after this."

"Only if tomorrow morning goes the way we hope it will. If she doesn't go and get the money . . ."

"I think she will, otherwise she would not have arranged to meet her anonymous caller in the first place."

"Supposing she flits tonight?"

"That would be a greater admission of guilt than being caught with the money, wouldn't it? No, I think she'll come, but I'll suggest to Inspector Whetstone he puts a watch on her house, just in case."

I breathed a big sigh of relief. "So you will make all the arrangements with dear Digby tomorrow?"

He chuckled. "Don't worry, I will. Do you want to come along to the Conference Centre and view from afar?"

"No thanks. I'll stick around at home. The tension would kill me. Just promise you will ring me the second you know any outcome."

"I promise. I may be a few hours though. We will want to interrogate her thoroughly. By the way, how the hell did you get Mr Lynch to co-operate?"

"We did a deal, but you must never tell a soul."

"Cross my heart."

"I promise to say, if the outcome is the release of Adam Longhurst, which, please God, it will be, that he and I sleuthed together from the start."

"I see. Mr Lynch isn't just a pretty legal face, he's an astute businessman, who knows how to use others to further his reputation."

"Precisely. Does that description ring any home bells, Sexton?"

"Touché!" Blake laughed, and I felt happier than I had done for weeks. Especially as, soon after I'd put the phone down, I received two big kisses from two of the bluest-eyed blondes you'd care to meet around Osmington way. But I did remind both Lana-Lee and her daughter that their lips might be being a trifle premature.

There was only one problem with going to see Muir: I was stuck with Gus, for I was his only transport to get home. What's more, we had both had the odd drink at Lana-Lee's, which had rendered Gus rather more intractable than he normally is, as he drinks at about twice the rate of any other sane human being, when the tipple is free. Luckily, the more modest amount I had imbibed had been pretty beneficial—it had somewhat dulled my worries about the morning to come, it had increased my childish excitement at seeing my first model creation, and it had pushed into the background my apprehension about encountering, yet again, Muir and his wife's solemn moralizing.

So, other than being apprehensive about Gus, I was feeling pretty good when I pulled up outside Muir's place.

"Now, I promise not to be very long. Don't get out of the car."

Gus nodded reluctantly, then asked with a grin, "What if I need a leak?"

"Then get out. Do what you have to—I won't be very long."

"All right then but don't hang about. Me legs ache if I sit too much in one position."

I left him grumbling, and went excitedly up the path to see my beloved Flamingo.

I was certainly not disappointed. Muir had done an expert job, and I was amazed how much the final detailing of the brass model had added to both its realism and its charm. When I had spent some considerable time inspecting it from every angle (it looked particularly good when viewed from the same angle as the old Meccano magazine photograph— in other words, when slightly looking down at it, half frontal), Muir pointed to the lower part of the right wing.

"I don't know whether you mind, Mr Marklin, but I have not incorporated the word 'die' in 'die-cast.'"

I turned the model over and read in clearly defined lettering, "Cast in Dorset by P.M."

"You see, Mr Marklin, we need to be very honest, don't we, in life?"

What could I do, shake my head?

"And I doubt if you will be actually die-casting this model, in the strict sense, will you? It would be prohibitively expensive, I would have thought."

"Oh, I see what you mean," I said. "If I use rubber moulds, or whatever, I would be misleading the public."

"Or perhaps even contravening an Act. We have to be careful. But I can always replace the lettering, if you don't agree with me. I should have mentioned it on the phone, I suppose, but I only made the modification this morning."

"No, I think that's fine. 'Cast in Dorset by P.M.' is quite sufficient, even if it was die-cast. My mother would approve, anyway," I grinned.

"How so, Mr Marklin?" Hell, he was taking me seriously. I should have known.

"She always used to tell me, 'Never say die,' that's all," I blushed.

"Oh." Muir luckily was lost for words.

"Can you advise me on casting?" I slipped in quickly. "I know next to nothing about the methods."

"Probably. My father often used to experiment with little models of his own of an evening, after he had returned from work at Dinky's factory in Binns Road. That's in Liverpool, you know."

I knew, and so does every die-cast collector in the whole wide world. Binns Road is as famous to them as Detroit is to a car enthusiast.

"I still have some of his creations somewhere. In the attic, I think. You might like to see them sometime, and I'll tell you how he made them, the different methods . . ."

At that moment, the door of the sitting-room opened to admit the rather frail figure of Mrs Muir. I was amazed and concerned to see the change in her appearance. Whilst she had not exactly looked well on my previous visit, now she looked positively ill, her face ashen and her eyes troubled and seemingly without life or hope. I rose from my seat.

"No, don't get up, Mr Marklin. I only came in to get my book to take up to my bed."

Muir started ferreting behind the cushions on the chairs, found the slim volume almost immediately, and handed it to her. I noted the title, *The Agony of Faith,* and its dust jacket had an amateurish feel about it, as if it were the publication of some small religious society—the kind of thing you sometimes see clerics or maiden aunts reading on trains.

"Your husband has created a marvellous master for me, Mrs Muir. He's extremely talented."

Her rheumy eyes looked up at me. "My husband is a very dedicated man. He doesn't rest until he has achieved the exact results he wants, however long that may take him."

"I wish more people were like him," I said, smiling, but she didn't smile back.

"You go upstairs, my love. I am sure Mr Marklin will understand." There was an edge in his voice I had not heard before, and Mrs Muir turned, tucked her tract under her arm, and slowly left the room, shutting the door behind her. Somehow, I sort of felt it wrong even to say goodbye, and suddenly I decided I'd had enough of the Muirs for one evening, so I remained standing.

"Well, I'll catch up on the different casting methods maybe next week."

"Oh, won't you stay now?"

"No, thanks, but I've—ere, had a very busy day, and I'm sure you'd like an early night. I'll take your beautiful model with me, though, if you don't mind. I'd like to sit at home and admire it for a bit. Oh, I nearly forgot, I've brought my cheque book."

"Oh, don't worry now." Muir looked rather embarrassed, but I insisted and wrote him a cheque which would mean another telephone call to my bank manager, as I had neither got round to selling any of my recent tinplate investment nor banking the cash I had received from Gus's surprising salesmanship.

As we shook hands at the door, Muir suddenly asked, "Any more news on poor Adam Longhurst?"

I shook my head. "He's still in custody, awaiting trial. But I believe the police may have discovered some new leads now."

"Do you have any idea what those might be?"

"No," I lied. "I just heard it around, that's all. Could be nothing in it."

Muir shook his head, sadly. "The whole Maxwell affair is most tragic. So many people caught up and tainted by his evil."

"You mean John Saunders?"

He hesitated for a split second. "Ah, yes, John Saunders, and God knows how many others."

And the way he said "God," for some reason, sent a shiver down my spine.

I was glad to run down the path to my Beetle, but less glad when I reached it. There was no sign of Gus, not a whisker, not a ruck of a sweater. I looked over towards the hedge bushes that lined the field opposite, but it was too dark to see anything except their vague silhouettes. There was nothing to do but get in the car and wait. It was a full ten minutes before he surfaced, and when he did, he looked more than a little scared.

"What's the matter, Gus? Seen a bogey man?" I laughed. "Serves you right for being so long."

He clambered into the car and shut the door with more than usual force.

"Next best bloody thing."

"Where the hell have you been? I could have had a whole row of leaks in the time you've taken."

"Wasn't just the leak, was it?" he muttered. "Decided I'd have a nosy around whilst I was out of the car. Wish I bloody hadn't now."

"Why, what did you meet?"

"Thought I'd met a sodding ghost, I did. In a large shed at the back of the house."

"What did you say? A ghost?"

"Well, it's like this 'ere. I'd had me leak, and decided to stroll around his garden. Thought he wouldn't mind, considering I was a friend of yours. And I came across this large shed thing. Thought it was some kind of weird greenhouse at first; it had a lot of glass, you see, in the roof. So, being a curious bugger, I tried the door to see what kind of strange plants he might be growing in there. It opened and I went in. Couldn't see much at first, until I struck a match. And then I saw it. Bloody great white thing, tall as a house . . ."

"What the hell was it? Did you find out?" I asked excitedly.

"Well, I dropped my match in me fright, and ran out. But then I plucked up courage and thought, come on, Gus, and went back in."

"And?"

"And I struck another match, and saw it was some funny statue thing covered in a big, white sheet. So I went up to it, still a bit scared like, and pulled a corner of the cloth. Bloody thing began falling off. I couldn't stop it."

"What was underneath?"

"A huge, gold, shiny figure with great wings and a terrible look on its face."

"An angel?"

"Devil, more like, by its expression."

I suddenly remembered what Muir had told me on my earlier visit, that he had been commissioned by his old church in Buckinghamshire to make an altar-piece. I patted Gus's hand.

"It's all right, Gus, it's a big angel he's making, that's all. He's told me about it. Never seen it myself, though."

"Don't bother," Gus grumbled. "Must be a pretty strange idea Muir's got of heaven, that's all I can say, with angels looking like that."

"Looked more scary in the dark, I dare say," I said, and started up the car.

"Maybe. But there must be a devil in a man who can make angels look like that."

I thought about Gus's remark for quite a bit of the journey home.

Fourteen

For Gus and myself, that Thursday morning seemed endless. Whilst I had devised a way of discovering about the initial scene at the International Conference Centre by getting Arabella to go straight there before going in to her paper—she didn't take much persuading; she had visions of a scoop—we had no way of knowing about the real outcome until Blake phoned us.

It even seemed hours until Arabella called. We almost fought as to who should pick up the receiver. I won. Her first words were like liquid gold.

"They've just taken her away."

I blew kisses down the line. "Did you hear anything? Did she make a scene?"

"Not as far as I could see, and I couldn't hear a thing. I was kept outside the doors. I just saw her arrive, and vaguely through the glass, then saw her being escorted out by two police officers. They got in the back of a car and were driven away."

"How did she look? Could you see?"

"Shell-shocked."

"Was she handcuffed or anything?"

"No. She was walking quite freely. But one of the officers was carrying her handbag."

"I guess they just asked her to come down to headquarters for questioning. Can you get on down there?"

"I'm on my way. Phone you soonest."

And that was that. Gus and I did not dare celebrate because, as yet, all we knew was that the first necessary phase was over. It was the second phase that would either uncork our bottles, or jam the damned corks further in.

We didn't bother opening up shop. We just sat around in the kitchen, with Bing, alternately making coffee and pacing the room. When lunchtime came, I broke open a couple of cans of Heineken, but neither of us went back to the fridge for more, nor thought of getting together something to eat. And what made the waiting worse was the number of false alarms. Two of the calls were queries from collectors about various toys I had listed on my last monthly mail-out, one was from Lana-Lee anxious to know if we'd heard anything, and the last from Sebastian Lynch asking likewise, and saying he was off to police headquarters, just in case.

However, our nail biting did at last end—at a quarter to two. It was Blake. I held the receiver so that Gus could hear, too. His first words were even more welcome than Arabella's.

"Well, you can go back to being a toy dealer again, Peter. She's confessed."

"To being at Osmington Mills the night of the murder?"

"Better that that. She's confessed to the murder."

"*Lavinia* murdered Ben?" I said, in some disbelief. "I thought she must be involved in some way, but I never really dreamt she did the actual killing."

"You won't like this, but Whetstone was right about one thing. It wasn't a big conspiracy, or a devious plot. It was all very simple. 'Domestic,' as he puts it."

"She killed Ben because he wanted to throw her over?" I tried.

"That was a part of it, she claims, but only part."

"And the big part?"

"Drugs. She states it was all triggered by that anonymous phone call when she learned about the drug smuggling. She was horrified. She could see her and her husband's whole life-style being put in jeopardy if it continued, so she decided to try to put a stop to it. First she rang her husband in Paris, but couldn't make much headway. Then she phoned Maxwell, but was told he would be out until the evening. In the end, she waited for him, hiding in that clump of trees opposite the Manor gates. When she heard his car, she waved him down, and said she had to talk to him urgently. He was unwilling at first, saying their affair was finished, but she insisted. So he reluctantly let her in the car and they drove down to the quiet of Osmington Mills beach for their talk.

"After a short while, he insisted they get out of the car and go to the far end of the beach, so as to draw less attention to themselves. She pleaded with him to stop the drug smuggling operation with her husband, even if he would not resume his affair with her. He laughed at her, apparently, and said she had as much brain in her head as she had between her legs.

"She lost her temper and picked up a rock. He laughed, turned and began walking back to his car. It was then she struck him on the back of the head. He fell and she went up to him and felt his pulse. When she realized she had killed him, she was horrified. She threw the rock as far into the waves as she could manage, then climbed back up the beach, praying she wouldn't meet anybody. But it was very dark, and the one person she did see in the distance, didn't seem to see her. By the time she had got back to the main road, she'd devised a crazy scheme to throw suspicion elsewhere. She went home and immediately rang Longhurst . . ."

"Imitating Lana-Lee?"

"That's right. That way, she threw two red herrings into the mix, got back at a previous lover who had ditched her, and his new American lady friend. She hadn't prophesied how loyal Longhurst would be to Lana-Lee in not revealing who he thought the call was from."

"Do you think she would have eventually let Longhurst be convicted?"

"I don't know. I get the impression today that she is not so much horrified at being caught out, as relieved at being able to confess the truth at last. I don't think she is fundamentally a wicked woman, somehow. Just very unpleasant."

"But she did bash Maxwell's face about a hell of a lot."

"That's an interesting point. She swears on everything that's holy, that she only gave him the one blow, on the back of the head. In fact, she became quite hysterical about it."

"Do you believe her?"

"I don't know. I'd like to, but . . ."

Gus suddenly grabbed the receiver. "Somebody else could have done it, couldn't they?"

Blake chuckled. "Well done, Gus. They could have, but only if they had come up on the body almost immediately after Lavinia had left. The medical evidence indicates that the facial injuries were inflicted only a very short time indeed after death."

"Well, maybe someone followed her. Who knows?" said Gus, and handed the receiver back to me.

"Anyway, I've got to have a meeting with Whetstone now. As you may imagine, he's feeling very edgy, and I mustn't delay things. Meanwhile, you should grab yourself a glass of champagne."

"I will. I must ring Lana-Lee first. Does this mean Longhurst will now be released?"

"When all the formalities have been cleared, yes in all probability. Would you like me to ring Lana-Lee later and let her know when?"

"Please. Thanks for all your help, Blake."

"Thank *you*, my friend. Dinner Saturday—on me?"

"Dinner Saturday—on you."

I didn't bother putting the receiver down. I pressed the tit with my finger, then dialled Lana-Lee's number. Her gratitude poured over us like nobody's business, and I could only break off the call by reminding her she should leave her line open for Blake. Then Gus and I popped along the road to the off-licence to buy some champagne—two bottles, in fact, one extra for when Arabella came home, hot foot, no doubt, from Inspector Whetstone's second press conference to announce his candidate for the murder of one Ben Maxwell esquire.

The Rutan roared off down the close-mown grass strip, and I waved to Arabella in the cockpit. I had a funny feeling in the pit of my stomach as I watched the futuristic tail-first shape of the Rutan soar into the air in a steep climb. I turned to Lana-Lee.

"He's a good pilot, isn't he?" I asked to reassure myself.

Lana-Lee nodded. "Do you know, this morning is the first time I've been allowed up with him? I hope Adam doesn't only allow me to fly with him when he's celebrating."

I laughed, as I watched the Rutan, tiny now against the cumulus clouds skudding across the sun, bank steeply to start what I guessed would be a high speed run across the strip, before proceeding out to sea to hug the coast to Lyme Regis and back.

"He must have felt that he would never ever feel the freedom of flight again," I said, and Lana-Lee came nearer and grasped my hand.

"He wouldn't have, if it hadn't been for you, Peter."

"Oh, the police would have discovered their error, sooner or later. Inspector Blake reckons Lavinia was so tired of lying that she would have eventually given herself up without any pressure."

"How long is 'eventually'? It could have been a lifetime." She squeezed my hand. "Anyway, Peter, we owe you a hell of a lot. I wish you would let us repay you properly, instead of just settling for a holiday."

"But what a holiday," I smiled. "You don't realize what a free trip to Hollywood and back with, no doubt, over-generous hospitality from your agent, Chester Austin, means to English folk like Arabella and me. We can't wait to go west, ma'am." I tipped my forelock, as the Rutan sped across the grass strip in front of us and made off south-westwards towards the sea.

Lana-Lee looked at her Cartier watch that was as thin as a platinum crisp. "I hope he gets back when he said he would, otherwise we will be late for lunch. I've prepared something rather special as a surprise."

"Dare I ask what?"

"It's a full Thanksgiving dinner, American style. I know it's premature for Americans, but not for Adam's release. And we've made a special dessert, cholesterol-filled cake in the shape of his Rutan aircraft."

"That's nice. He'll love that. So will we," I said, though I groaned inwardly at the thought of having two rich meals in one day, for we had Blake's dinner in the evening.

"I hope so. And Tara-Lee put the candles on it this morning, didn't you, darling?"

I looked around to where Tara-Lee had been only a few minutes before. There was no one to be seen.

"Where is that child? She's always wandering off. I think it's because she was always cooped up when we lived in Hollywood for fear of kidnapping. It's not much fun being the child of someone well known over there . . ." Lana-Lee broke off, as both she and I realized the inference of what she had been saying. We both feverishly scanned Longhurst's field in every direction, but there was no sign of Tara-Lee.

"Perhaps she has wandered back to Adam's house," I said in order to prevent Lana-Lee panicking. "You go back there. I'll search these fields." I pointed beyond the hedgerows that bordered the landing strip.

"You don't think . . . ?" Lana-Lee began, as she started running back towards the house.

"No," I shouted, lying through my teeth and cursing myself for having exorcized ghosts from my mind after Lavinia's confession to Maxwell's murder. As I stood alone on that landing strip, I felt as small as I must have looked to Arabella from the soaring Rutan.

"I wish you wouldn't try to confuse the issue, Marklin," Digby Whetstone sweatily observed, "with these apparitions of yours."

I moved away from looking out at the moonless night from the huge French windows and returned to the centre of Lana-Lee's drawing-room.

"Look, Inspector, I'm not trying to give you a hard time. I'm just trying to help, that's all. Exactly as I was doing over Maxwell's murder, although you wouldn't believe it then."

"Calm down. I'm grateful for what you did to bring Mrs Saunders to a confession, Marklin."

"Not as much as I am," Adam Longhurst muttered from the fireplace, where he was standing with his arm protectively around Lana-Lee, whilst Arabella held her hand.

Whetstone forced a flabby smile, and then continued, "But even if these ghosts of yours actually existed—and nobody can be sure they did, can they?—I don't believe they have any bearing on Tara-Lee's disappearance."

"Why bloody not?" I came right up to Whetstone's chair.

"Because, Mr Marklin, we know quite a bit about this fellow who has been terrorizing children over the past few months, and in none of the other reported incidents has the question of ghosts, white sheets or whatever, arisen. From the few sightings, he seems to be a Caucasian male, of around thirty-five, of medium height with what seems to be a cockney accent, certainly not a local one . . ."

"So, supposing there are *two* different people involved. It's not beyond the realms of possibility, is it?"

Whetstone rose, with a sigh, from his chair.

"Possibility, no. But what about probability?" He came up to me, and put his arm on my shoulder. "Look," he whispered, "I don't think we should distress Miss Claudell any further by discussing the affair in front of her."

"So where do you suggest?"

"My office in the morning."

With a glance at Lana-Lee, I moved with Whetstone out into the hall.

"Well, the speed with which you work, she could be . . ."

"I've got men searching the area with a fine-tooth comb, Mr Marklin. I've ordered them to continue into the night wherever possible, with torches and mobile floodlights. I've ordered detectives to carry out house-to-house calls in the vicinity right now. They'll continue until ten or so, then resume first thing in the morning. I've circulated Tara-Lee's description to every police force in the country. We're not just sitting on our jacks, as you . . ."

"Okay, okay. But don't dismiss this ghost thing out of hand, Inspector. I have a funny feeling they're real. Too many people have seen them now—me, Tara-Lee and Maxwell."

"The Maxwell affair is over, as you know. This unfortunate disappearance of Miss Claudell's daughter is a quite separate issue, a most tragic coincidence. Calamities often come in twos and threes. If we don't treat them as separate issues, we may even delay the discovery of the little girl's whereabouts."

"So Tara-Lee is locked tight in the child molesting computer, right, and can't escape to mingle with all the facts in the murder computer, the drug peddling computer, the Interpol computer . . ."

Whetstone's tiny moustache trembled with annoyance. "Everything is being done, Mr Marklin, that can be done. Now I must get back to headquarters, if you don't mind, after I've said goodbye to Miss Claudell. We've got a long night ahead of us." He moved back towards the sitting-room door.

"I'll see you in the morning sharp at nine. Okay?" I said.

"If we haven't by then located Miss Claudell's daughter, by all means. I'll be happy to see you. But, as I say, I don't just want to talk apparition talk."

"I'll say what I bloody think, Inspector. I can't help it. I'm made that way."

He disappeared into the sitting-room, leaving in the magnificent hall, with its two suits of mediaeval armour flanking a wonderful Elizabethan refectory table. I went up to one of them and tapped it, but it rang back hollow as a drum.

"Welcome to the club," I said, and then looked at my watch. It was half past eight. I suddenly realized it was the time we should have been meeting Blake for dinner. I went to the other end of the hall and picked up the phone.

By the time I had finished my call (Blake had apparently been ringing the Toy Emporium constantly ever since he had heard about Tara-Lee's disappearance), Whetstone had left, and Arabella and I had a chance to be alone with Lana-Lee and Adam for the first time.

I decided to plunge in head first, even though Lana-Lee looked as if she was very near total collapse. Whilst Adam Longhurst poured a drink, I took Arabella aside and ran through what Blake and I had discussed on the phone.

"We have to eliminate it from our enquiries, to use Blake's words, just in case it has a bearing on Tara-Lee."

"I suppose so," Arabella conceded and sighed. "But let me ask her. You keep Adam busy somehow."

I indicated I would like to speak to him at the other end of the vast room. So we repaired, as they say, but quite unnecessarily as it turned out. For the moment after we had moved over to the door, Arabella and Lana-Lee exited from it, and we heard their footfalls ascending the staircase.

"What's all that about?" Adam asked in his usual boyish directness of manner.

"Checking on a loose end," I replied. "There are one or two still in the Maxwell affair, you know."

"Such as?" he asked with some surprise, then double took. "Oh, you mean the ghosts?"

"No." I hunted round for a substitute for the subject Arabella was actually raising upstairs. For I wasn't sure Lana-Lee would like Adam knowing.

"No, there are one or two others." I sipped my scotch to try to stimulate my little grey cells. But to no avail. Longhurst was just about subtle enough not to probe further, and changed the subject.

"It's ghastly, this whole bloody mess following on the other. What poor Lana-Lee must be going through." He too drained his scotch, then looked at me. "Do you think they are connected?"

"I don't know. I really don't. If it hadn't been for those ghosts, I wouldn't have, I guess. Maybe Whetstone's right."

"For once," Longhurst added, and went to freshen my drink.

211

"Gosh, we're lucky." Arabella clung to me, and her naked body moulded itself to mine, contour by beautiful contour. But we clung, not through libido, but for comfort and refuge, I suppose, from the harsh world outside.

"Yes, we are," I whispered back. "It's not quite fair, is it? With all our troubles, we've led charmed lives, compared to hers." Her cropped hair tickled my chin as she shook her head. "I just hope, when all this is over, Adam will be good enough for her." She continued, "She deserves some peace in the world now, somebody strong on whom she can rely, really for the first time in her life."

"You're talking as if Tara-Lee won't ever be found."

She sat up in bed suddenly, and turned on the bedside light. I blinked.

"No I'm not. She *has* to be found alive. No woman should be asked to suffer like Lana-Lee has over her life. Some of the things she told me, I just can't begin to tell you. At the time, I wished I'd never asked."

"You had to. We had to know why she let Ben Maxwell back into her life—just in case it was connected with Tara-Lee's disappearance. Blake said we would only find out if we hit her whilst she was still shattered about Tara-Lee. He was right."

Arabella snuggled down beside me once more. She looked even more wonderful in the light.

"She never found the videotape, you know."

"Lord knows if Ben even actually had one. But imagine his reaction to the possibility of its existence. A lever like that almost guaranteed that Lana-Lee would accept him back into her financial fold. It would have been altogether too damning. Imagine—her foster-father forces her to appear in a pornographic film when she was only fourteen. Ben knew she would do anything to prevent such a film's release on the hard-core circuit, revealing its existence to the public via the press, so just the possibility of his having transferred the sixteen-millimetre film to videotape would have been enough. Poor Lana-Lee. She'd managed to keep it a secret all these years and then suddenly, out of the blue, returns her hated husband with the news he has unearthed a copy. No wonder she took him back. Everything was put at risk: not only her personal career and reputation, and the Reinhardt contract, but, above all, her relationship with Tara-Lee. Maxwell was sick."

"Not only Maxwell. What about her foster-father? He didn't only force her to do the film, he apparently raped her as well. Early struggle for stardom in Hollywood is apparently carried out more on your back than on your feet."

"As Marilyn Monroe is reputed to have said. And I gather *she* made a hard-core movie as well, or so they say."

"But at an older age than fourteen."

"Sixteen or seventeen, I think it was."

"And nobody forced her."

"Just ambition."

Neither of us spoke for quite some time. Then Arabella rose on one elbow and asked softly, "What are you thinking of?"

"All the other loose ends, since that one proved abortive."

"Ghosts?"

"Yes. Those, and that anonymous phone call Lavinia claims she received, and Maxwell's facial injuries. I can see Lavinia losing her temper enough to crash a rock on his head, but I can't see her mangling his face."

"His mouth mainly wasn't it?"

"Mouth—face; I still can't see her doing it."

"So someone, or *something* else, must have caused it."

"Blake says it must have been only a minute or two after the fatal blow, according to the post-mortem findings."

"So someone followed her?"

"Or him. Or both. Or something." I sat up straight. "You know, whatever Whetstone says, I can't help thinking that all those factors must be linked in some way. I have no evidence whatsoever. It's just this nagging feeling that Tara-Lee's disappearance is not just a tragic coincidence, or the work of a thirty-five-year-old Caucasian of medium height."

"Because of the ghosts?"

"Partly."

"What's the other 'partly'?"

"Well, whilst I was as happy as a sandboy that in the end we got Lavinia to confess to Maxwell's murder, I sort of felt, on reflection, that there were just too many loose ends for the whole thing to be wrapped up that neatly, but I kept all my fears to myself and forced them to the back of my mind. After all, my work was done. I had freed Adam Longhurst."

"Okay. Stop trying to expiate your feelings of guilt." She smiled at me, then snuggled her head in my lap. "Sorry," she whispered.

"You're right.. I do feel guilty. The instant I looked round on that landing strip and found Tara-Lee gone, those fears came flooding back—enough to drown me." I looked down at Arabella, and stroked her face gently. "I've got to find Tara-Lee, my darling. I've *got* to find her. If I had spoken out earlier, I might have been able to . . ."

"You couldn't have prevented it." She sat up once more.

"I could, maybe, if I hadn't kept my fear to myself."

"It was by keeping it to yourself that you got around to Lavinia."

"I had time then," I said. "It's all different now."

I woke so many times in the night that in the end, I called it a day, got up quietly and dressed. It was still only 5.45; Bing couldn't believe his luck in getting Whiskas that early.

I went into my dining-room and sat at the table, glassy-eyed, looking at the ranks of tinplate toys I'd bought in Weymouth. With all the celebrations marking Longhurst's release, I still hadn't got round to sorting out the ones I had to sell to make the ones I wanted to keep affordable. After a while, I realized staring at them was becoming the opposite of a placebo, as even they began reminding me of the terrible Maxwell via his motoring past.

I went into the sitting-room, and stared at the mantelshelf on which I had placed the beautiful brass model of my Flamingo albeit without propellers and wheels, and it reminded me that, at some point, I had to go and see Muir again to glean some advice on casting methods. I wondered when that would be now. Restless, I went into the kitchen and made myself a cup of coffee—three, in fact—but they didn't help. I looked into Bing's blue eyes, but they just blinked.

I sat at that kitchen table for ages, until Arabella came down and kissed her way into my consciousness. The kiss revived me somewhat, and we shared a little early breakfast together, then she went up again to dress. To fill in time before I went to see Whetstone, I opened the post I had been neglecting for the last few days. There were four bills and a letter from Poole. I left the former and opened the latter. I should have done the opposite, I felt at the time, for it was from D.E. Weatherspoon of Poole, postmarked four days before, who happily informed me that he had heard from a friend of his who worked at a local box manufacturers, that I was producing a model Flamingo to 1/200th scale just as Dinky had planned to do. (So much for all my attempts at secrecy.) He went on to say he might be able to help me, as he had worked at Binns Road, Liverpool, in the late thirties on the aeroplane lines and remembered the wooden proto-type of the Flamingo being prepared. Would I ring him, but before Sunday midday, as he would be away for a month for a bit of a break after that.

Normally, despite the blowing of my cover, I would have been pleased to receive a letter of that sort as all knowledge is useful in the old toy game, but that Sunday was hardly a normal time. I was going to ignore it, when Arabella suggested I might like to pop in on him on my way back from banging my head against Whetstone's in Bournemouth.

"It's not out of your way. You practically pass his door, and it shouldn't take more than a few minutes, should it? You'll kick yourself when all this is over if you don't. Who knows, he might have some information that could influence that brass master of yours before you commit it to produc-tion."

In the end, I submitted to her advice. Lucky I did—and not just to cheer me up after Sunday morning's completely un-productive meeting with Digger Whetstone.

Fifteen

Mr D.E. Weatherspoon proved to have some very vital information—but none of it was about my beloved Flamingo. And surprisingly, I found myself on my way to the village of Jordans. It was nestling in that executive belt in Bucks which has Gerrards Cross as its rather anonymous buckle. I cursed the distance, and looked at my fuel gauge. It was only a quarter full. I swung out of Poole and made for Ringwood to get onto the A31 going east. There I filled the tank up to the rim (or rather a surly youth did) and used the public phone opposite the garage to ring Arabella. She wanted to come with me, but I said every second counted, and it would take her too long to get to Ringwood. She reluctantly agreed, and suggested a simultaneous plan of action of her own. I told her to forget it with a capital F until I got back in four hours or so. She wished me good luck. I said, "Thanks. I'll need it, but not as much as Tara-Lee."

Thereafter, I don't think I've ever been so indebted to the genius of Dr Ferdinand Porsche, for that Beetle of mine almost literally flew up the M3, and via the M25, across the M4 to the Slough turn-off. From there on, curse it, I had to proceed at Sunday-driver snail's pace until I pulled into the village of Jordans. It was lunchtime, and the place seemed uncannily deserted, church services over, and roast beef and Yorkshire pudding, no doubt, keeping the inhabitants off the streets. I decided my only hope was to knock on a door and interrupt somebody in mid Yorkshire.

I pulled up beside a large thirties house pretending to be Tudor, and knocked at the door. It was eventually opened by a military-style gentleman, whose gruff and clipped delivery matched his appearance. I apologized for intruding, and asked where the local vicar lived. He gave me the directions as if he was still commanding a battalion on D-Day, and as I walked away, I felt I really should have saluted.

The vicar's house was Victorian and looked like a giant ivy bush with holes in it for windows. My flesh creeped at the thought of all the tiny examples of God's creatures that must be crawling through its rooms. The vicar himself came to the door, a gravy-stained napkin in his hand. I went through my apologies (standard version) and then explained why I had called. After a moment's hesitation (he licked his lips at this point, no doubt thinking of his favourite joint getting cold), he invited me into the darkest study I've ever seen in daylight. What's more, he was obviously not the local electricity board's biggest customer, with the result that my interview with him was like a scene from those mindless modern movies, where lack of content is hidden by shooting in almost total darkness. However, I digress. At least I could hear what the vicar said.

"Very sad affair, Mr Marklin, very sad affair. That's why they moved away and changed their names, you know. Down to Dorset. I hear from Mr Wall occasionally. He's making a figure for our church, you know." The vicar made a steeple with his fingers. (His church didn't have one.)

I couldn't hide my excitement at my hunch being proved correct. "What was sad about the Walls? What happened? You must tell me. It may be very important."

"Mr Marklin, I'm not sure whether I should. Private grief should remain private, should it not? If you know the Walls, or Muirs as they now call themselves, as you claim to, then surely they would have told you all about it already, if they wanted you to know."

"Look, I must know right now what happened. It may literally be a matter of life or death." I was sorely tempted to tell him my suspicions, but decided he would be so horrified that he would have thrown me out of the house—if he could have found me in the dark. "If you don't tell me, I'll knock on every door in Jordans until someone does."

"All right, Mr Marklin. I suppose you could look over back editions of our local paper anyway." He dismantled his steeple, and leaned towards me as if he were just about to hear my confession.

"It must be getting on for a year ago now since she died. Lovely girl she was. I christened her. She was the apple of her father's eye, and rightly so, brought up in a sound Christian tradition, brilliant at school. Took eleven o-levels at just fifteen, including, would you believe, Russian. Her father, I remember, was very concerned about that choice in case she developed left wing leanings, you understand."

"You're talking about Muir's, sorry Wall's, daughter? I did not know they ever had a child."

"She was their only child. That was what was so tragic. I can't imagine, even now, what made her change so. Maybe her father was too strict, I don't know, but suddenly, when she was seventeen, she seemed to change. It started when she took up with a local boy who was mad keen on motor racing. She started neglecting her A-level work and spending all her time at race meetings and with the racing set.

"Then, one day, quite out of the blue, she announced she wanted to go to Monte Carlo that spring for a Grand Prix race—and with her boyfriend. Naturally, her father was very upset, and they had a terrible row before she left, according to what Mrs Wall told my wife at the time. And it was at Monte Carlo that she was first introduced to drugs, the drugs that were to take her young life."

"Was her boyfriend into drugs?"

"No. That's the tragedy. He tried to stop her experimenting, but she had fallen under the influence of another man, very much older, for whom, eventually, she gave the boy up. Anyway, he came back to England without her, and she remained with the racing team in Monte Carlo, and then seemed to follow them around Europe."

The vicar shook his head sorrowfully. "I'm told there are quite a few young girls who are drawn to the excitement generated by motor racing, and to the drivers themselves, no doubt."

"Yes," I said. "It's a familiar scene. They're called groupies. But tell me, do you know the name of the man she fell for? It wouldn't have been a Ben Maxwell, would it?"

"I'm being very truthful, Mr Marklin, when I say I don't know. Mr Wall only confided in me so far, you know, and it's not a vicar's role to pry. Suffice it to say, by the time she eventually returned to England at the end of the racing season, she was a confirmed drug addict. I never saw her, of course, at that stage. Indeed, her family saw almost nothing of her. She lived in London in some sort of commune." I could see him literally shudder as he said the word.

"How long ago was that?" I asked.

"I suppose, around two and a half years ago."

"And then what happened?"

"It must have been about a couple of months after her return that she had the accident. It was something called LSD, I believe. She suffered, what do you call it now . . . ?"

"A bad trip?"

"That's the expression. She leapt out of the window of where she was staying. It was quite a few floors up in a tower block. She thought she could fly, so a friend of hers told her father. Anyway, she hit the ground."

"She wasn't killed?"

"Killed? Oh no. In a way, it might have been better if she had been, for the next two years were ones of almost unbelievable pain and anguish for the Walls. She remained in a coma, on a life-support system the whole time. Can you imagine what her father and mother went through, visiting her hour after hour, day after day, looking in vain for the slightest sign of her regaining consciousness? I was with them on quite a few occasions at the bedside, and we all prayed together. But to no avail, I'm afraid. God walks in mysterious ways."

"Yes, yes," I said, I'm afraid rather impatiently. "And she died and soon after, the Walls packed up and moved away?"

"Correct. Not right away, but after a time, they abruptly

left. They felt they had to start again, where memories were not so razor sharp. I was sorry to see them go. They were such devout members of my flock. But . . ." he raised his hands as if to his Maker, ". . . I understood their feelings. If they were to have any kind of life before them, to live their remaining years in any kind of peace or serenity, they had to try and leave part of their pain behind them."

The vicar smiled a beatific smile. I didn't like to tell him that the Walls, alias the Muirs, might have devised a very different way of alleviating their agony.

Directly I'd left the mass of ivy that passed as a vicarage, I made for the first phone box I could find, which was on the outskirts of Slough. But the Knoll House Hotel reported Blake had checked out that morning and wouldn't give me his home number. Nor would Bournemouth CID, nor Scotland Yard. I toyed with ringing Whetstone, then realized real evidence for my theory just did not as yet exist, and he'd laugh me off the line in seconds. So I called on all the powers of the Porsche engine once more, and dared the police to stop me, but they must have been taking Sunday snoozes. (The only patrol car I noticed was standing in a garage forecourt with its bonnet up.)

It was only when I was back in Wareham that I made my final decision not to involve Arabella, for the temptation to turn left to Studland and pick her up was strong, and I was naturally anxious to tell her of my discoveries. But the caution that had prevented me ringing her when I tried to ring Blake won the day, and I continued straight on. I had no idea what I might meet when I arrived at the cottage. After all, if my theories were correct, Mr Wall (I wondered if he had chosen the name "Muir" because the tragedy that had befallen his daughter had originated in France) and, maybe, Mrs Wall, were probably desperate enough in their grief to add another act of violence in the name of God's avenging angel. And I loved Arabella far too much to give her up to God right now, or indeed, any lesser being, immortal or mortal.

I parked some distance from the cottage and made my way cautiously on foot the last few hundred yards. I stopped by a clump of trees, from behind which I could scan the house and its garden. The garage doors were unfortunately shut, so I could not tell if the Morris Minor Traveller was there or not, but I prayed at least one of them had decided on a Sunday afternoon stroll.

I waited for around five minutes, but I could detect no movement of any sort in the house or in the garden, though that still left the shed on which Gus had reported, with its huge figure of the devilish angel, and this was totally obscured by the house and a high hedge. I decided this should be my first objective, for if I was going to meet Muir, I could get away with entering a garden shed more than with breaking into his house.

I Pink-Panthered (fast motion) across the road, and then crept stealthily along, keeping the hedge as my cover, until I came to a small gap through which I could crawl. The shed was now very visible as the rays of the dying sun flared off the considerable area of glass in its roof. I waited a further minute or two, but, hearing no signs of any activity, I ran across the smallish lawn and flattened myself against the side of the shed. I had no means of seeing inside without opening the door, as the only windows were too high up, so, taking a deep breath, I approached the only door I could see and tried the latch. It gave with a click, and I pushed. Inside, I instantly saw what had so upset Gus that night. Given that he had exaggerated its height by at least the power of three, it was a fearsome figure even without its white shroud, which now lay in folds at its feet. I wondered if the vicar at Jordans had any idea what he had actually commissioned for his church, and how disturbing its presence would be for his flock.

I walked quickly round the brass figure, which seemed to be almost finished, and at the back of the shed discovered what I thought was another sheet, which, on further inspection, turned out to be a white surplice of some kind, with voluminous wing-like sleeves such as priests and bishops sometimes wear on formal religious occasions. As I replaced it on the garden table on which it had been draped, I spotted a small white bundle in an old-fashioned hat box, tucked between the table's cast-iron legs. Directly I lifted the bundle, my hand shook like a leaf, for it unfolded into a white hood with holes cut out for the eyes, as penitents sometimes wear in countries where Catholicism has its deepest roots. I dropped it instantly, and looked back in fear towards the door. There was no one, but my eyes caught an inscription that was almost complete on the reverse side of the awesome figure.

> And if a man cause a blemish to his
> neighbour; as he hath done,
> So shall it be done to him;
> Breach for breach, eye for eye,
> tooth for tooth; as he hath caused
> a blemish in a man, so shall it
> be done to him again.
>
> *Leviticus 24:19–20*

I closed the shed door as softly as I could, then ran back across the lawn in order to make my getaway through the hedge. But as I did so, something seemed to draw me inexorably towards the cottage itself, but I stayed by the hedge for some time, my heart racing, before I finally plucked up enough courage to give in to its call.

When I came opposite to what I remembered as the dining-room, I sprinted across and cautiously peered in the window. It was darkish inside, but sufficiently light to show no one was there. I then ran past the front door to the next mullioned window, which I knew to be that of the sitting-room. Again, at first, there seemed to be no one, but then I saw a figure slumped over an open desk in the far corner of the room. I pelted around the side of the house (luckily, no windows on the ground floor), and peered in the windows at the back of the room. It was then I saw it was a woman. And that woman was Mrs Muir, and she was as still as a tomb.

At first, I felt like running the fastest mile on record away from that chill place, but then realized that Mrs Muir might yet be alive but unconscious, perhaps due to a stroke or some illness, so I picked up one of the stones that marked the border of the flower-bed, and crashed it against the nearest diamond of glass to the window catch. The glass tinkled inward, down on to the window-sill and floor as I released the catch, and in my hurry to climb in I scratched my hand. I dropped on to the floor inside. As blood began welling from the small cut, I ran to the inert figure slumped over the desk, but within a few seconds, realized my haste had been in vain. Mrs Muir's ashen face said it all, and the lack of pulse confirmed it. She was dead. In front of her right hand was an empty medicine bottle and a glass of water three-quarters empty.

As I moved away from the desk, my foot kicked something across the carpet. I bent down to pick it up. It was a Biro. I held it in my hands for a second, and then had a thought. I returned to the desk, and forced myself to lift her torso a few inches from the desk top. But all that was underneath her was a traditional blotting-pad. I was about to lower her down when the slanting evening light from the window showed up some indentations on the top sheet in the blotter. Holding her body with my arm, I pulled out the sheet, and was relieved to find a similar coloured one underneath. I lowered my burden then folded the sheet of blotting-paper carefully into a size that could be concealed in my trousers pocket.

Then I moved over to the sitting-room and went out into the hall, where I'd noticed the phone on my previous visits. I was about to dial for an ambulance, when I heard the unmistakable click of a Yale key in a lock. And a few seconds later, I was looking straight into the close set and intense eyes of Mr Muir, alias Wall.

I instantly moved back from the telephone towards the sitting-room door.

"Good evening, Mr Wall."

His stare did not flicker one iota.

"Good evening, Mr Marklin. May I ask how you got into my house?"

"I broke in, Mr Wall, because I saw your wife slumped at the desk in there." I pointed into the sitting-room.

His eyes left mine for the first time. "Slumped?"

"Yes, Mr Wall. I'm afraid I have bad news for you. I was just about to ring for an ambulance."

"She's ill. Had a stroke?" He rushed towards me and I instinctively held my hands up in some form of self protection, although, of course, it was the door he was making for.

I watched as he crossed the room to the desk, and carefully lifted his wife's left hand to feel for a pulse. He looked more like an ordinary local GP on his rounds, than a grief-stricken husband or a crazed and tormented avenger, self-appointed in the name of his Lord. My initial fear at his arrival evaporated enough for me to walk slowly into the room towards him.

"It looks like she couldn't take any more suffering, Mr Wall. The pain of your daughter's death, or was it more the horror of watching you exact your vengeance on Ben Maxwell and *his* daughter?"

Wall moved as if in slow motion away from his wife's body, and sat down on the edge of his usual hard chair.

"Mr Marklin, I would like to ask just how you discovered about our terrible tragedy."

"From a man who used to work with your father up at the Dinky factory at Binns Road, Liverpool. He said no one he knew there was called Muir. So I got him to describe every one of his colleagues who had worked on the preparation of new models. Eventually he mentioned a Mr Wall, who, in his words, was a bit of a religious nut and had retired to the village of Jordans in Bucks. I asked if Wall had any children, and he said, yes, one son. And he vaguely remembered from a newspaper cutting his sister-in-law had sent him—she lived near Jordans, in Chalfont St Peter—that son had suffered a personal tragedy in the death of his daughter from drug addiction. I remembered you came from Bucks, and, suddenly, a lot of things that had puzzled me became dazzlingly clear. So I drove up this morning and had a word with the vicar for whom you are making your avenging angel."

Wall rose from his chair, and said quietly, "We should ring for an ambulance, Mr Marklin."

"And the police, Mr Wall."

"If you care to. But you've got it all wrong. Yes, I changed our name to Muir, because we wanted to start a fresh life in a new part of the country, where nothing and no one could remind us of the prolonged pain of our daughter's passing. But if, as I gather, you're also trying to connect me with Ben Maxwell's terrible death, and his own daughter's disappearance, about which I only heard this morning on the local radio, then I'm afraid you will have to think again."

He moved past me. "Now, pray let me ring for that ambulance."

I followed him to the phone, and watched his bony fingers dial, fingers that I was a thousand per cent sure had exacted to the letter, the biblical injunctions of Leviticus 24: 19–20, an eye for an eye, a tooth for a tooth. His voice was calm on the phone, as he described how he and a friend had discovered his wife dead, slumped across a desk in his house, and would they please send an ambulance, together with the police (he looked hard at me as he said that word) as quickly as possible. It was the calmness of a man who knew quite well that he could never be brought to temporal justice on the few facts I had so far collected.

The rest of that evening and night was a nightmare—of frustration. Two local constables I'd never seen before turned up a few minutes before the ambulance, and refused to listen to anything until I had recounted, in detail, how I had found Mrs Wall, who, of course, they continued to call Mrs Muir. When I, at last, managed to include my conviction about Wall's part in the disfigurement of Maxwell's face, and in Tara-Lee's disappearance, I could see from their expressions that they thought I was a prime candidate for the Raving Loony Party. In the end, they suggested that I

225

come down to the local Weymouth station and make a statement. I said I'd do better than that: I'd contact Scotland Yard direct, into the bargain. They didn't even raise a bloody eyebrow. So I kept my piece of blotting paper in my back pocket for later.

"Come back to bed. You can't go on pacing the room all night. It's helping nobody." Arabella patted the white and empty space beside her.

"How can they all be so stupid?" I ranted. "I mean, the local constables wouldn't really take me seriously down at the station, Whetstone wouldn't even speak to me on the phone, and I still can't get hold of Blake, because it's sodding Sunday. Meanwhile, that crazed man, I'm convinced, knows where Tara-Lee is, and we're wasting precious time, every second . . ."

"Do you think she might be already dead?" Arabella asked, almost in a whisper.

"I don't know. I've got a funny feeling even Muir, Wall, wouldn't kill an eight-year-old child."

"But you think he's capable of smashing up a dead man's mouth and gouging out his eye."

I had to admit Arabella had a point, but it was a point I'd forced myself to forget.

"Look," I said, suddenly sitting down on the side of the bed, "Wall and his wife suffered two years of agony, waiting for their child to die. It could have been that Wall intended to make Maxwell suffer for a long period, in retribution, couldn't it? And all that dressing up as a hooded angel was to unnerve and torment Maxwell until one day he . . ."

". . . killed him. Only Lavinia got there first," Arabella interrupted. "A convenient coincidence."

"Yes," I said, and then a thought hit me. "Or quite the opposite."

"What do you mean?"

"Well, if we are right, Wall must have planned the persecution of Maxwell, and maybe his murder, over a hell of a time, and there is not much satisfaction in vengeance if

226

someone else exacts it, is there? The satisfaction is in striking the blow oneself."

"You mean, he must have felt robbed?"

"Could be. So he mutilated Maxwell's face, instead. And maybe even that wasn't enough. He had to get at Maxwell's child, as Maxwell had got at his."

"And what about poor Mrs Wall? Do you think she knew?"

I pointed to the piece of blotting paper resting on the bedside table.

"Probably. She was just as much a religious fanatic as her husband. Trouble is, you can't really tell from what little we can decipher of that missing note."

"Only that she seemed to have suffered some mental problems for years. All that 'ills made during the war' bit. I wonder is she was injured or affected by air raids or something."

"Who knows? I wish she'd written her suicide note fair and square on the blotter, rather than at an angle. Then we'd have had all of it."

"Where do you think the note went?"

"Well, either Wall had already discovered her body earlier that afternoon, and destroyed the note for some reason, or perhaps she had destroyed it herself, or it's still somewhere in the house."

"Or she'd posted it to someone."

I leaned forward and picked up the piece of blotting paper. "I know you'd like to get a little sleep, but do you mind if we look at these indentations just once more?"

Arabella shook her head. "Read it out again."

"Okay. First bit of a line, '. . . d's sake . . .' That could be 'God's sake.' Then, second bit of a line, '. . . on the edge of a cliff . . .' Third line, '. . . ills made during the war . . .' Fourth line, '. . . late to save me now . . . .' Last line, '. . . ngel . . . .' Must be 'angel' and 'Please God forgive me." I sighed. "I can't make anything more of it than I did before, really. Something like, 'For God's sake, I'm on the edge of a cliff,' or 'have been living on the edge of a cliff,' something, something, maybe, 'all due to ills made during the war. Far too late to save me now.' Ending with a plea for forgiveness to some unspecified angel and her Maker."

"Curious use of words, sometimes."

"Maybe she was already succumbing to her overdose by then."

"Maybe, but the handwriting, though erratic, doesn't tail off, nor does the pressure of the pen. The indentations in the blotting paper aren't any fainter at the end than at the start of the note."

I rose and began pacing the room once more. "I'll read it out to Blake on the phone in the morning."

"Meanwhile, it might mean more by then if you slept on it, you know." Arabella smiled, patting the sheets beside her. It was at that moment that the events of that dramatic Sunday finally caught up with me, and, on my next circuit, I just collapsed on to the bed beside her. She said I went out even quicker than a Citroën rusts.

The three and a half hours' rest had not made the blotting paper any more meaningful, despite an extra half hour's examination after tiptoeing down the stairs so as not to wake Arabella.

Bing greeted me with hooded blue eyes, and an expression that said, "Whiskas at dawn is becoming too much of a good thing." I subsided into a chair with a Nescafé. I had hardly drained it to the little brown bits, before I was shattered into red alert by a hammering on the front door that could have woken the dead. My immediate reaction was a raising of the heartbeat to a million a minute, until I realized there could be only one person with a knock like that at such a frail hour of the day. And when I unslid the bolts, there he was, strong as an ox and twice as smart.

"Where the hell have you been?" Gus asked as he trod his usual mud into the kitchen. "Arabella wouldn't bloody tell me yesterday."

"It wasn't a case of wouldn't, it was couldn't, Gus. Honest, all she knew was that I had gone to make some enquiries in Buckinghamshire."

"Yeah," he sniffed, "she told me that bit."

"Well, that's all she knew. She didn't hear from me again until after I had left Weymouth police station."

Gus raised his hedge-like eyebrows and smiled. "And what, old lad, were you doing down there, might I make so bold?"

So I told him. "And I'm just sitting here now, Gus, tapping my fingers, whilst Tara-Lee rots away somewhere, Inspector Blake has his three Shredded Wheats before going to the Yard, and Wall stares with the rivets of his eyes into a mirror and says, 'Who's the cleverest lunatic in the world, then?'. Really, if I was a bomb, I'd be in a thousand pieces by now."

"Calm down, old son," Gus said, and went over to the toaster. "Can I make you some breakfast? You look as if you need something."

I smiled weakly. "Okay, Gus, go ahead. I like three thick slices of toast, half an inch of butter, marmalade like it's going out of fashion and four cups of coffee, half and half."

"That's funny," Gus winked, "that's exactly how I like it." He cut two slices of bread and popped them in the toaster. "I'll do yours in a minute. We've got a lot of thinking to do."

"We've?" I queried.

"Well, I'll do it on my own, if you like." Gus smiled broadly. "Now let me see that bit of old blotting paper." I gave it to him, and his only response was, "Well, go on then."

"Go on with what?"

"Make that call."

I looked at my watch.

"It's still too early to catch Blake."

"Not Blake, you great berk. Muir, Wall, *him.*"

"What to say?"

"Get him going. Worry him. Torment him a bit, like you think he was doing to Maxwell."

"But what good . . . ?" Then suddenly I saw the sense in

what Gus was suggesting. I told you everyone should have a pain in the arse like Gus as a friend.

"I'm on my way," I smiled.

It took a little time for him to answer the phone.

"Muir here."

"Wall there," I retorted. "How are you feeling this morning, Wall?"

"Tired, Mr Marklin, tired. I didn't get back from the hospital and the police until 2.30 or so. Mind you, that was mainly my fault. They would have let me go earlier, but because of your wild accusations, I was determined to give as full and frank a report of our tragic past."

"Forget all that sanctimonious garbage, Wall. Remember your eye for an eye, a tooth for a tooth? Well, I'm taking a leaf out of another book, the gospel according to Marklin, Chapter One, verses one, two, three and four. They read as follows: 'And if a man cause a blemish to a little girl of eight; as he hath done, so shall it be done to him. But twice over, breach for breach, eye for eye, tooth for tooth. And he shall be given no rest, no peace, no, not for a single moment of a single hour, until judgement day . . .'"

"Don't be blasphemous, Mr Marklin."

I laughed out loud. "That's wonderful, Wall, coming from you. You're a living, breathing, walking, talking blasphemy. And I can prove it." I waited for a reaction to my lie.

There was silence for a moment, then he said, still as cool as ever. "The fact that my daughter had met Maxwell once, you mean. That's not proof."

"I wasn't referring to that, Wall. I found a note your wife had written before her death."

"A note?" For the first time I detected a tremor in his voice.

"A note, Wall, and guess what it said?"

"You can't have. There wasn't a note."

"Oh yes there was."

"There wasn't. The police searched everywhere."

"I'd found it first."

Another silence, and then he said, "A suicide note?"

"No," I tried.

I heard him draw in a breath.

"It said you had taken Tara-Lee."

Another gap, then he muttered: "Mr Marklin, if you persist in presenting me with your wild accusations and inventions, I shall have to file a complaint with the police."

"File it," I said, and put the receiver down with a crash. I turned to Gus with a smile of my own.

"Well?" he asked.

"*Very* well," I said. "*Now* I'm pretty sure that blotting paper has a little more to offer than an apology for suicide."

Sixteen

It was Arabella who cracked it. Gus and I had been working on the note for over half an hour when Arabella came downstairs and joined us over yet another (for us) cup of coffee.

"We need a cloning machine," I said, as she poured milk on her muesli.

"Like Woody Allen had in *Sleeper*," she grinned, "when he was asked to clone a whole president from just the nose."

"Precisely. Then we could clone the rest of the note. It's very important we do because . . ." And I told her about my telephone conversation with Wall.

"Hell! Let me have it," she said, "and let's see if my few more hours' sleep have added any charge to my brain cells." I gave her what we had made of the note so far, which was basically the same as we had deduced the previous evening. I wondered how she could think over the noise of Gus slurping, but suddenly she remarked, "Maybe we're missing a trick. We're assuming only the obviously unfinished words are incomplete—for instance, 'ds' being 'Gods' and 'ngel' being 'angel.' " She looked across at me. "But take that odd phrase 'ills made during the war.' It's puzzled me since the beginning. Wouldn't it be more usual to have said 'ills created during the war' or 'caused by the war' or 'originated through the war,' if she was referring to some mental or physical problem caused by it?"

"What are you getting at, dear?" Gus mumbled.

"Well, it's occurred to me that 'ills' could be an incomplete

232

word too. I mean there are quite a few words that end in 'ill.'"

"Thrills," I said. Then more seriously, "Pills."

"Ah," Gus perked up. "She could have been referring to the pills she took."

"I would doubt they were made as long ago as the forties, Gus."

"Lots of mine are," Gus grinned. "Me cascara tablets, for a start."

"Drills. Sills. Tills," I continued, ignoring him. "It has to be a noun."

"Gills. Hills," Arabella continued.

"Hills. That would go with the 'cliff' of the line above, wouldn't it?"

"But hills weren't made during the war."

"Only little ones," Gus smirked, "for gun emplacements."

I suddenly sat bolt upright. "What did you say, Gus?"

He looked startled. "Only mentioned little hills, old lad, gun emplacements, you know. Ones made in the war, like at Osmington . . ."

". . . Mills," I shouted. "That could be it, don't you see?" I leapt up from the table. "From Muir's reaction to my mentioning the possibility of another note, about Tara-Lee, I guessed his wife might have been writing a note about her. And that note, if we were lucky, might mention where she might be found."

"'On the edge of a cliff,'" Arabella read out, "at Osmington Mills. That makes sense. But 'made during the war' still doesn't."

"It might," I countered, "if more of the note was missing than we assumed. For instance, it could be something, something, something 'on the edge of a cliff,' like, 'You'll find Tara-Lee hidden' etcetera. Then the 'somethings' before 'ills' might be 'in a gun position' or whatever 'at Osmington Mills made during the war'—almost like Gus said just now about little hills."

Arabella leant over and kissed Gus. I missed his reaction,

as I was hell-bent for the phone. For I knew I had some vital calls to make.

We went in Arabella's Golf. Not because it was pouring with rain, but because it was fast and Wall had never seen it. Gus, naturally, insisted on riding in the front. I didn't mind so much this time, as I saw from the bulge near his crutch that he had brought along his clandestine Colt that a soldier had sold him for a fiver during the war.

We took the first of the turnings down to the sea, the one that led to Ringstead Bay, for the gun emplacement we had earmarked for exploration was the one on the cliff that formed a bridge between there and Osmington Mills itself— the very emplacement near which Tara-Lee had spotted the ghostly white figure the hide-and-seek afternoon. For, whilst even that route would not afford us much of an element of surprise, we guessed it was a tidy bit more discreet than climbing up from Osmington itself—the route that Wall would most likely assume we would choose.

We parked opposite one of the holiday homes by the beach, all now locked and shuttered and rather eerie, waiting for the spring to bring back laughter and light, cars for their garages, dinghies for their drives.

"Now, you must promise to stay here, Arabella," I climbed out of the car after Gus, and saw him wince as his gun obviously caught on something it shouldn't. (I prayed he had the safety catch on.)

"But it's safer with three. He wouldn't kill *three*, would he?" she said, in reality, knowing the answer.

"If he'll kill two, he'll kill three. And, anyway, you will be needed here. If there's an emergency, Gus will fire his gun into the air. You'll hear it."

"You're a stubborn idiot, you know," she said, through the open driver's window. "You should have let the police handle the whole of this. If Tara-Lee's there, that's it. You didn't need to stick your neck out."

"It's not it, and you know it." I leaned forward and kissed her. "If a battalion of police storms the place, and he's there,

234

he's crazy enough to kill her, if he hasn't done so already. And secondly, when he sees them coming, he can pretend he's just on a cliff walk, and what a coincidence, Tara-Lee is found just as he's passing."

"The last bit he could bluff out with you, too."

"I don't think so. If he thinks I've come alone . . ." I stopped suddenly, as I could see the alarm mounting on Arabella's face. "Anyway," I said quickly, "we're wasting time. Now, remember, stay by the car. That's where you'll be of most help."

I waved, and then Gus and I sprinted along the dirt road in front of the empty homes, which soon narrowed into a foot-path to start its curve up the cliff. The bushes each side of the path thinned, Gus and I parted as planned, and I continued alone along the main path up the incline, but now at only a brisk walking pace.

Although the rain had now eased off into that thin, grey drizzle that is so typical of the south-west, drips constantly ran down my face, sometimes blurring my vision for a split second, as they welled around my eyes. And I remembered the night it had really all begun, the night of the party, of Longhurst's outburst and the night of the first ghost. As I climbed, my confidence began ebbing, the confidence that I would find Tara-Lee at all, let alone alive, that I could force a confession out of Wall, and even that I would survive any kind of encounter. Suddenly a shrill cry startled me. I peered ahead, but it was only a sea-gull complaining that winter was on its way. I wondered who might be the next to scream.

The gun emplacement seemed to be embraced by its very own veil of mist, almost like a ghostly halo, and I shivered, but not from the wet and the cold. I maintained my pace towards it as if I were some late autumn tourist, fascinated by the relics of wars long over. I looked around carefully, but there was no sign of life, just the mound, the concrete and the black slits through which death would have been delivered, had an enemy dared to land on the coast.

Before I actually attempted to enter, I looked over to the left towards Osmington Mills, nestling in the valley beneath, but it was shrouded in mist, and I cursed the fact that visibility was now reduced to only about two hundred yards, and rapidly getting worse. I crossed my fingers, prayed Gus knew what he was doing, and dropped down into the shadowy concrete interior.

I took a torch out from my anorak pocket, and shone it around. There was some straw, an old Coke can or two, and the inevitable old rubber sheath, but no sign of anything that indicated Tara-Lee might have been there at any time. To say I was disappointed was certainly the understatement of my time. I peered out of each of the slits to check whether anyone was about, but the mist now had closed in even more, and I felt unbelievably isolated and alone. I shone my torch once more around the graffiti-covered walls, but there was no place a child or a body could have been hidden that I could see. But, though sick with disappointment and frustration, I was not over surprised, as I realized the gun emplacements could well have been searched already in the police hunt for Tara-Lee.

I was about to return outside to check the turf in the immediate surroundings of the pillbox, to see if it had been recently disturbed, when I spotted something that seemed slightly odd. The straw on the floor came from a bale that some local farmer had obviously placed there many months, or even years, before. What was left of it (about half) was propped up opposite one of the gun-slits, through which rain was driving, leaving the floor in that area dark with damp. But it was obvious the bale had been moved very recently indeed, as the damp area alongside it was very uneven.

I bent down and moved the bale a foot further along. It was even wetter under the bale than beside it. I got up again, put my arms around the straw, and lifted it across to the other side of the pillbox. Then I knelt down and explored with my torch the area of floor where it had been resting. When I brushed away the damp pieces of straw and debris, the floor seemed to be composed of large concrete sections, cemented together, but the pointing around one smaller section seemed to have been disturbed. I took a small penknife from my pocket, and inserted it along one edge. It sank in without resistance. But before I could fully appreciate my discovery, I heard a grating noise behind me. I whipped my head around and saw, with horror, that one of the gun-slits was now being used for its original purpose—only this time, the firearm was not pointing out. It was pointing in—and at me.

"Come on out, Mr Marklin, there's not enough room for two down there."

There was little else for me to do. I came on out, and prayed Gus had seen Wall's figure approaching the gun emplacement. For Wall was dressed from head to toe in white in the surplice and hood I had seen in the work-room in his garden, and could have easily merged with the swirls of mist. I knew I had to play for time.

"You feel above all human laws, don't you, Wall, when you're in God's fancy dress?"

"Is it a sin to obey God's laws, Mr Marklin? If only the world obeyed the teachings of the scriptures, sentence by sentence, word by word, then we would have a glimpse of heaven upon this earth, rather than the hell we have now."

He wagged his gun at me, which I saw was an army issue .38 pistol, similar to Gus's, which, no doubt, Wall had retained legally or illegally from his army days.

"You're wasting time, Marklin. I want you to take a little walk over this way." He wagged the pistol once more, and I got the message. I was to have an unfortunate accident whilst out walking. That's the trouble with cliffs—it's quite a way down to the rock-strewn sea below. I knew I would have to start moving, if only as slowly as he would allow.

"Before you push me over the edge, Wall, can I have the privilege given to all men under sentence of execution?"

He prodded me forward, his close-set eyes seeming the

more deranged, isolated in the small round cut-outs in his hood.

"Last request?"

"Just a few questions, that's all."

He prodded me again. "You will not have time for too many. But may I ask you one first? How did you find out about the pillbox? From the blotter? I noticed the top sheet was missing. You see, there was an ink blot on the top sheet that was not on the second sheet. I remember everything, Mr Marklin, everything."

I turned my head back towards him as I plodded inexorably towards the edge of the cliff, now only some hundred feet away. "Yes, it was the blotter. But now let me start my questions. It was you who anonymously rang Lavinia Saunders about her husband being involved in drug smuggling, wasn't it?"

"Yes, Mr Marklin. Question number two?"

"How did you find out about the drugs?"

"I overheard Maxwell and Saunders discussing it when they thought they were alone in the Manor grounds."

"A ghost with big ears?"

"Precisely, Mr Marklin. It was a pure coincidence, not part of my original plan, I can assure you."

"Why did you tell Lavinia Saunders?"

"Because I thought if Saunders knew the cover was blown, he might pull out of the scheme."

"Leaving Maxwell up a gum-tree." I stopped for a second, and turned around. "You intended to plague and torment Maxwell, didn't you? Let me guess for how long—the exact number of days your daughter survived in a coma?"

Wall pointed the Colt at my belly button. "Right again, Mr Marklin." His voice hardened. "Now turn around and keep walking."

As I did so, my eyes scanned the mist for any sign of Gus, or anyone—Superman, Spiderman, Supergran or even Lassie.

"And Lavinia spoilt it for you, didn't she? Were you plaguing Maxwell that night, too?"

"That was my intention. I was on my way to the Manor, when I saw Lavinia Saunders wave Maxwell's car down. I followed them down to the beach."

"So you were the figure Lavinia claimed she saw."

"Was I? I thought she hadn't seen me."

I stopped once more, as the cliff was now clearly visible, and horribly near, about fifteen feet away.

"Look, Wall, Lavinia may have robbed you of the pleasures of killing Maxwell, but she also *saved* you from committing murder, because that's what it would have been, Wall—murder. Not God's divine and, oh so just vengeance. And Tara-Lee is still alive, isn't she? I know you checked this morning. Did I interrupt you?"

"God will take her life, Mr Marklin, in His own good time. I'm surprised He has not already. More air must be filtering into that old ammunition space I excavated than I'd imagined. Now walk on. You have not far to go now. God is awaiting you too."

I turned and took three slow paces towards the edge, and had to shout over the noise of the waves breaking on the jagged rocks beneath the cliff.

"You haven't murdered anyone yet, Wall—except perhaps your wife."

I heard the squelch of his footsteps cease. I turned around.

"I didn't murder my wife. I could never have murdered my wife."

"Maybe not directly," I said, "but indirectly. She took her life, didn't she, because you'd not been satisfied with mutilating the body of Maxwell? You had to take his daughter, as he had taken yours. But Maxwell was dead by then. The only person you were hurting was Tara-Lee's innocent mother."

He laughed out loud and it seemed to echo across the void ahead of me.

"No woman of the screen can be innocent, Mr Marklin. They were all evil—Miss Claudell, Mr Longhurst, the Saunderses, all evil in their own ways."

He came right up to me and I felt the pressure of the pistol

239

in the small of my back. "Now, only three more steps, Mr Marklin, if you would . . ."

I took a deep breath, closed my eyes and threw myself down sideways on to the ground. As I did so, I heard a deafening report but was amazed to feel no pain. I rolled over and got on my knees. Muir was now facing away from me, gun still in hand, but with his arms raised on high, the sleeves of his surplice billowing out like great, white wings. Behind him, through the swirling mist, came the unmistakable silhouette of the most wonderful pain in the arse this world has ever seen, and behind him again, some six silhouettes that could only be Dorset's daring constabulary.

A voice shouted, "We'll take over now, thanks, Mr Tribble." And from the voice, I recognized one of the plumper silhouettes as Digby Whetstone. I rose slowly to my feet. And as I did so, the white figure turned, his arms still held high and wide, and taking two quick steps forward, leapt into space off the edge of the cliff. He seemed to soar, as the thermals caught him, filling out the loose white folds, and I watched his free flight for what seemed like an eternity, until the rocks and the sea claimed the fallen angel as their own.

"It was quite a cute trick of yours to get Sebastian Lynch to phone Whetstone," Blake observed smiling, "with all the guff that you had found Tara-Lee's hiding-place but were anxious to keep the police out of it so you could get all the kudos for yourself."

"Well, I knew Whetstone was likely to poo-poo almost anything I reported to him, if it were person to person, but he could hardly ignore a legal beagle."

"How did you persuade Lynch?"

I grinned. "He sort of owed me a favour, that's all."

Arabella came and sat on the arm of my chair. "He's not exactly alone, is he? But, my darling you still took a terrible risk going up to that pillbox alone."

"I wasn't alone," I corrected her. "I had Gus."

"Better than the US cavalry, wasn't it, old dear?" Gus sniffed and held out his glass. I rose and refreshed it.

"Wouldn't say better, Gus. Equal, maybe. But to be honest, you needn't have left it so bloody late."

"That was Whetstone's idea. He wanted me to overhear more of Wall's confession, before he charged in. Don't forget, we only picked up the last few exchanges between you and him anyway, so we didn't know what had gone before. And you told me to keep out of it until you had wormed some kind of confession out of him."

"The mist probably saved my life. And I bet Whetstone was enjoying seeing me in a cliff-hanger situation so much, he didn't really want to end it too quickly."

"He's not that bad," Blake said. "He's a pretty professional officer with a reasonable track record, you know."

"I bet that track runs in a straight line," I muttered. "He seems to me to be painfully lacking in lateral vision, if you'll excuse the jargon."

"Policemen, by nature, normally have tidy minds, Peter," Blake continued, "so they tend not to like untidy cases with loose ends. And what's more, they don't feed into the computers quite as easily. So they . . ."

". . . cut off the ends to make them neat. So Wall was a Caucasian male around thirty-five with a cockney accent."

Blake didn't need to comment, so changed the subject. "By the way, I heard tonight, just as I was leaving to come to you, that Whetstone has recovered Mrs Wall's last note. It was in Wall's wallet and was recovered with his body. He must have found her just before you arrived at the house, pocketed the note, then perhaps, seen you go into the shed in his garden."

Gus shivered. "I wonder if that vicar is ever going to get that God-awful angel now."

"Let himself out of the house," I continued, "hid somewhere, watched me break in, then, let himself in the front door. He could have killed me any time he wanted to."

"I guess he didn't want to, because he reckoned there wasn't any need. After all, he did not really know the purpose of your visit, and once he had pinched the note, your finding his wife's body, in a way, was no bad thing."

I sat back and savoured my Johnnie Walker, for Arabella's arm had now crept round my shoulders, and I liked its warmth.

"Tell me, Inspector," she asked, "how did he get Tara-Lee to that gun emplacement without anyone seeing?"

"Apparently, he and his wife kept her in the house for some time after Wall had enticed her away that morning. We've found evidence of that upstairs. It seems she was kept strapped to a bed. They kept her drugged most of the time; Mrs Wall used to be an army nurse. But, I'm told, Tara-Lee does dimly recall being bound hand and foot in a car in the middle of the night."

"I suppose, in the wee small hours, they could get away with it," Arabella admitted.

"Especially if he drove down to Ringstead Bay, and carried her up the route you took, Peter. The police search would have been called off for the night, and Ringstead is dead from October to Easter, I would imagine."

I nodded. "Yes, and that's in the daytime. At dead of night, it would have been a doddle." I stopped, for I suddenly felt very tired. Then I said quietly, "Anyway, let's stop talking about the poor, crazed, fanatical Walls. I just hope they're at peace now, wherever they are, and that they're reunited with their beloved daughter."

"Talking of beloved daughters," Arabella beautifully picked up my mood, "it's good news from the hospital. Lana-Lee phoned us just before you arrived, Inspector. Tara-Lee seems to have come to no real harm from her ordeal, although they are keeping her in overnight, just for observation."

"More for mental reasons than physical, I suspect. Almost thirty-six hours tied up and gagged in total darkness in that small ammunition pit that Wall had half excavated would be enough to unnerve an adult, let alone a child."

"Don't forget, children are more resilient," Arabella smiled and patted me on the head. "Just like Peter, here.

He's looking a bit like death warmed up at the moment, and I'm not at all surprised, but by tomorrow . . ."

". . . he'll be playing with his toys again, just like normal," Gus grinned, and raised his glass. "Here's to you, old lad, and never grow up. For remember, it's the sodding adults who are always screwing up this wonderful world."

Blake raised his own glass. "Can I join in? We've talked so much about the case since I arrived that I haven't really got around to the purpose of my visit."

"Which is to see if I have any Schucos in stock for you," I interrupted, laughing.

"That, of course," he smiled, "but also, unofficially, to express the relief of, first and foremost, Scotland Yard and the Dorset Constabulary for . . ."

". . . us solving their bloody cases for them," Gus interjected, but Blake shook his head.

"No, Mr Tribble. Not so much for solving our external problems, perhaps, as helping solve our internal ones, and without too much bloodshed."

"You're all one big happy family again," I remarked, rather irritably, "to all intents and purposes. And, what's probably more important—appearances: Whetstone's mistake over Longhurst corrected without any internecine warfare, or even a dirty memo to go on any police records, and Tara-Lee found alive by a posse, led by the same dear old Whetstone storming the hill. What's he going to get now, bless his cotton socks—promotion? You know, I'm beginning to suspect, Sexton, that every branch of government, and that includes law and order, is more obsessed with the peaceful resolution and hushing up of its internal politics than solving any external problem, however grave. Come to think of it, someone should write a new television series to follow up on *Yes, Prime Minister* called *Yes, Commissioner*. It would be a riot."

"Yes, Peter Marklin," Blake laughed and saluted, then looked at his watch. "Meantime, if you're not all too tired, would you care to pick up that rain check of the other day? We could almost write the first episode while we're eating."

I thought for a second, then said, "Great, thanks, but only if you are willing to drive us all to the restaurant and drive us back, in your glossy white car."

Arabella looked at me in surprise, but Blake got the message immediately. "Can I use your phone?" he smiled. "It sounds as if I'd better order up the first round of drinks right now."

And so life slowly started to return to what I call normal. (Loads of others, I'm sure, term it downright eccentric.) That is, the Toy Emporium opened more or less on time on more or less its designated days, my mail orders were wrapped and despatched, and Bing saw much more of me (and stopped having his breakfast at sparrowfart), and I also, at last, sorted out what I could afford to keep of the tinplate collection I had bought, and set the rest aside for the next big Sotheby's or Phillips' auction—or, maybe, for sale in Hollywood on our trip. Americans are as crazy about old toys as us Europeans. Arabella was getting the cream of the reporting tasks on the *Western Gazette* since her graphic piece on the Maxwell affair, written, as you may imagine, beautifully, but with the utmost discretion, so as to leave no after-taste in any participant's mouth, particularly those mouths below which chin-straps often go.

By special request, notably his and mine, Sebastian Lynch's role was flatteringly re-written, and mine was watered down to almost that of a helpful friend of Miss Lana-Lee Claudell who happened to be around now and again when trouble brewed. I really didn't want any of that kind of publicity.

A month after Tara-Lee was restored to her loving mother, Digby Whetstone actually caught the thirty-five-year-old Caucasian with whom he had been obsessed. He proved to be a mobile-home minder, Durdle Dor way, and had been apprehended in Swanage offering sweets to, would you believe, a local policeman's six-year-old daughter, as she was playing in her garden. So all Dorset (or rather, all Dorset's mums and dads) has breathed a great sigh of relief, and gone back to preparing the county for the next on-slaught of other people's children, buckets and spades akimbo, this coming spring and summer.

There was also a curious little item in a national paper the other day, that caught my eye. It was at the end of a news report on the latest terrorist outrage in Beirut. It read, "The only one so far identified amongst the British dead is G.M. Truscott of Windlemere Manor, Windlemere, near Salisbury, Wiltshire, a well known international arms dealer. He leaves a wife and two children." I guessed he'd never found that original Dinky Flamingo for which he had offered me fifteen thousand pounds. And even if he had, and tried to take it with him, where he had now gone, the metal would have melted in the heat.

As for my reproduction of the Flamingo aircraft, the boxes for it duly arrived from the printer and box maker the day after our rather riotous evening out with Blake—a hundred of them, matt blue and wonderful. I have them still stacked in the attic, but as far as I am concerned, they will never have any contents. For, to me, the joy of toys, modern, antique or reproduction, is their very innocence, their freedom from taint and the often twisted values and desires of the so-called grownup world.

So, one afternoon, after Arabella and I had spent another wonderful morning at Osmington with an ever adoring Tara-Lee, and her now sublimely happy mother and prospective stepfather (the only embarrassment of our mutual visits is their ceaseless display of gratitude towards us), we beetled on down the coast to Charmouth, where so many of my childhood dreams had been formed. The day was, as my mother used to term it, "bracing" (in others' parlance, "cold and windy"), but our walk up the cliff paths to the towering Golden Cap warmed us sufficiently to make the trek very pleasurable. At the very top, Arabella and I inched our way as near to the edge as we dared, and then I reached in my pocket for the object of our mission. It felt cold as death to the touch. As I withdrew it, a shaft of wintry sun caught the golden surface of a wing, and flared back into my eyes. I must have reacted in some way, for I suddenly felt Arabella's steadying hand on my arm.

"Do you really want to do it?" she said quietly.

"I have to. It's where it belongs now."

She put her arms around my waist and I could feel her lean backwards, her heels dug into the turf.

"Just don't forget to let go," she breathed.

I held the brass Flamingo in my right hand and looked at its fineness of detail and purity of line for the last time. Then I swept my hand back slowly behind my head, holding the fuselage of the plane with my thumb and forefinger, just as I had with so many flying model aeroplanes in my youth. I held it there for a moment, then projected it sharply forward and opened my hand. The tiny golden airliner seemed, at first, to defy gravity, and held its outward course in straight and level flight. Then, as natural forces caught up with its attempt to cheat them, the shape started tumbling, downward and outward, betraying its imbalance and reverting to its base reality.

Soon it was lost to sight and we never saw or heard whether it hit rock or water. But I felt curiously elated; somehow, now, for the first time for what seemed like an eternity, free to return to the life I and Arabella had chosen for ourselves in this normally so peaceful and rewarding corner of England.

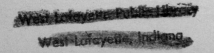